THE GIRL WITH THE WINDUP HEART

THE GIRL WITH THE WINDUP HEART

Kady Cross

 HARLEQUIN®TEEN

ISBN-13: 978-0-373-21119-7

THE GIRL WITH THE WINDUP HEART

Copyright © 2014 by Kady Cross

This edition published by arrangement with Harlequin Books S.A.

For questions and comments about the quality of this book, please contact us at CustomerService@Harlequin.com.

Printed in U.S.A.

This book is for everyone who has supported and followed this series beginning to end. You all rock. So, if anyone asks, you can say this book was written just for you. It's okay—I'll back you up.

And this book is for Steve, because he supported me— not only through this series, but through every book that came before and since. That's a lot of crazy to deal with! Thanks, babe.

Chapter 1

There was a most villainous killer on the loose. For weeks the nobility of Great Britain had been terrified—particularly the gentlemen. More than usual had fled to the country to their family homes, and those who hadn't family seats had gone with those who had to hunt and have lavish parties. They thought they were safe away from London, but they weren't. There'd been three murders outside of the city over the past month—two in Derbyshire, and one in Leicestershire. All three had happened at house parties where the guest lists contained almost exactly the same names. Two more deaths had happened in London, also at parties.

The victims were all men and they had all been burned to death. From the *inside*. That fact made the murders odd enough that Her Majesty Queen Victoria had requested that Griffin King, Duke of Greythorne, investigate. The only clue Griffin had to go on were two loose pearls found at the scene of one of the Derbyshire murders. Based on that scant evidence, the press had decided the killer was a woman, and dubbed her "Lady Ash" because ash was exactly that to which her victims were reduced.

Griffin had a particular dislike for the press but unfortunately they seemed to be correct. It seemed the killer was indeed a woman, but who? And why?

"I've never seen people madder than the aristocracy," Finley Jayne remarked as she lounged on the sofa in the library of King House, nibbling on shortbread. An audio cylinder of Beethoven played softly in the background. "Excluding you, of course."

He smiled at her. "Of course." Griffin treasured these quiet moments when it was just the two of them doing mundane things. True, they were trying to catch a criminal, but tea and biscuits made it seem normal. Any moment now he expected someone to come barging in, but for the time being he was content—a feeling he rarely experienced anymore.

He wasn't an idiot. He knew that he had to confide in Finley that The Machinist, Leonardo Garibaldi, was haunting him. Everyone had expected something of that nature to occur after the villain had died. Even from beyond the grave, Garibaldi was hell-bent on destroying Griffin and everything he held dear. The Machinist gave him no rest. He'd appear at any time of day, during any sort of function. Sometimes Griffin could send him back to the Aether, or ignore him, but other times…

Garibaldi was getting stronger. Very strong. Being dead had only made it easier for him to harness Aetheric energy and use it for his own dark purposes. Soon, the ghost would make his move, but with any luck not until they found and apprehended Lady Ash.

What would happen when Garibaldi came for him was anyone's guess. Griffin worked on strengthening his own abilities, but it felt more draining than empowering. He was tired all the time, and all he wanted was to commit Finley's smile to memory—just in case. He wasn't being maudlin, just prepared. Death didn't frighten him, but imagining all the things Garibaldi might have in store for him before and after…well, that was disconcerting. Still, he wasn't about to go without a fight, and even if Garibaldi did his worst, Griffin would find a way out—and defeat his nemesis.

He reached out from where he sat on the sofa beside Finley and stroked a lock of black that ran through her honey-blond hair. It had appeared shortly after they'd amalgamated the two sides of her Aetheric self. She'd rather been like that Jekyll and Hyde character before, though much prettier.

She glanced at him, amber eyes troubled. "What?"

He shook his head. "Nothing. Just wanted to touch you."

She snuggled closer. "You can touch me whenever you like."

"That's an interesting invitation," he murmured, trailing his fingers down her neck. She was wearing a violet frock with long sleeves under a black leather corset. Even though he'd helped lace the corset that very morning, there was something tantalizing about possibly getting her out of it…. He pressed his lips to her throat.

The door to the library burst open.

Finley swore. Griffin chuckled. Of course the others would choose this moment to show up. Their timing was, as always, terrible.

They filed in one after the other—Emily in front, followed by Sam, Wildcat and Jasper. A motley bunch if ever there was one. Emily carried a stack of papers, and had that expression on her freckled face that said she believed she'd solved a puzzle. Griffin loved to see that look.

"What did you find?" he asked as Finley sat up, putting a little distance between them. He wanted to pull her back, but she wasn't much for flaunting their relationship in front of other people, even their friends.

Emily flopped down in a nearby chair, spreading the papers out on the tea table. "Lady Ash, I think."

Sam snatched a shortbread from the plate and shoved the entire biscuit in his mouth. "She's a genius."

It always amazed Griffin to watch Sam eat. His friend loved food so much that somehow he managed to talk without spraying crumbs—as though his mouth knew better than to waste them by spitting them out.

"That goes without saying," Griffin agreed.

"Just let her speak, will you?" Finley was peevish—and it was obvious. Griffin patted her thigh. He'd make certain they had some time alone later.

Emily arched an eyebrow at the other girl's tone and Wildcat and Jasper shared a glance. Maybe Griffin should speak to the cowboy and ask him how he managed to find time to sneak away with Cat. They never seemed to have a problem spending time together. In fact, there had been times when they'd been impossible to find. People always seemed to find *him*.

"I used the Aether engine to compile a list of possible suspects," Emily informed them in her Irish lilt. "I compared the guest list to all the gatherings with the Scotland Yard accounts of recently reported burglaries."

Finley frowned. "But Lady Ash hasn't stolen anything. Has she?"

Emily grinned, seemingly unaware of just how foul the other girl's mood was. "No, but I reckoned she might be intelligent enough to realize someone would look into her ruined pearls. Two aristocratic women reported having pearls stolen as of late, but only one was invited to—and attended—each of the parties."

They all stared at her—waiting. She sat there, smiling at them as tension built.

"Emily," Finley growled. "Just tell us who the bloody hell she is."

"She's in an ugly mood, Em," Sam added. "Best not to poke too much."

The little Irish girl sighed. "I stayed up all night compiling this data—the least you all can do is allow me to bask in my success."

"Bask later." Finley sounded as though her jaw was glued shut. Griffin hid a smile. It was cruel of him—childish even, but how could he not love knowing that she was so sour because they'd been interrupted?

"Just tell us, Em," he urged. "And then we can praise your hard work and genius."

That seemed to appease her. She lit up like Guy Fawkes Night. "Lady Grantfarthen."

Grantfarthen. It wasn't a title Griffin knew well, but

then, he wasn't exactly a social butterfly. As a young noble, especially a duke, he was a person that many sought to know, curry favor from or shove their daughters at. He had more important things to do than dance and drink champagne. Although, perhaps if he'd done a little more of that, his life wouldn't always seem to be in peril.

"Her husband was a viscount," Emily went on. "They spent most of their time at their country estate in Lincolnshire until Lord Grantfarthen shot himself over gaming debts, and the new heir tossed Lady Grantfarthen out."

The new lord must be quite the peach indeed. "Let me guess. The victims have all been people to whom the late viscount owed money?" It wasn't a brilliant deduction, so Griffin didn't pat his own back over it.

Emily nodded. "Two of them had called in their markers, as well. When Grantfarthen couldn't pay, they threatened to ruin him publicly."

It was enough to make Griffin ashamed of the society into which he'd been born. If the thought of ridicule was enough to make you eat a bullet, what sort of world did you live in? Not a very pleasant one. "So the widow uses her abilities for a little revenge and claims her necklace was stolen to cover her tracks."

"She's not stupid," Wildcat commented. "Would have been smarter not to wear the pearls at all, though."

"Appearances," Griffin said, absently. "One must keep up appearances. Not wearing the pearls might make people speculate that she'd taken to selling off her jewelry. Did you look into the lady's finances?"

Emily puffed up like a little bird. "On a whim, I did. Turns out she had her own fortune as her father's only child, but her da had put a stipulation on her dowry that Lord Grantfarthen couldn't have access to it without written permission from his wife and his father-in-law. The old man's in trade apparently, and rich as Midas. He refused to sign over any money, but he did offer his son-in-law a loan."

"Which he refused," Griffin concluded with a grimace. For many men—especially titled ones—pride was a terrible thing. Having a man "beneath" him deny him what he saw as rightfully his must have driven the viscount to distraction. "Do we know where the father is now?"

Emily consulted her papers. "I have an address for Mr. Peabody in Cheapside. He's been out of the country, though."

"When's he due back?"

She looked again. "This morning. What are you thinking, lad?"

Griffin smiled without humor. "I'm thinking that our fiery lady might decide to pay a visit to her papa. She might decide she's had enough of him controlling her money—and she might want his, as well."

Some of the color left Emily's cheeks. She was already very pale. "You don't think she'd kill her own father?"

"I think she's insane, very powerful and drunk on the fact that she's gotten away with it for this long. I also think we'd better make haste to Cheapside if we're to save Mr. Peabody from a grisly death." He rose to his feet and offered Finley his hand. "Let's go."

Her fingers entwined with his as she rose to her feet. She wasn't happy, he could tell—and he didn't blame her. Since they'd met, their lives had been one adventure after another. Some of it had been fun, but most of it had been dangerous. They could use a little quiet time together. He wanted to give her that, but not at the expense of a life—especially not when it was a life they could save.

"We'll go away after," he told her in a low voice. "Spend some time alone."

She shot him a doubtful glance. "All right." But there was no conviction in her tone. She pulled her hand free of his and walked toward the door.

"I don't blame her," whispered a voice near his ear. *Garibaldi.* Griffin didn't turn his head. Didn't even acknowledge that he'd heard. No one else seemed to have either.

"She knows you don't mean it, Your Grace. More importantly, *you* know you don't mean it."

Griffin's jaw tightened, but he remained silent. Clenching his hands into fists, he followed his friends.

The Machinist chuckled—the sound echoing in his head.

"I'm coming for you, Griffin King."

"Why do I need to learn to dance?"

Jack Dandy smiled as he guided Mila through a turn. She was a good dancer, despite her whining. "Because it's something every well-bred young lady knows how to do, and because it's enjoyable."

"I'm not well-bred. I was built. I suppose I could be well built."

She was at that, he thought with a touch of irony-laced guilt. She was very fit, and her tailored trousers and waistcoat showed that off to brilliant advantage. Add her mane of wild red hair and wide amber eyes and she was a girl a fellow didn't easily forget.

"You don't like to dance?" he asked, turning her again.

"You could have just given me a book on it. As soon as I read the instructions I'd know how to do it."

His lips quirked. "So, you don't like dancing with me, is that it?"

Her cheeks flushed at his teasing. "No. I'm sure you know you dance very well—otherwise you wouldn't do it. I just think this is a waste of your time."

"It's not." And that was as much conversation as he intended to have on the subject. He wouldn't admit—not even to himself—just how much he enjoyed dancing with her. She felt comfortable in his arms—as if she was made to fit him.

Which was ridiculous. She'd been made—engineered—to house the brain of a madman, only those plans had gotten all mucked up by Griffin King. Because of an injection of some sort of goo that apparently gave a kick in the bollocks to the evolutionary process, Mila the automaton had become Mila the girl, complete with a sharp brain and all the blood and organs that went along with being human.

She learned at an incredible rate, which was good, because, though she looked like a woman, if she were human, she wouldn't even be old enough to crawl yet. She'd learned so much already—more than he'd ever thought possible, but there was still so much she didn't know.

"Are you enjoying *Romeo and Juliet?*" Shakespeare was practically required reading in England.

Her winged ginger brows knit into a frown as she moved. Her dancing had dramatically improved in the past five minutes. Remarkable. "No. It's foolish and contrived."

Both of Jack's brows shot up. He misstepped and almost trod upon her toes. "Apologies," he muttered.

Mila easily moved around his clumsiness and kept the dance going with effortless grace. Then again, he could have fallen on his arse and she would have simply swept him back onto his feet. It was enough to emasculate a fellow, her strength. "You're surprised."

"I am. Most girls quite enjoy the romance of *Romeo and Juliet.*"

Her frown grew. She was adorable when she scowled. "I don't find tandem suicide the least bit romantic, Jack. Why didn't they just stand up to their families?"

"Because that just wasn't done."

She snorted. "Ridiculous. If I was in love with someone, I wouldn't let that stop me."

"You haven't lived your life by a strict code of rules."

The gaze she leveled at him was so direct it was unsettling. "Neither have you."

Were that true. "I did for a little while—when I was younger."

"If you so dislike the rules, why are you imposing them on me?"

Oh, she was getting far too smart. To think that when she came to live with him she was more like a child. Now…well, there was nothing childlike about her. "Because I want you to have a better life than I had."

Mila glanced around at the opulence of his drawing room. It looked like a brothel—an expensive one—with its crimson walls and dark furniture. "Yes, your life has been little more than tragedy and want."

He never should have taught her sarcasm. It was yet another thing at which she excelled. He also never should have revealed to her that the atrocious cockney accent he often used wasn't his true manner of speaking. That had opened up a whole slew of questions—and hurt her feelings when he told her he didn't want to talk about it.

"My life has been what I've made of it, and it wasn't easy." That was the bluntest, least dramatic way to phrase it.

"You want my life to be easy?"

Yes, damn it. "I want your life to be exactly as you deserve."

"But you're the one deciding what I deserve."

He whirled her around. This conversation was becoming tedious. They'd been having it quite often of late. "Just making certain every option is available, poppet."

She whirled him around—to make a point, no doubt. "No, you're making certain every option you want me to have is available."

"Now you're just splitting hairs. *Put me down.*" And she did, because he'd put enough will behind his gaze to give himself a headache. Mila took more of a push than normal people to bend to his will. It wasn't an ability he used on a regular basis—not anymore. He preferred winning the old-fashioned way these days.

Mila stopped dancing and shook her head as if to clear it. "I hate it when you do that."

"Not a big lover of being picked up like a rag doll either, love."

Her eyes brightened. She was spoiling for a fight—and he was prepared to give it. What was happening between them? It seemed just a few days ago she was still his sweet, curious Mila. Now she was this difficult, argumentative creature that challenged him at every turn. So, why did he find this new her so bloody interesting even when he wanted to throttle her at times?

He stared at her and she at him. They were perfectly still—tense. The music continued to play in the background as they stood with their fingers entwined, his hand on the small of her back, hers on his shoulder. A few inches and they'd touch. He could haul her right up against him. What sort of reaction would that get?

The doorbell rang. Swearing, Jack stepped back, releasing her. He consulted his watch. It was ten o'clock. "Lesson's over, poppet."

"My heart is broken," she drawled. "Expecting company?"

"As a matter of fact, I am." He slipped his watch back into his pocket. "Off to your room."

"I don't get to meet your friend?"

Never would he use that word to describe Darla. "No." God, the last thing he wanted was to have to explain Mila's presence in his home. Normally he'd say she was his ward, but the changes in her lately had made that more difficult. At least one of his companions had gotten very jealous of the other girl—foolish chit. Mila was his responsibility, not his lover. There was no reason for any other woman to be threatened by her.

"Why not?" she demanded.

"Because you insulted my last visitor."

She frowned. "I did not!"

"Hmm, you did. You commented on her hair color."

"I simply wanted to know why the hair close to her scalp was a different color than the rest of it."

Jack walked toward the foyer. "You don't ask women such questions."

"I'll add it to the list."

Cheeky baggage. He paused near the door and shot her a pointed gaze. "Upstairs. Now."

Mila sighed with the gusto of an elephant expelling water from its trunk. She stomped from the drawing room to the stairs.

"Easy," Jack warned. "Break my staircase and you'll be cleaning the water closet for a week." The girl didn't know her own strength sometimes. Shortly after he'd taken her in she'd ripped two doors clean off their hinges by accident.

She glared at him, but her steps were light as she huffed and muttered her way upstairs. He heard just enough to decide to watch his language around her. She knew more profanity than most sailors.

When she was gone from sight, and he'd heard the door to her room slam, he greeted his visitor.

Darla arched a brow. She was a tall willowy woman, with hennaed hair and brown eyes and a feisty disposition. "Kept me waiting long enough."

He stepped back to let her enter. "Apologies, pet. I was 'avin' a bit of an issue with me cravat."

She glanced at his throat as she crossed the threshold. "You're not wearing a cravat."

"Issue solved." He closed the door and flicked the lock. "Drink?"

"Of course." She removed her coat and handed it to him to hang up on the stand by the door. "Gin if you have it."

Vile stuff. "Got a little bit of ev'ryfing." At least his gin was top quality—not that Darla would know, or care. "Do come in."

Her skirts swished as she entered the parlor. Jack immediately went to the bar to pour their drinks. She didn't sit down, but glanced around, as though expecting to find someone hiding under a piece of furniture. She knew about Mila, but the two of them had never met. That was how he intended to keep it.

"'Ere you go, pet." He handed her a glass.

"Thanks." She took a sip. "I didn't know you like music."

"I like a lot of things." Perhaps he should have turned the cylinder player off, but this way there was less chance of hearing Mila thumping about in her room.

"Are we going to dance?" she asked with a saucy smile as she took another drink.

Jack grinned in return. "No," he informed her as he slipped an arm about her waist. "That's not what I had in mind at all."

Chapter 2

When they arrived at Peabody's, the house was already on fire, with Peabody and his daughter inside.

Finley took a moment to collect herself. She was angry…and hurt and mad at herself for it. She oughtn't be angry at Griffin for helping people—it was one of the things she adored about him, but it would be nice to have a bit of a break from the intrigue. A little extended time together—alone—would be nice. She loved her friends, but they were always around.

Sam kicked the door in so they could enter. The trail of smoke led them to a small parlor near the back of the dark, but well-appointed house. Peabody had money but he wasn't loose with it, judging from the economy, but quality of decor. Sam kicked in that door, as well. Jasper rushed in, nothing more than a blur as he rushed to create a vacuum around the flames, stifling the fire that had already consumed draperies and a sofa.

Mr. Peabody lay gasping on the floor, a cloud of smoke hanging over him that rose toward the high ceiling. His daughter stood over him. The skirts of her beautiful gown were singed. Her dark hair was a mess, and her eyes and hands glowed like coals in a furnace. Finley could feel the heat coming off her.

"Greythorne," she snarled.

Finley wasn't surprised that the woman knew Griffin. Sometimes she forgot he was a duke, but this wasn't one of those times—not when he stood there, staring down his nose at "Lady Ash" as though she was little more than dirt beneath his shoe. "It's over, Lady Grantfarthen. The killing stops here."

The older woman—she was perhaps in her midtwenties—smiled. "No, Your Grace. It does not." And with that pronouncement, her right hand ignited into a ball of fantastic blue flame.

"Get him out of here," Griffin instructed to Emily and Sam, gesturing at Peabody.

Lady Ash drew back her arm to throw her fire, but Wildcat dived into her, taking her to the ground. Out of the corner of her eye, Finley saw Sam scoop the old man off the floor and head outside. That was when she leaped into action to help Cat. Both of Lady Ash's hands were burning now, along with her eyes. Finley didn't think, she simply grabbed the pitcher from the small washing pedestal—obviously Peabody liked to be able to scrub the ink from his hands—and tipped it onto the woman.

She actually sizzled.

Swearing and sputtering, the woman struggled beneath Cat, who straddled her, trying to trap those flailing arms with her knees. As Finley bent to help—Lady Ash grabbed for the pistol strapped to Cat's thigh. It happened so fast that Finley barely had time to shout at Cat to move. But it wasn't Cat she should have worried about. The pistol discharged at the same second Jasper pulled his own. That was the exact same second that Peabody's home security automatons burst into the room, their own weapons engaged.

Being shot hurt. It hurt a lot.

Finley cried out as Lady Ash's bullet tore through her upper chest and exploded out her back. She staggered under the impact. The second bullet—from one of the automatons—drove her to her knees in breathless silence.

"Finley!" It was Griffin. She could hear the terror in his voice. He must really care about her to be so afraid for her. Stupid that *would* be what she thought about at a time like this.

Not going to die. She clung to that thought as she struggled to breathe. Punctured lung? Blood soaked her shirt, ran down her front and back in hot little rivers. Both bullets went through. Good. At least Emily wouldn't have to go hunting for them inside her. At least her body wouldn't try to heal around them.

She just had to heal before the wounds killed her. As she fell forward onto her hands, she prayed for the abundance of Organites in her system to get to work. It seemed the reconstructing process of her body had intensified as of late. Now was not a time to regress.

Lifting her head, she sought out each of her friends who were involved in the fight. The scene before her played out like one of those moving pictures—one frame at a time. Emily was back and using her ability to communicate with machines to make one of the large automatons fighting them dismantle itself. Sam took another down with his incredible strength. Jasper used his amazing speed to grab Lady Ash and bind her limbs. He'd shot her in the arm.

She tasted copper as her gaze turned to Griffin. Finley opened her mouth, but only blood came out. Griffin wasn't watching her. He was watching Lady Ash and he…he was *glowing*.

Griffin's power was the ability to harness the Aether—the energy expelled by all living creatures, and the realm of the dead. It was a terrible power, one that he fought to control every time he used it. A power that had brought so much pain upon himself—and his friends—as of late. It was power he rarely directed at a person, and now he directed it at Lady Ash.

She'd made short work of Jasper's restraints, burning through them like they were spider silk. Even with soot and blood on her she was beautiful. She looked like a china doll, not the destructive witch she'd proved herself to be. Finley watched as flame ignited in Lady Ash's palm and slowly licked its way up her arm, until her entire body was engulfed. The flame didn't harm her, dancing just above her skin. She watched in horror as the flame took on the form of a long whip in her hand.

The automaton that had shot her stomped toward Finley, pulling a large sword seemingly out of his very back as he walked. The floor between them trembled with every step. She'd be worried if those holes in her body were already starting to close themselves. Finley took two tiny capsules from her pocket, broke them open and jammed one into each entry wound, wincing as her ripped flesh protested. Organites in their pure form immediately set her insides tingling as they worked their magic. They were little beasties from the very cradle of life itself, responsible for the evolution of life. Putting them into her body might take her abilities up another notch and she didn't bloody care.

She forced herself to her feet. She wasn't bleeding quite so heavily now, couldn't feel the gurgling in her chest. She was going to live.

Too bad she couldn't say the same about the automaton. She punched her fist—with the brass knuckles Emily had fashioned for her—through the creature's chest, smashing its logic engine and dropping it in its tracks.

Lady Ash screamed—a ragged, eardrum-piercing sound that brought them all to a standstill. All but Griffin, that was. He was the one responsible for the woman's anguish.

Finley had no idea how he'd done it, nor how it was even possible, but somehow Griffin was using his own abilities to turn Lady Ash's power against her, so that her fire actually began to scorch her flesh and clothing. The awful smell of burning hair began to fill the air as Griffin seemed to glow from within—as though a light had been switched on inside him. Tendrils of power radiated from him, swirling around him like opalescent ribbons. That was new. The rest of the ribbons wrapped around Lady Ash.

It was also terrifying.

"Griffin!" She cried. He was going to kill the woman

if he didn't release her. Lady Ash might deserve to suffer for all she'd done—she'd killed people—but Griffin wasn't the law and he wasn't God. He'd already been haunted by one death this year; his conscience didn't need another. *"Griffin!"*

He still didn't acknowledge her. He began to lift off the ground, pulled up by his own power. Bloody hell, this was not good. She had to stop him.

But before Finley could help Griffin, she needed to take care of the automaton advancing on him. Her wounds were healing quickly, but she'd lost blood, and was still sore. She was nowhere near her peak fighting condition, but it was going to have to do. She had to stop that machine before she could stop Griffin from making a horrible mistake.

She oughtn't have worried. The metal hadn't even touched Griffin when an arc of sizzling blue light danced along its fingers, all the way up to its shoulder. The polished body began to convulse and gears ground and screeched. Sparks flew, and Finley raised her hands to protect herself from them. The automaton clattered to the ground, just as Finley saw what it was that had felled it.

Griffin had built a sort of energy field around himself and Lady Ash.

She wasn't going to make the same mistake of touching it.

"Griffin!" She cried, "You have to stop!"

And he did. Suddenly, the flames around the woman flickered out, and Griffin's feet touched the ground once again. She ran to him, but he held up a hand stopping her from coming any closer. "Don't," he said. When he turned to face her, both of his eyes glowed an eerie blue—no pupil and no iris, just blue. "Finley, don't come any closer."

She was dumb at times, but she wasn't stupid. If he told her not to come any closer it was because he was afraid of hurting her, and she would stand her ground. A few feet away from her Lady Ash crackled and smoked, her body slowly turning into her namesake. Griffin had killed her.

Finley stared at the charred corpse in horror, not because the woman was dead, but because Griffin wouldn't be able to live with himself for the death.

"Take a deep breath," she told him. "Just calm down."

"Get out of the way, Fin." His voice was quiet and hard. *"Now."*

"No." She shook her head, putting herself between him and the body. "You won't hurt me, Griffin. I know you won't."

"But I will," came a dark whisper from behind her. The threat slithered down her spine, but she refused to shudder. Instead, her gaze locked with Griff's. It was terrifying, that blue fire in his eyes, but not as terrifying as the realization that a ghost had just spoken to her.

"Garibaldi?"

Griffin nodded.

"You're more clever than you look," the voice whispered. Now that she knew who it was, Finley could hear his faint Italian accent.

"Thanks," she replied dryly, not making any sudden moves. Every instinct demanded she whirl around and put her fist through the villain's head, but that was the problem—her fist would go right through his head, and that was only if he was visible.

"Finley?" Emily asked, glancing from her to Griffin. "What's going on?"

Finley barely glanced at her. It looked as though the others had defeated their opponents, as well, but thankfully there was only one corpse. Every bit of machinery was still. Garibaldi obviously hadn't lost his touch when it came to controlling metal. "We've company."

"Behind you?" Emily asked. She wouldn't be able to see Garibaldi unless he wanted to make himself visible. She hadn't heard him either. None of the others had, except for Griffin. Finley had only heard him because she'd spent some time in the Aether with Griffin and had begun to become attuned to it.

"Right behind me." If the bastard had breath she'd no doubt feel it on the back of her neck.

There was a high-pitched whine and then a blast of white light so strong Finley was momentarily blinded. What the…?

Garibaldi swore—impressively. "Little bitch almost hit me!"

Another blast. This time Finley covered her eyes and dived to the ground. Emily wielded what looked like an Aether pistol, but she had modified it. This thing had a larger barrel, a smaller grip, and a flashing red light on the side. "Missed." The Irish girl was obviously not pleased. "Where is he now?"

Suddenly, a frigid weight slammed down on Finley's back, driving her face into the sooty carpet. She managed to turn her head at the last second to avoid being suffocated. Being able to hear and see Garibaldi—and there had been plenty of times when she knew he'd been there and she couldn't see him—came with other issues: it made her susceptible to attack by creatures of the Aether. But if The Machinist thought she wouldn't risk herself to bring him down, he was sorely mistaken.

"E-Em," she called through chattering teeth. The

chill of death seeped deep into her bones. "He's on me. He's on my back!"

But before Emily could shoot, Griffin charged. One moment she was cold as ice, and the next, the weight was off her. She flipped onto her back—a motion that was far clumsier than it ought to be thanks to every muscle in her body being frozen stiff—and saw Griffin take Garibaldi to the ground. His power made The Machinist visible. He pummeled the ghost with his fists as his eyes blazed. Garibaldi laughed with every blow. "That's it, lose control. It feeds me, you know."

The chill in Finley's heart had nothing to do with Garibaldi's touch and everything to do with his words. "Em, shoot here!" she placed her hand on the ground near The Machinist's head. All her friends would see was Griffin's fists flying, not what he struck. She whipped her head around as another blast struck, narrowly missing her thumb.

It also missed Garibaldi, who pushed himself up, taking Griffin with him, until they were both on their feet and The Machinist had his hands wrapped around the younger man's wrists.

"Got you now," he said, chuckling. "You're mine, Your Grace."

Finley jumped to her feet and leaped at The Machinist. She grabbed at him, but her arms took only air, and she slammed into the ground once more. Emily opened fire again, the blast aimed right at the spot where Garibaldi stood. It would have hit him if he hadn't disappeared.

And he had taken Griffin with him.

Mila lazed on the sofa, her boots propped up on the arm as she popped grapes into her mouth. She liked grapes very much. In fact, they were one of her favorites of all the foods she'd tasted thus far. Almost as good as that Indian chicken dish Jack had bought her last night.

Stupid Jack.

She was still learning words, as well. *Stupid* was one of the newer additions to her vocabulary. She'd been using it a lot lately, especially where Jack was concerned.

Two months she'd been living in this house with Jack. Two months of incredible food, interesting words, extraordinary books and plays and music. Two months of filling her mind with so much information she thought she might explode, and she kept wanting more.

Two months of Jack being so stupid she wondered how he managed to function in the world. At first she thought the fault lay with her own brain, because she'd been an automaton once, but then she realized that, no, Jack was simply defective. That was bothersome, because he seemed completely adequate in many other ways. In fact, he seemed so smart in many other ways.

Just not when it came to women. Not only did he seem completely ignorant of the changes she'd gone through since coming to live with him, but he chose the most annoying, foolish, idiotic, pretentious, untrustworthy women. He had one upstairs with him right now. And judging from the noises—and the pictures she'd seen in a naughty book he'd since hidden from her—she had a pretty good idea what he was doing with her. It was enough to make even the sweetest grape sour on her tongue.

If Jack's stupidity ruined her palate for grapes she'd gut him like a…well, whatever people gutted.

Above her head she heard a thump—her hearing was most exceptional. Apparently everything about her was exceptional, or at least that was what Emily told her. Emily was terribly smart, so it must be true. But if she was so bloody exceptional, why didn't Jack realize it? He seemed to think of her as a child or a pet—she had yet to work out the subtle differences between the two. She knew it was something pertaining to biology and such, but emotions were complex and she didn't completely understand them yet.

She only knew that no one could make her happier, angrier or sadder than stupid Jack Dandy. And she was stuck in the bloody house listening to him entertain another woman with dubious hair color. It didn't matter where in the house she went, she'd hear. She could go out, but Jack didn't like her going out at night, especially alone. What did he think would happen to her? If anyone came near her, she was physically capable of defending herself—more than capable. She wasn't naive enough to just go off with someone, and it wasn't as though she'd would go looking for trouble. She just didn't want to be there, in that house. Listening.

Thump. She glared up at the ceiling. It would serve the two of them right if she climbed up on some furniture and smashed her fist through the floor. How fast would that painted-up…*tart* run away when she realized that Jack's houseguest, the one he hid away but sometimes referred to as his "ward," was not normal?

Another thump—followed by a trill of laughter that made Mila's teeth ache, or maybe it was the clenching of her jaw that made them hurt. She swung her feet off the sofa and stood up, setting the bowl of grapes on the table. She had to do something to distract herself. She could get a book, but she didn't feel like reading. She could listen to music, but Jack had taken the phonographic cylinder player upstairs with him.

Pity he hadn't put some music on, but even if he had

she'd still hear. The tart was loud enough she could be heard over the scream of a steam whistle.

She glanced at the polished mahogany bar in the corner. Bottles of liquor were neatly placed on shelves beneath it. She knew this because she'd seen Jack take them out. He'd taken a bottle upstairs with him earlier.

What was so amazing about the stuff? She'd tried to take a sip once and he'd torn a strip off her for it. Well, he wasn't there to stop her now. A little smile curved her lips as she walked over to the bar and behind it. Yes, tonight seemed the perfect time to do something Jack didn't like. *Spite,* she believed it was called. It was a good word, and she was full of it.

Crouching, she withdrew one of the bottles, uncorked it and poured herself a full glass of the contents. She took a sniff. Not too bad. Then she raised the glass to her lips and drained it in several long gulps. She set the glass back on the bar and waited.

Nothing happened.

She repeated the process again. And again. The third time she paused to enjoy the warmth that filled her belly. Hmm. Perhaps she oughtn't have drunk it so fast—the bottle was empty. Well, that was a short diversion. She went back to the sofa and her grapes. A few moments later, as she lifted a grape to her lips, it wavered slightly. She frowned at it. No, there was only one grape in her fingers, not two. But two would be better, wouldn't it? She plucked another one with her other hand and held them up side by side.

"Jolly fine weather we're having, is it not, Mr. Grapeypants?" she asked in a low voice, bouncing the left grape up and down.

"It is indeed, Lord Cabernet," "replied" the right grape in a higher pitch. "Nary a cloud to be seen. And isn't it a travesty, the price of tea these days?"

"Highway robbery. We've taken to using the same leaves over and over until the pot runs clear."

"A sound notion."

Mila laughed. Now, this was a diversion!

Another thump from upstairs. More laughter—and this time she heard the familiar sound of Jack's chuckle. It ruined her fun, and made her angry.

Very, *very* angry, which was surprising because she'd heard that wine was supposed to make a person happy. The laughter continued. Mila reached behind her and took a candlestick from the small table. She tested the weight of it in her palm and then tossed it upward with all her strength. It broke through the ceiling, trailing plaster dust as it tore through the floor of Jack's bedroom. The doxy screamed. Jack swore. From where she sat, Mila could see through the hole the candlestick created, to where it had lodged itself in the ceiling above.

She grinned. She was still grinning when a portion of Jack's scowling face appeared above the hole.

"What the bloomin' 'ell was that all about?" he demanded. "'Ave you gone completely mad?"

Completely mad? That implied that he thought her *somewhat* mad, didn't it? Her grasp on language might not be as good as it ought, but she knew what *mad* meant. She tossed Lord Cabernet and Sir Grapeypants into the bowl with their society friends and set it aside. Then she jumped up on the sofa. Another big jump and she was able to grab a handhold in the hole she had made. Jack backed up—good thing, too. She drew back her arm and snapped her fist upward, knocking another chunk of ceiling loose.

More screams from the woman. Mila was going to shove the woman's own knickers into her mouth just to shut her up. She punched again, and this time a large enough chunk fell—onto the sofa—that she was able to bring her other hand up and haul herself through the jagged opening.

Jack stared at her as though he truly thought her insane. As if he thought she was a monster. Mila had never wanted to hit him before, but she did now. How could he look at her as if he didn't know her? As if he didn't understand?

"Wot the 'ell?" He was on his feet now—clad only

in a pair of black trousers that weren't fastened all the way. His naked flesh was quite captivating, though Mila wasn't certain why. She'd seen him undressed before, but now she wanted to put a shirt—or her hands—on him. Behind him, his "companion" tried to hide her nudity with her garish gown. Her naked flesh was not so captivating. In fact, the sight of it made Mila want to toss her out the bloody window.

Instead, she turned to Jack. "You're stupid," she informed him. Her tongue felt thick and heavy in her mouth. "Stupid, stupid, stupid. You're a stupid-head. And you're loud, and pretty and…" Her attention went back to the woman. "Your laugh hurts my ears like a screeching door hinge."

"Are you drunk?" Jack demanded.

"How should I know?" Mila shot back. "I don't know what drunk is!"

"Right." He took her arm. "You're wasted."

Waste. That was bad, wasn't it? Mila jerked free of his hold. "I am not. I'm angry. How can you *seem* so smart and be so *not* smart?" She ran a hand through her hair; it came out covered in plaster dust. Blast.

Jack frowned at her. He was pretty even when he frowned. "I told you to stay away from the liquor cabinet."

Mila scowled back. "You told her—" she pointed at

the woman who had since donned her shift and was climbing into her gown "—that she was pretty. Obviously you are not consistent with the truth."

The tart—Darla—gasped and Mila rolled her eyes. Surely the woman had heard worse insults than that.

"Go to your room," Jack instructed sternly. "Later the two of us is going to 'ave a serious chat."

"I hate it when you talk like that," she shot back. "Speak per-properly."

He grabbed her arm again and propelled her toward the door. Honestly, she wouldn't have been surprised if he'd shoved her back through the hole. "Get out."

Jack yanked open the door to reveal the new housekeeper he'd hired for Mila. Why he thought Mila needed someone to look after her when she had him, Mila had no idea. He'd said something about propriety that she didn't understand and still didn't quite comprehend. Basically he'd hired the woman to make sure he didn't treat Mila like one of his "ladies."

What if she wanted him to treat her that way?

"Beggin' your pardon, Mr. Dandy, but is everything quite all right?" the older woman asked in her Northern accent.

Jack forced a smile. Mila knew it was forced because it looked nothing like his real smile. "Goin' to need someone what to fix that 'ole, missus. Be a love and take care of that would you?"

"Of course, sir." She continued to stand there. Mila grinned at her and waved. The housekeeper—Mrs. Brooks—tentatively waved back. "Are you unwell, child?"

"Wasted," Mila replied with a grin. Jack, she noted, winced.

"Be a love and escort Mila to her room, missus." And then, to the doxy he said, "You best be on your way, love."

"Yes," Mila chirped. "Do be on your way."

"Oy." Jack poked her. "Don't be rude."

"That wasn't rude," she protested. "Rude would be—" And then she threw up all the lovely wine and grapes all over Darla's skirts.

Where was he?

Griffin tried to sit up, but thick straps over his chest, arms and legs kept him from rising. The spots where the straps touched him felt cool—wrong. There was something about them that separated him from the Aether, made it impossible for him to use his abilities in any way. What were they made of? It bothered him that he didn't know what they were or how to combat them.

He was too tired to panic. He'd never gotten into a

situation he couldn't get himself out of, and he'd get out of this one. He just had to keep his wits about him. Garibaldi would want him to be afraid and off balance.

He closed his eyes. Was Finley all right? At least Garibaldi hadn't taken her, as well. When he saw Lady Ash, and then that automaton, shoot her…well, he'd lost all reason. If he lived to be one hundred he would never regret killing that woman—something he'd never thought himself capable of feeling, but he'd slaughter an army to protect Fin.

She was probably ripping London apart looking for him.

But he wasn't in London.

Griffin's eyes snapped open. He was in the Aether. How was that possible? How could Garibaldi imprison him there and render him powerless? It was his element, he should be strong, but instead he was as weak as a newborn kitten trying to hold its head up. He reached out for any hint of power and felt the bands around him tighten. There was pressure on his head, as well—like a set of fingers digging into his skull. He could feel his power being siphoned through those conduits. Garibaldi was leeching the Aether from him to keep him weak. Helpless.

Still refusing to panic, he glanced around at his surroundings. The implements digging into his scalp prevented him from turning his head much, but he could see that he was in a house. Garibaldi was strong enough to construct within the Aether. Bloody hell, that was not good. The man would be practically a god in this world, while Griffin's power was being slowly drained—probably to strengthen Garibaldi, the bastard.

Leonardo Garibaldi was a villain in every sense of the word, and the closest Griffin had ever come to having a nemesis. Not only had the man been responsible for the death of Finley's father, but he had instigated the deaths of Griffin's own parents, with whom Garibaldi had once been close. He had also tried to turn Sam against his friends and used him as something of a spy. They thought they had defeated him and his plans to build sentient automatons, but he'd come back again, kidnapping Emily and almost killing Sam. Some of his friends had thought Garibaldi's death put an end to his criminal career, but apparently death only served to make him stronger, something Griffin had feared might happen.

He was trapped with a vengeful madman in the land of the dead, a land of pure energy. He'd known only one other living person who had been able to access this dimension—Nikola Tesla. Tesla had built a suit that allowed him to put himself into a deathlike state so he could access the Aether. The man had been attacked by some of Garibaldi's "demons" and had given the suit to Griffin for safekeeping.

The suit was at his house, and if he knew Finley half as well as he thought he did...*damnation*. The girl was mad enough to put the suit on and come looking to rescue him. If she did that there was no way that he could protect her—not that Finley was the sort of girl who would count on that anyway. Still, the idea of her at Garibaldi's mercy was enough to tighten his gut and seize his heart. Physically she was a match for anyone, even Sam. But in the Aether she would be at a disadvantage, vulnerable.

He had to escape before she decided to come looking for him. He pushed against the restraints, digging his booted heels into the mattress. The straps didn't even budge and he fell back panting and sweating. A wave of dizziness washed over him, bringing with it a flush of sick heat.

"Struggling won't do you any good."

Griffin went still at the sound of Garibaldi's voice. The older man drifted into the room, a gray-hued pantomime of a human. In death he'd made himself "more" than he had been in life. His hair was thicker, his face more chiseled. He might even be slightly taller. Regardless, he was still a vain madman with delusions of grandeur.

He smiled at Griffin. "I designed those restraints just for you, Your Grace. They'll not let you go now that I've got you."

"What do you want?" The straps around his head made it difficult to move his jaw so the words came out slightly slurred.

His enemy's face darkened. "I want to be alive again, but you made certain that could never happen."

Griffin simply stared at him. His silence obviously angered the ghost, whose eyes filled with black. He lunged forward. Griffin tried not to flinch, but it was impossible.

Garibaldi chuckled—a dry, rasp. "And so, I'm going to make you suffer, young Greythorne. Suffer like no one has ever suffered in the history of the world."

Still Griffin said nothing.

The Machinist leaned down and whispered close to his ear, "I'm going to make your little band of misfits suffer, as well. I'm going to make you watch."

He couldn't help it—Griffin tried to rise up, but all he did was jerk hard against the restraints.

Garibaldi laughed again. "That's what I want. I will so enjoy the pain their deaths will bring you."

"Bastard."

Dark eyes bore into his, and all trace of amusement

vanished from that cruel face. "You need to learn some respect, and I need to teach you who is in charge here."

As he spoke, he drew one of his fingers through Griffin's face—it was like an icicle being driven through his skull. The dead weren't tangible, but Griffin wasn't dead. The rules of this world didn't apply to him, especially when he couldn't use his abilities. Garibaldi's fingers slid through his flesh right into his chest, grabbed hold and squeezed. It hurt. Oh, hell, it *hurt*. He ground his teeth. He would not give the bastard the satisfaction of making a sound.

Blackness edged his vision, blurred it. His mind burned. Nothing existed but pain. Such pain.

Garibaldi smiled, cruel fingers searching. "Ah, there it is. I've always wanted to hold someone's heart in my hand." His fist tightened.

Griffin screamed.

Chapter 3

Gone.

Griffin was *gone*.

Finley stood in the doorway of the room they shared and looked around. She'd hoped to find him here when she came running up the stairs—hoped that he'd escaped Garibaldi and found his way back home. Honestly, she'd known he wouldn't be here the moment they arrived. He hadn't come to greet them and let them know he was all right.

Which meant that he wasn't all right at all.

Griffin was the strongest person she knew. If Garibaldi was strong enough to imprison him, then the madman had finally achieved the power he sought during the twisted course of his life. There was no telling what the villain might be able to do now.

Her heart kicked hard against her ribs, seized by a terrible fear that refused to let go no matter how hard she pushed. Garibaldi might kill Griffin. No, there was no *might* about it. Garibaldi *would* kill him, just as he had killed Griffin's parents and her real father. The only question was how long did she have before the terrible event took place?

The Machinist wouldn't do it quickly, and that was as much a blessing as it was terrible. He'd want to make Griffin suffer, and that meant kept keeping him alive. Didn't it? Or would Garibaldi decide to torture Griffin's soul for eternity instead? God, it was too much to even think about—too many wild and awful places her imagination could go. She couldn't think of what might happen, she had to concentrate on what she was going to do about Leonardo Garibaldi's insane ghost. Were they never going to be free of the man? First he'd tried to take over England with a false queen, and then he'd tried to implant his brain into an automaton. Now he had Griffin.

She was not going to cry, no matter how much her eyes burned or her throat tightened. Her eyeballs could ignite and she'd still refuse to cry in order to drench the flames. Griffin didn't need her tears, he needed her help. So, no—she was *not* going to throw herself on the bed they shared, bury her face in his pillow and sob herself dry. She would *not* bawl and snot and pray for him to return to her. What she was going to do was figure out how to bring Griffin home and rid them of Garibaldi once and forever.

But how? It wasn't as though she could simply kill Garibaldi either. Despite all her concern about Griffin killing Lady Ash, she knew she would find it incredibly easy to kill The Machinist. The problem wasn't whether or not she could stand to kill him, it was the fact that the villain was already dead. Unless someone figured out a way to kill a ghost, the pleasure of ending the bastard's life would not be hers. Never mind that killing him wouldn't necessarily save Griffin. She needed to find him first, and how the bloody hell was she to do that? It was only because of Griffin that she could see what little ghostie bits she could, so it wasn't as though she could trust her eyes and search for him. Maybe Emily had some sort of contraption that could isolate his unique Aetheric resonance—if he had such a thing, whatever it was.

Not like she could simply kill herself and go into the Aether to rescue Griffin.

Couldn't she? The thought came to her as though sent via divine messenger, and latched on to her mind with sharp and certain claws.

Finley pivoted on the thick heel of her boot and left

the room. Her dress and tailcoat were dirty from the earlier scuffle, but she didn't take the time to change. Clean clothes could wait; Griffin could not.

Her friends had gone to check other rooms in the house just in case Griffin had returned, but she didn't find them in any of the rooms, which meant they were probably in Emily's laboratory beneath the house, their search having turned up as empty and fruitless as her own. Finley took the lift down and stepped out onto the stone floor. Everyone was already there, just as she suspected.

No one asked if she'd found Griff. The fact that she was there alone meant she hadn't.

"What are you doing?" she asked. They were all gathered around Emily at one of the worktables. The walls and shelves throughout the vast space were covered with tools, bits of machines and automatons and other bits and bobs. A large vault contained the remains of several dangerous automatons, including the one that had almost killed Sam, and the Victoria automaton Garibaldi had created.

Wildcat lifted and turned her head. Her full lips curved into a slight smile. "Emily's trying to adjust a portable telegraph so it will pick up Aetheric transmissions."

So Aetheric resonance just might be a thing after all.

The portable telegraphs already utilized the Aetheric realm for communicating with one another, so it was a sound idea as far as Finley was concerned. However, she understood the Aether about as well as she understood the secrets of the Javanese, which was to say, not at all. However, she'd gargle while standing on her head, reciting the Magna Carta in Latin if someone told her that was the way to get Griffin back.

"How do we know he's even in the Aether?" Jasper asked. He'd removed his cowboy hat, and the tips of his hair stuck out like little wings. "That scoundrel could've taken him anywhere, right? I reckon Griffin's abilities could make that possible."

They all looked at Emily, who was uncharacteristically vexed. "Oh, right. Ye all look to me for the answer, well, I don't have a single one! I'm going on pure assumption and grasping at straws. Being dead, it's most likely Garibaldi has Griff in the Aether—it's the one place he knows we can't look, and the place he has more power. Unfortunately, I know next to nothing about the Aether—that was Griffin's area of expertise."

"You know more than the rest of us," Sam reminded her in a gentle tone. He placed one of his big hands on her shoulder. "No one's putting the responsibility of finding him on you, Em."

"No," Finley agreed. "In fact, I plan to take that responsibility on myself."

Now they all turned to her, in unison like a monster with four heads. "Do ye now?" Emily asked, arching a ginger brow as she crossed her arms over her brocade waistcoat in a challenging manner reminiscent of a school matron confronting a naughty pupil. "Would you care to explain how and why to the rest of us, who I wager want him back just as much as you do?"

"Of course," Finley replied, ignoring her friend's attitude for the sake of their friendship. "You're going to kill me."

"Are you out of your ever-loving mind?"

Finley opened her mouth to speak, but Emily cut her off—the girl loved a good tirade. "Kill you? That's your bloody solution? And then what do we do when we get Griffin back?" She banged a spanner against the workbench. "Tell him that killing you was the best we could manage?"

This time when she opened her mouth, Finley put her hand over Emily's to prevent another detailed account of how idiotic she was, because she knew it was coming. "No, that's when you wake me up." Her gaze locked with her friend's. Emily's bright eyes snapped with annoyance, worry and fear. Emily was always the smartest person in the room, and at that moment, Finley reckoned her friend had no more answers than she did. "I'm going to use the Aetheric Mortality Disambiguation suit to go into the Aether and find Griffin."

They gaped at her. She felt Emily's jaw drop beneath her hand—only then did she remove her fingers.

"Oh," Sam said. "I see." A man of many words, he was.

Wildcat frowned and looked to Jasper, feline eyes bright against the dusky hue of her complexion. "What the heck's an Aetheric Mortality whatchamacallit suit?"

"That Tesla fella made it," he explained in his American drawl, casting a perplexed glance in Finley's direction. "Don't know much more about it than it kills folks so they can go into the Aether."

Black curls bobbed as she shook her head, her scowl deepening. "Who'd want to die?"

His lips quirked on one side. "Says the girl with nine lives. Some folks want to know what happens after we die."

She made a face. "Who cares? You're dead."

Finley would have chuckled if her stomach wasn't in knots. "Em? Will you do it?" She intentionally chose *will* rather than *can*. She had no doubt her friend could kill her and bring her back, but whether or not she would...

Emily's ginger brows were knit tight, the edges of each almost meeting over the bridge of her pert nose. "You know I will, you daft baggage. As if we have any other option."

Relief struck with such force Finley almost doubled over. She wanted to fall down on her knees before her friend and babble her thanks, but she couldn't move. Couldn't speak. She would find Griffin. She would. She would find him and get him out of the Aether. They'd worry about Garibaldi later.

"Tesla only used the suit for a few moments," Sam said. He'd actually been present in New York when the genius inventor showed off his creation. "Is that enough time for her to find Griff?"

That was an annoyingly astute question for the big brute to ask. Should she pinch him for asking, or herself for not? A few minutes might be enough time to find Griffin, but the Aether was a big and vast dimension— its own world. Garibaldi would have him well hidden. The villain didn't know about the suit, but he had to know they wouldn't just let him win.

Then again, maybe he thought he already had. In which case it might be very easy to find them. But then there was the fact that time moved at a different pace there… Oh, damnation. She had no idea how long it would take or how long the suit would give her.

Apparently Emily did, however. "The suit has a cooling system to safeguard against loss of oxygen, as well as an Aetheric field that slows down all metabolic functions. When used properly, and if monitored correctly, it acts as a bubble, or stasis field, putting the body into a near-death state."

Sam smiled at her before turning to the others. "That means that Finley can stay in the Aether for a long time."

Emily patted his arm like a proud mother. "That's right, lad."

Arching not one, but both brows, Finley resisted the urge to shake her head at them. "How long will I have?"

The little redhead turned to face her and shrugged. "Forty to sixty minutes if I had to guess."

"And if you didn't have to guess?"

"For most people I'd be certain of forty, but you're not most people. You're ability to heal and your physicality may afford you more time."

"But there's no way of knowing?"

"I could equip the suit with some sort of safety feature that would sound an alarm once your brain activity and oxygenation levels began to drop. It would trigger the Lazarus switch."

"Resurrection," Finley murmured. She wasn't having second thoughts or cold feet, but dying was a risky thing, and she had heard about the Aether demons that had attacked Tesla when he wore the suit. They were Garibaldi's creations and they would come for her, as well. She'd already tangled with some of his creatures before. It would not be easy. It would be dangerous and she would be totally alone.

But Garibaldi had Griffin, and she would die a hundred times to save him. Too bad she only had to die once for everything to fail.

"How quickly can you make the changes, Em?" No sense in thinking about what bad things could happen. She had to concentrate on the task at hand.

Her friend looked at the suit, as though she could take each section and devise a dependable schedule. She probably could. Lord, Emily could probably estimate right down to the quarter hour. "Three hours and ten minutes," Emily responded.

Better than the quarter hour. "No faster?"

Her friend shot her a cross look. "No. No faster. That's fast enough. Maybe you're fool enough to risk your life, but I'm quite committed to making certain both you and Griffin come back from this."

"Fair enough."

"However, the process would be easier, and possibly a bit faster with an assistant."

"I'll help you," Sam said.

Emily wrapped her arm about his waist and squeezed herself against him. "I know you would, but your hands are too big for the delicate work." She tilted her head back and smiled up at him. "Besides, I need you to keep me sane, not drive me mad."

All this romance was well and good, but Finley felt it like a thorn under her fingernail. "Could you stop batting your eyelashes at each other long enough to help me save Griffin?"

To her credit, Emily didn't seem the least bit irked by her snotty tone—which only drove the thorn deeper. What if she never got to touch Griff again? "Plus, Finley is in need of someone to fight with, and you've always been very good at that."

Well, that was a bit of a surprise. Finley never thought Emily would suggest she and Sam fight especially after that time she almost killed him.

Sam regarded her thoughtfully—another aggravation. When did Sam Morgan become someone who was thoughtful? Usually she thought him fairly vacant of thought, the big dunderhead. Although, he had been surprisingly ingenious on occasion. "I can do that."

No doubt he could. It was like fighting a mountain, sparring with him. Was it wrong that she was a little excited at the prospect? All that fear for Griffin turned so easily to bloodlust, itching to be indulged. At least she wouldn't be sitting around feeling useless. She had to be calm when she went into the Aether. Her temper wouldn't do her any favors when she needed to keep her wits about her.

"Run along, then," Emily told them in her best school matron voice. "Jasper, I don't need you right now, but I will when it comes time to engage the stasis field. Wildcat, I'd like you to stay and assist me."

Cat looked surprised, but didn't protest. The American girl was with Jasper now, but the two of them sometimes went off and had their own adventures outside of their group. No one begrudged them for it, but it had made it a little harder for her to become part of their little family. Hopefully this would change that. After the events in New York, it was only since Cat's arrival that the cowboy seemed like his former self. He was one of them, and if they wanted to keep him, they needed to welcome the girl he cared about, as well. If Emily was opening up to the idea, then Sam would follow shortly—he was always the last to trust anyone, taking his role of "family" protector to new levels of over-the-top. Finley liked Cat—they trained together on occasion. Direct and honest, Cat was exactly the sort of solid person Jasper needed in his life, and she wouldn't allow him to dwell on the past.

Although, there was something disconcerting about those fangs of hers. Sharp, they were. Then again, Jasper didn't seem to mind, and Finley had caught them kissing once, so it couldn't be an issue. Still, there were reasons they called her *Wild*cat, and Finley was pretty certain she didn't want to know all of them.

Sam stepped in front of her, blocking out the rest of the room. "Let's go."

Finley peered up at him. She barely cleared his shoulder and she was tall for a girl. "Itching to go toe-to-toe with me, Goliath?"

He smiled—actually smiled! "You're not?"

He had a point. She needed to do something about this fear simmering low in her gut. She was afraid— more afraid than she had ever been in her entire life. It threatened to take over completely, like when her other self would come out before Griffin taught her how to merge the two sides of herself. He had saved her, given her purpose, and he accepted her for who she was, flaws and all. She had a great number of flaws, but then again, so did he.

And she wanted more time putting up with them.

As she turned to follow Sam and Jasper to the lift, Finley paused. Her gaze sought out Emily, who opened the door to the locker where the Tesla "death suit" was kept. She must have felt Finley's attention because she whirled about.

"Thank you," she whispered.

Emily must also have a talent for deciphering the movement of lips because she smiled ever so slightly, but not before Finley saw fear in her eyes, as well. This had to work. She couldn't let Griffin die without knowing she loved him.

But she *was* going to die; Griffin's life depended on it.

Mila woke up to the sound of her brain beating out a tenacious rhythm against the inside of her skull. There was a sour taste in her mouth and her tongue felt as though it had been replaced by a dirty wool sock. A few days ago she would have actually felt her tongue to make certain that hadn't happened. Was it odd that she was disappointed she didn't do that now? She knew her tongue was exactly as it was, and that was good, but she missed…she missed the not knowing, and the need to find out.

Regret was a word she was becoming more and more familiar with.

Cautiously, she opened her eyes. *Bloody hell!* She closed them again. Her brain throbbed. Her stomach rolled. There was that regret again! And Jack was sitting in a chair just a few feet away, watching her like a cat watching a newborn mouse.

So this was what the morning after a night of too much drink felt like.

Summoning all her strength, she cracked one eye open again. It didn't hurt so much this time. She focused on him—and there was only one of him, unlike the two she'd seen after puking all over his lover. He was dressed entirely in black, as he often was, but his shirt was unbuttoned at the throat and he wasn't wearing a waistcoat or a jacket. His dark hair fell in waves about his shoulders. No bloke—Finley had taught her that word—should have such lovely hair. No bloke should be so lovely to look at either.

She ought to have vomited on him.

"She wakes," he commented dryly, long fingers following the scroll carved in the wooden arm of the chair. "How's your head, poppet?"

She tried to scowl at him but it was hard to do with only one eye open and her brain trying to come out her ears. "I think you know very well how my head is." She'd seen him the morning after indulging a little too much the night before. He looked then like she felt at that moment.

"Probably better than I ought" was his reply. He even smiled a little. He couldn't be too angry at her, then.

"Now, let's discuss how you're going to apologize to my friend for ruining her gown, and to me for pulling such a destructive, impulsive, childish stunt."

Or maybe he was.

Mila pushed herself into a sitting position. Her head was starting to hurt less—the benefit of having a metal skull and a fast metabolism. She also, she realized, had her pride. Or maybe it was stubbornness. She hadn't figured out the difference between the two yet, despite careful reading. She supposed she'd understand once she'd experienced both enough times to discern between them. "I'm not apologizing to your doxy, so you can just forget about that. I am sorry about the floor, but if the two of you weren't making so much noise I wouldn't have done it."

Jack arched a brow. The expression made him look somewhat sinister. Lucifer before the fall. Such a fascinating story. "Where did you learn the word *doxy?*"

She scowled as she took a peppermint from the crystal bowl on her nightstand and popped it in her mouth. "I heard one of your friends say it, so I looked it up in the dictionary." She'd started reading the huge books for something to do, in order to learn, but words were easier to learn when a body had examples to which to apply them. "And don't talk to me like I'm an imbecile or a child. I'm neither of those things."

His gaze flickered over her before glancing away. Was he actually flushed? That was an indication of fluster. Jack Dandy was never flustered. "No, you certainly are not." He cleared his throat. "I'm sorry you…overheard. That was wrong of me. You shouldn't be subjected to such things."

It was fortunate she couldn't frown any harder because her eyes would disappear under the onslaught of her lowered forehead. "Now you're talking like I'm some sort of fine lady. I'm not that either."

His head tilted to one side as his gaze came back to her. "What are you, then, poppet?"

Sometimes she hated that damn pet name. It was better suited to a small child. And she hated that condescending tone, as though he knew her better than she did. She might still be new, but she was the one who spent time in her own head, not him. "I'm a girl, Jack. I might have started a machine, but I'm still a girl, and I've got a girl's mind and a girl's heart…." She stopped. What was she saying? "I've got a girl's pride and a girl's feelings. If I was up here banging the headboard against the wall with some bloke, how would you like it?"

Jack's jaw hardened, as did his gaze. "That's never going to happen."

"Why not? You have your doxies, why can't I have mine?" How had their conversation taken this turn?

Mila didn't know and she didn't care. A fight was just what she was spoiling for, and she knew Jack was game to give it to her.

"You will never, ever have a man in your room, Mila. I forbid it."

Forbid? Heat rushed to her face. Indignation was stronger than common sense, because the look on his face should have silenced her. She should have at least wondered why he looked as though he'd kill anyone who touched her. "*You're* in my room."

"That's different."

"So, it's not having a man in my room that's the issue. It's having a man in my bed."

He leaped to his feet and moved toward the door. "We're not having this discussion."

Mila followed after him. "Why not? Why can you do it and I can't?"

"Because no one is going to treat you that way."

"But you treat girls 'that way.'"

That stopped him—just a step or two away from the door. He froze as though she'd tossed a bucket of ice water on him. "Yes, I have," he murmured. "But that doesn't mean it's right. And no one's going to do it to you."

"That's a bit of hypocrisy, don't you think?" She'd just learned that word yesterday. What a perfect time to use it! "And it's stupid. If you can have such 'friends' I should be able to, as well." But she didn't want those sort of friends. She wanted…

She wanted Jack.

Mila recoiled as though someone had punched her in the chest. That's why she was so upset over Jack and his girls. Why she got so angry. She was…what was the word? *Jealous*. She didn't want Jack to be with other girls because she wanted him for herself, and she didn't want to share him.

"I know it's hypocritical," he explained, oblivious to her epiphany (another timely word!), "but it's the way of the world. Girls are expected to behave with more propriety than fellows. Feminine virtue is something to be respected and saved for marriage, which is a load of rot, but it should at least be reserved for someone you love. Someone worthy."

Virtue. She had heard the word before, but wasn't clear on its meaning. "You mean virginity? I'm not even sure I have one of those."

"Oh, bugger." Jack ran a hand over his face. Were his cheeks actually red? "That's not the point."

"Then what is?"

"The point is that you deserve better than a meaningless tussle. You're worth more than that."

"What am I worth, Jack?"

He turned on his heel. She stepped toward him, closing the distance so that their chests were almost touching. He was maybe four or five inches taller than her own considerable height. There was something in his eyes she couldn't comprehend, but it made her want to grab him by the shirtfront, haul him close and press her lips to his—press her everything to his. Maybe make a little noise of their own. A wave of warmth rushed up her neck.

"You're worth more than I am, poppet. Worth more than any bloke, and don't ever let anyone tell you different. You deserve a good life and a good man."

"What if I don't want a good man?" She knew from remarks he'd made during their time together that Jack thought of himself as the very opposite of good. He sometimes seemed to wear his underworld connections as if they were badges of honor, something to be proud of.

His eyes widened. "You're obviously still drunk. We'll discuss the floor and whether or not you'll apologize when you're sober."

"Jack." He kept walking toward the door. His hand closed around the crystal knob, started to turn it.... "Jack!" She moved fast—incredibly fast—and slammed her palm against the heavy oak. The wood groaned under the impact—splintered just enough to poke the tender flesh inside her hand.

He didn't look at her, didn't speak, but they both knew he wasn't getting out of that room until she allowed it. He was no match for her physically. Emotionally, however, was a different story. When he finally turned his head, his eyes were like glistening pools of darkness that cast a soothing spell over her, tugging her deeper and deeper into their depths until she'd do whatever he asked.

The bounder.

Mila shook her head, clearing the fog Jack had created. He'd almost had her—almost made her open the door. Jack had a talent for getting his way.

"Not fair," she said from between clenched teeth.

"No less than you using your strength against me. Open the door."

"No."

He drew his shoulders back, anger tightening his features. "Mila, open the damn door. I've had enough of your sulking and pouting. Sober up and I'll take you for an ice. We can do whatever you want."

She stared at him. He thought she was pouting? And did he truly believe a bloody ice would fix it? "You really are stupid, aren't you?"

Jack's brows lowered. "What the devil is wrong wit—"

Mila didn't think, she just wanted to shut him up. She grabbed him by the shirt and lifted herself up on her toes.

And then she kissed Jack Dandy. And it was wonderful.

Chapter 4

Three weeks earlier…

"I need you to explain something," Mila announced as they left the little theater. They had just seen a production of *An Ideal Husband* by Oscar Wilde.

Jack buttoned up his long, black frock coat. "All right."

"Why didn't the wife just tell her husband she'd gone to visit his friend? Why was it such a terrible thing?"

"Because he was a single gentleman and she called upon him at night without a companion."

She shook her head. "That still makes no sense."

"Ladies aren't supposed to call on gentlemen at their homes, and certainly not without a chaperone."

"Can a gentlemen call on a lady without a chaperone?"

"Yes, but he shouldn't if he really likes her. People might think ill of her."

Mila kicked at a pebble with the toe of her shoe. "That's stupid."

Jack laughed. "It is." He shrugged. "But, that's how it is."

"But why?" She knew she asked a lot of questions, and Jack had been very good about answering them, but the world was just so bloody confusing. Sometimes she didn't think she'd ever understand.

"Because a lady's virtue is her greatest possession, apparently. And a gentleman might lose control of himself and take advantage of her."

Virtue. That was pureness. It was a synonym for virginity, as well. "Do men usually lose control of themselves?"

He opened the door to his steam carriage for her, so that she might climb in. "I'd like to think that they do not, no."

She waited until he'd walked around and climbed in the other side. "You have ladies visit you."

Jack paused, and she knew he was trying to think of a way to lie to her. He did that sometimes. "That's different." That was what he always said when he didn't want to talk about it.

"Do you take advantage of your ladies?"

He made a strangled sound as he ignited the engine. "No."

"What do you do with them?"

"That's really none of your business, poppet. Not something you need to know about."

"Do you have intercourse with them?" She'd read about intercourse in a book she'd found underneath the sofa.

His head turned, and he looked at her with an expression of…surprise? Horror? Bloody hell, she couldn't tell! "How do you know about that?"

If she told him, he'd take the book away. "That's really none of your business."

"It is so my business!" Jack's eyes were wide and black in the dim light.

Something in his tone made her fold her arms over her chest and glare out the window. "I don't like how there seems to be separate rules for girls and boys. It's not fair."

Jack steered the carriage out into traffic. An old-fashioned carriage pulled by four automaton horses, their brass gleaming, raced past them. "No, it's not. But it's the way of the upper class."

"Then, I don't want to be part of the upper class."

"I don't think you'll have much choice. That's the sphere into which His Grace will introduce you."

"I don't understand why I can't stay with you."

"Because I'm exactly the sort of fellow a girl like you should avoid. Someday you'll see that."

Out of the corner of her eye, she glanced at him. "But you said you don't take advantage of those girls."

He kept his gaze on the road. A muscle in his jaw flexed. "I don't, but that doesn't mean I'm a good man, poppet."

"But you're the best person I know. I love you."

The carriage swerved. Jack yanked on the steering mechanism to correct it again. "You don't know what love is." He didn't say it meanly, but she resented it all the same. She couldn't argue, though. Maybe she *didn't* know what love was. But Emily had told her that love was when you cared about someone very much, and she did care about Jack. He was her whole world. The idea of being without him scared her.

"Do you know what love is?" she asked.

He shook his head. "And I don't want to. I've seen what love does to people."

"What?"

Jack sneered—it was an awful expression on his lovely

face. "It makes them weak. Makes it easy for other people to hurt them, use them and toss them aside."

"Did that happen to someone you know?"

"Yes."

"Who?"

For a moment she thought he wasn't going to answer her—that meant that a conversation really was over. "My mother. She thought my father loved her, but he didn't. Unfortunately, she loved him, and it ruined her."

Mila didn't quite grasp the depth of his mother's disappointment, but she knew when Jack was upset, and when he was angry. That his father had been mean to his mother upset him and made him really angry, and that was a bad thing. "I'm sorry."

He flashed her a slight smile before returning his attention to the street. "You're sweet, you know that? You're probably the nicest person I've ever met."

Warmth blossomed inside her. It was like pleasure, but more—as if her heart were being blown up like a balloon. She smiled—and then remembered her manners. "Thank you."

"That's why I'm going to make certain you are never in a position to be dependent on a man. You'll never go hungry. No one will look at you as less than what they are. No one will ever take away your sweetness."

She looked at him. "Like your father did your mother?"

"Yes."

"I don't understand. Why would you even want me to marry someone of the upper class, then?"

"They're not all awful. His Grace is all right. I want you to be comfortable and taken care of."

"I can take care of myself," she said, as the lamps of the carriage illuminated familiar streets. They were almost home.

Jack chuckled. "Physically, yes. But there are still a lot of things you need to learn about the world, poppet."

"Like what?"

"Like that people lie. They steal. People can hurt you emotionally as well as physically. It's worse than being hit."

Mila frowned. "Who hurt you, Jack?"

For a moment, there was an odd vulnerability in his eyes, but then it was gone. "No one." He reached across the leather seat and took her hand. "I promise you that I will never hurt you—not intentionally. No matter what happens now or in the future, you can always come to me. I will always be here for you. Do you understand?"

She nodded. "I understand."

But she didn't, not really. If she had, she would have known that Jack was lying again.

★ ★ ★

For the first time in the two decades he'd been alive, Jack Dandy couldn't think.

Jack could *always* think. Thinking—plotting, playing out every scenario—was what had kept him alive and built him a fortune. He started thinking the moment he woke up and sometimes he even thought in his dreams. Certainly no girl had ever interfered with the process before.

Not even Treasure.

Mila's lips turned his brain to gruel. No thoughts, only instinct, and instinct told him to enjoy this a little while, even though his conscience screamed in protest. His arms went around her waist, pulling her tight against him. His hands splayed across her back, feeling the movement of her muscles beneath cloth and skin. She was warm and soft and tasted like peppermint.

And he was *not* a good man.

Her fingers twisted in his shirt, tearing through the soft cotton as if it were nothing more than candy floss. She could easily crush his bones with those hands. The thought vanished as quickly as it had appeared—nothing more than a flicker in his mind. One of his hands came up and fisted in her wild hair—it felt like silk against his skin.

A loud shredding noise filled the silence—she'd torn

his shirt completely open. Warm fingers found their way beneath to touch his chest, roam over his stomach and ribs. He shivered. Her hands moved up to his shoulders, shoving the ruined garment down his arms.

Mila was trying to undress him. *Mila*.

Mila, who he had first found in a box—not even fully formed. She'd been monstrous and heartbreaking. Guilt had made him take her in and look after her, but something else made him let her stay. Responsibility was only part of it. Watching her grow and change made his head spin, it had all happened so fast. He tried to keep up, but he had to constantly remind himself that, while she was childlike, she grew in maturity by leaps and bounds. She was gorgeous and looked like a young woman. Pretty soon she was going to be just that, but not yet. And he had no right to take advantage of her curiosity.

Logic and sense returned with a vengeance. It didn't matter that she felt and tasted like a dream. Didn't matter that she made his heart pound or his limbs tremble. She was his ward. His responsibility. It was his duty to protect her, not to treat her like one of his girls. She was so much better than that. Better than him. She was naive and sweet and good. He would not be the one who ruined that.

But bloody hell, he wanted to.

Jack put his palms against her shoulders and pushed. Her metal skeleton made her heavier than she looked, and stronger, too. Still, he managed to put a couple of inches between them, which was just enough to break the kiss. The moment his lips left hers he felt a profound sense of loss that was both awesome and terrifying. Damnation, what was that feeling?

"Stop, poppet."

"Don't call me that." She tried to pull him close again, but he stepped back, and she ended up with nothing but a strip of his shirt in either hand. She looked at him, eyes wide and full of hurt confusion. She didn't understand, did she? No, of course she wouldn't. So smart in many ways, but the subtleties of humanity still escaped her grasp. She wouldn't understand that he *couldn't* treat her like that; she would only know that he'd pushed her away.

"We can't do this, Mila," he told her. "Do you understand that?"

"But I thought you liked it."

A strangled laugh lurched in his throat. *Liked* it? *Liked* didn't even begin to describe how he felt, which was all the more reason to walk out of this room *right bloody now.*

"It doesn't matter what I like. What matters is what's right."

She frowned and shook her head. "I don't understand. You liked it. I liked it. How can that not be right?"

He swore to himself. How could he make her understand when she hated all the bollocks about rules and expectations? "You're right, you don't understand, and I don't know how to make you. I just can't."

"You could with your doxy."

"You're not like her." No, she certainly wasn't. "You're not the same as those girls." She had the world laid out before her. He could make sure she had an education, employment if she wanted. And when the time came, he'd pay all the right people to make certain she found her way into good society and caught the eye of a man who might someday deserve her.

Mila nodded. "No, I'm not. It's all right, Jack. I understand. I'm sorry about your shirt."

His shirt? He didn't care about his shirt. He had other shirts. He cared about her. "It's all right, poppet. I can't imagine what it's like for you, with all these changes that have been happening in the past weeks." She'd gone from machine to human—a miracle in itself. She couldn't possibly understand it all. "I know very little about womanly...things. I'll ask Finley to talk to you about...how these things work." He had to assume that by now Treasure's relationship with His pain-in-the-arse Grace had progressed to a certain level. Not long ago that would have made him jealous enough to drink. Now he hoped for it. Hoped that Finley would know how to make Mila understand that he respected her too much to use her.

Something sparked in her eyes but quickly disappeared. "I wouldn't want to bother her."

"It would be no bother." Besides, Treasure owed him a favor or two. "I'm going to let you rest now. We'll talk about this more later, all right?" Truth was he was a top-notch coward, running away from the situation because he had no bloody idea what to do or say. His gut told him one thing and his conscience told him another. He didn't want to hurt her, but he wanted to kiss her again. He wanted it very badly.

She just watched him with those big sad eyes. "Goodbye, Jack."

"It's not really goodbye, poppet. We'll see each other at dinner."

Mila nodded. "Right."

Jack walked over to her and kissed her forehead. "It's all going to be fine." And it would be. He'd do everything in his power to make certain she had the best life she could ever have. She was not going to be tossed aside like he had been. He would care for and protect her until the world wasn't such a danger to her.

Only then would he let her go.

★ ★ ★

A trip to the library was not what Finley had in mind when she followed Sam from the cellar laboratory. It was not the sort of room that invited violence.

"Is this a new form of fighting?" she asked, glancing around the familiar room. She remembered when she'd first come there, Griffin smiling down at her from the balcony that ran along each wall. That day she'd thought him the finest thing she'd ever seen.

Floor to ceiling was shelf after shelf of books, and the ceiling was very, very high. Griffin had more books than her stepfather's shop, and he was a bookseller! Large, multipaned windows provided ample reading light during daylight hours, and gave the room an almost churchlike feel. Of course, that might just be her imagination, having grown up believing that knowledge gleaned through reading was close to godliness. "Are we going to throw books at each other?" Of course, she was joking. She'd never risk harming a book by throwing it at Sam's thick skull.

"Funny," he replied dryly. "I wouldn't do that to a book."

Finley blinked. Sometimes she and Sam were uncomfortably alike. "I didn't know you read."

He shot her a sour glance. "Emily helps me with the big words."

Heat flooded her face. Sometimes she deliberately needled Sam, poked at him like a slumbering bear, but it was never her intent to offend him. Not really. "I mean, I didn't think you enjoyed books."

He shrugged before making his way to one of the shelves. "Depends on the book. Em likes to read, and she likes it when we can talk about a story. I like making her happy, so I read. Jane Austen's not exactly my cuppa, but that Dickens bloke is all right enough. No more Shakespeare, though. Not even for her. That's just rhyming nonsense to me."

She couldn't help but grin—and it was all right because he wasn't looking. "The things we do for love, what?"

Sam pulled a leather-bound book from a shelf by his head, his expression droll. "Like risking your own death? That's mad."

"You're a fine one to talk. If the suit fit you, you and I would be duking it out to see who got to go after him."

He paused, then turned to face her, certainty etched into his rugged features. His dark gaze was blunt and clear. "No, we wouldn't."

Right. Because, if it was Emily who was missing, she wouldn't even try to stop him from going after her. In fact, when Emily was kidnapped, Finley had known

Sam had to take the lead on bringing her home. She hadn't dreamed of getting in his way, even though Em was her best friend and she was worried sick about her. She played her own part, but let Sam do what he felt was best.

The big lad's understanding of this made her turn her gaze away, to the shelves of books before them. She didn't like that her feelings for Griffin were so transparent. It didn't matter that they shared a bedroom, feelings were so personal. Private. Love made a person terribly vulnerable, and vulnerability was a state Finley despised. That he understood this made her want to punch him, and then perhaps give him a hug for being more of a dear than he had any right. "Why did you bring me here, Sam?"

He grabbed another book from a higher shelf—one she would have required a step stool to reach—and took them to the large desk at the front of the room. "These are books on the Aether."

Finley was skeptical. "The Aether was only discovered a decade ago, give or take. Those books look ancient." Really, one of them looked about ready to fall apart from its bindings.

"This one is," he replied, pushing the less battered one toward her. "The other was written a century ago by a husband and wife who interviewed people who died and came back to life. Griff and I used to play with it as kids, that's why it's in such a state. Boys aren't taught to be gentle."

She didn't care what boys were taught. Girls were lucky if they were taught to read. "I don't want to read about people who resisted going into the light, or saw God or all their ancestors. I want to save Griffin, and you're wasting my time." So much for him being a dear.

"Remember when you told me I was smarter than I looked?"

She might have done that more than once. It certainly sounded like something she might say. "Yes."

"Well, you're dumber than you look. The Aether is where the dead go on the first leg of their journey. This book details what those people who came back experienced there. The Aetheric dimension is one of energy, and there are a lot of strange and dangerous things there for people who don't belong."

He was right: she was dumb. She should have thought of that—she'd seen enough bizarre things from the Aether to know better. "Like people whose souls are still attached to their bodies."

Sam nodded. "This is what you're going to be doing until Emily sends for you. When you go in there, you're going to be as prepared as you can be. I want both you and Griff back safely."

A lump settled in her throat, but she covered it with humor. "Aw, Sam. You must really like me."

One of his dark brows arched, but his black eyes sparkled. "Not usually, but I do care about you, so don't get permanently killed in there, all right?"

Finley blinked. She opened her mouth to speak, but nothing came out.

Sam laughed. "I wish I had a photograph of the look on your face right now."

She shook her head. "Just wasn't expecting such a declaration, Samson."

"You have a habit of calling me by Biblical names. Do you find me legendary?"

"In your own mind." Real annoyance poked at the edges of her mind. "All right, crack open those books. Griffin's waiting."

He did as she commanded, and together they skimmed through the narratives until they found the meat of each account.

"This one talks about the Aether demons," she announced, full of surprise. "I thought Garibaldi made those."

"Wraiths have been around for a long time," Sam informed her, turning a page.

"How do you know that?"

"I started reading these books when we got back

from New York, more so after we tangled with Garibaldi last time. The demons are nasty things—all hate
and anger—ranging in size from small spheres to man-
size."

The ones they'd already faced hadn't been that big,
but they did a lot of damage. They had cut Griffin up
pretty badly. What kind of damage would something
bigger do? They could be cutting him right now. Flay-
ing him. Tearing him apart.

Fear gripped Finley hard, crushed her lungs and
stopped her heart. God, she couldn't breathe. "I'm
going to be too late, aren't I? Garibaldi's probably already killed him."

Sam looked at her with an expression that offered no
hope, no sympathy, but neither was it morose. "He'll
be hurt, but you'll find him. The bastard's not going
to kill him quickly."

His words were as effective as a dagger to the gut
and just as painful. He was right. The Machinist would
torture Griffin patiently—he was too caught up in his
desire for revenge to rush things now. He'd want to
make Griffin suffer. In a way that was good, because
they had time to find him alive, but who knew what
sort of shape he'd be in when she found him. It wasn't
just his spirit in the Aether, it was his physical self, and
every injury would show. Would scar.

A large hand settled over hers and squeezed. She hadn't realized how cold she was until that moment. "Griffin is the strongest person I know—stronger than you or me. You will find him, and the two of you will send Garibaldi to hell, where he belongs." Finley's gaze lifted to his. There was an awful lot of determination in the black depths of Sam's eyes. "I mean it. You're going to destroy him, you understand me? And you're going to do that for me."

Out of all of them Sam had the most personal vendetta against The Machinist. The man had manipulated him, kidnapped the girl he loved and now had his best friend. The man was also responsible for the automaton that had ripped Sam apart. Maybe they weren't really friends, but they were family now, and Finley would get revenge for Sam.

"I will," she promised.

He squeezed her hand before letting go, and they went back to the books. It was difficult to concentrate when she kept waiting for Emily to come for her, but Finley did the best she could. She needed to learn as much about the Aether as she could.

"Someone should send for Ipsley," she said, the thought suddenly occurring to her. Ipsley was a new friend of Griffin's and a medium. He was able to communicate with ghosts, so it stood to reason he could communicate with anyone in the Aether. "He might be able to reach out to Griffin, and even if he can't, I might be able to talk through him."

Sam immediately picked up the handset for the telephone that sat on the desk and tapped out a number. Griffin had had the private telephone installed just a month earlier. It was a new design by Bell that eliminated the need for an operator, and connected Aetherically to the local switchboard, opening a line on its own. Fantastic little thing, but expensive. Finley couldn't believe how much it cost to have them installed throughout the house—more money than her stepfather made in a year.

Sometimes Griffin's wealth frightened her. Many young men would suspect someone of her background of sniffing around after his money, but Griffin never did that. Another example of how well he knew her— if she wanted money she could think of a dozen ways she could easily make a fortune, and most of them were legal.

She half listened as Sam spoke to Ipsley, and took from his half of the conversation that the medium was all too happy to help. Sam hadn't given him details, but he had mentioned that Griffin was in trouble. Ipsley was a good enough friend that he only needed to hear that to come running.

Finley was reading about the sorts of creatures she might encounter in the Aether when the library door opened and Jasper walked in. His green eyes were solemn. "Everything's ready for you, Miss Finley."

It didn't matter how many times she asked him not to call her miss he always went back to it. It usually sounded so very charming in his American drawl, but this time it sat like a weight around her shoulders.

Sam stood at the same time she did. Finley placed her hand on his forearm—it was hard as a rock beneath her fingers, and it wasn't completely because of the metal framework Emily had used during the reconstructive surgery she'd performed on him. The bloke was as solid as a brick privy. "Sam, just in case, I want to say…thanks." That was all she could manage without getting too choked up.

"Save it for later," came his gruff reply. Finley wondered what he would have said had Jasper not been there. The two men were getting on better than they had, but they still weren't best of friends. Maybe they would never be terribly close, but they each had a job to play within their little group, and each of them performed his job very well.

"I'll bring Ipsley down as soon as he arrives," Sam promised. "You tell Em that he's coming. He should be here soon."

Finley nodded and then joined Jasper, who walked her to the lift.

"I feel like I'm headed for the gallows," she joked—lamely—as the gate closed.

"I reckon you'd be a simpleton not to feel that way," her friend replied. "Ain't no pleasure in contemplating a body's mortality."

"But I'm not dying for good." Saying it out loud, it sounded so completely absurd. Challenging death, trespassing in that domain was not something anyone should take lightly.

Jasper chuckled. "No, you are not. I do wish you'd let me go instead."

"I've had more experience with the Aether."

"Yeah, but if Mei's still around, I could probably get her to help."

There was something in his voice—regret?—that broke her heart. "Mei's moved on, Jas. I haven't seen her since she helped me get Griffin away before." The girl's ghost had been manipulated by his family's nemesis, Garibaldi, into doing his dirty work, and it had been easy because of Griffin's regret for having caused her death when they were in New York. Mei had been an unfortunate victim of Griffin's powers.

The cowboy looked straight ahead. A lock of sandy

hair fell over his brow. "Then I s'pose that's the end of that."

"Is it?" He had loved Mei once. The girl had died in his arms. Was there ever an "end" to that sort of thing?

He turned his head to shoot her a wry glance as the lift jerked to a stop. "Got me a future to look forward to—there's no sense in living in the past."

"Sound advice. Is Cat your future, do you think?"

He smiled that crooked smile that charmed practically everyone he met. "Indeed she is."

Emily and Wildcat waited for them by what appeared to be a modified dental chair. It was bloody terrifying, whatever it was. It had clamps and tubes, needles and valves. There were restraints for her arms and feet and a framework to keep her head in place as she reclined.

Finley's courage wavered a bit. She couldn't get cold feet now, not with Griffin depending on her. Everyone was depending on her. She was the only one of them who had seen the Aether, let alone been sucked into it. When Griffin helped merged her two selves, a bond had formed between them. Everytime she brushed against the veil between the dimensions it got a little stronger. She would be able to find Griffin because of that bond. She would find him, save him and bring him home. And she would see Leonardo Garibaldi destroyed forever.

Emily must have seen the doubt in her expression. "You all right, lass?"

She nodded. "The Machinist has enough of a head start on us. I don't want to give him any more. Ipsley is coming to lend his assistance. Help me into the suit."

Jasper held the heavy canvas-and-wire-mesh suit as Finley stepped into it. It was an odd-looking thing, with dials and switches, valves and hoses attached. There was a headpiece, as well, with a glass front so her face could be seen. Emily put a small glove designed to monitor heart rate and body temperature on Finley's left hand. Once in the suit, her friends helped her into the dentist chair and began attaching the various loose bits together.

It was a good thing she didn't suffer from a fear of small spaces, or she'd have a fit. It was like being inside a snow globe.

"In a few seconds you'll begin to feel sleepy," came Emily's voice via a small amplifier near her ear. The disambiguation suit was equipped with communication devices that went both ways—an addition Emily had made to it just in case the wearer ever got into trouble or needed instruction. She certainly had put a lot of work into the bloody thing given that she'd proclaimed it too dangerous for use. "Are you ready?"

Finley nodded and drew a deep breath. Emily flicked

a few switches and adjusted a couple of dials on a control panel just a few feet away. As the machinery connected to the suit engaged, a slight hum began inside the helmet. She could feel a low vibration in her limbs. Then a hissing sound as the sleeping agent was released and the cooling system started. Cool air surrounded her as Finley's eyelids drooped. She forced herself to take deep breaths so the process would be that much quicker.

"May God hold ye in the palm of his hand, Finley Jayne," Emily whispered in her ear.

It was the last thing Finley heard before she died.

Chapter 5

"You have a most impressive tolerance for pain."

Griffin gritted his teeth at Garibaldi's mockery. Behind the "compliment" was the certainty that the bastard would crush that tolerance, push him to the point of begging for mercy.

He would not beg. Even if he thought it would matter, he wouldn't do it. Begging would only give his enemy pleasure. He'd die before he let Garibaldi know just how effective a torturer he was.

Blood dripped from beneath his fingernails. The Machinist hadn't ripped them off—yet—but he'd stuck needles underneath and pried skin from nail. He had burned him, cut him. He'd dripped water in his face until Griffin thought he might scream. The worst was the device used to drain the Aether from him. It felt like claws in his brain, scraping and digging. He didn't know if it was tears or blood trickling from his eyes.

Garibaldi's face loomed over him. He'd made himself look younger in death—a man in his prime rather than the broken shell that had slumbered in that large glass canister guarded by machines. A sly smile curved the man's lips—a slash of mirth in his rugged face. "Your friends. Do you think they worry about you? Do you think Samuel is worried?"

The man had an unnatural interest in Sam. It made a kind of twisted sense—Sam was part human and part machine, something The Machinist held in great fascination. He'd been playing God long before his dark path crossed Griffin's.

"What about Finley?" Garibaldi pressed when he got no reaction. "I'm sure she must be very worried. Is she a crier, your girl? Her mother was always a bit of a limp rag, but her father could be a very hard man when he wanted. Never showed any emotion. Only time I ever saw genuine feeling in his face was when he was dying. Your father was the same way."

Griffin ground his teeth. He'd probably wear them down to bloody stumps before Garibaldi killed him. Would the torture stop there, or would the monster continue after he passed? Would he spend eternity strapped to the table, impotent and helpless? His body ached from all that had been done to it since his capture, but he knew his soul would suffer even more.

So, no. He would not spend eternity on that table. He'd find a way out of this. Death might be his only option. At least with death he could slip free of his mortal shell. He'd be stronger then, in this place. If only he'd spent more time testing his powers rather than controlling them. If only he was as certain of his abilities as was the bastard trying to scramble his brain.

"It won't take her long to find someone else," Garibaldi told him, hovering above the head of the bed. He flipped a switch and Griffin stifled a cry. It was like hundreds of bees swarming about in his head—stinging and battering their wings against the inside of his brain—trying to burrow through his skull. "It didn't take her mother long to get over her father. Then again, there's not much choice for the women, is there? They must have a man to look after them."

He'd tell Garibaldi to shut the hell up if he thought he still had the capacity for speech, but if he dared open his mouth, Griffin knew all that would come out would be guttural, animal sounds.

"I'm going to wait until she finds a new man before I kill her," whispered The Machinist in his ear, his Italian accent giving the words drama. "I will wait until she's happy, so that when I reunite the two of you, you will have her with you for all eternity knowing she loves another."

It was beyond cruel—and more torturous than anything else the man could have done to him. Griffin could handle anything Garibaldi threw at him, but not Finley. If she found someone who could make her happy, he'd be fine with that—more than fine—but to take that away from her... Garibaldi would ruin her life, as well, just to get to Griffin.

Griffin forced his eyes open, even as wetness leaked out. Red blurred the edges of his vision. It was blood, then. He stared up at his enemy and set his jaw. "Go to hell," he growled.

Garibaldi chuckled. "Of course, dear boy. But I'm taking you with me."

Then everything went black.

Jack wasn't just stupid—he thought she was, too. It was the only way Mila could explain why he'd say those things to her. He dismissed her feelings, and then suggested she talk to Finley about "womanly" things. That was a lie...no, that wasn't the right word. Joke— that's what it was. Jack didn't see her as a woman, he saw her as a pet.

But when he said he'd never see her as he saw his

doxies, that she wasn't like those girls…well, she knew there was only one thing she could do.

Leave.

That part of her that was still fairly analytical knew it was ridiculous—running away because her feelings were hurt—but that other part of her, the one that was still new, and all girl, couldn't spend another moment under his roof, knowing he would never feel the same way about her that she did about him. It was simply too painful. She told herself that she wouldn't repeatedly smash her fingers with a brick, so why should she continue to watch Jack with his girls, knowing she was never going to be one of them.

No, not one of them. She wanted to be *the* one. The pain was knowing that Jack wasn't going to let that happen. He didn't see her as a real girl, and he never would. He saw her as a child, or worse—as a *thing*—and that she could not bear.

There was this emotion she'd begun to experience a lot as of late—it was the one called pride. Like most things, her understanding of it that day was better than it had been the day before. What a surprise to discover that she'd had an abundance of it long before she knew what to call it! But she did have it, and Jack…Jack had ground his boot heel into it when he'd basically accused her of not knowing her own mind. If there was one thing Mila knew it was her own mind. It might not always know her, but she was always well aware of it. Maybe other girls said things they didn't mean and pretended they weren't as smart as they were, but Mila didn't understand the motivation behind such behavior, unless it was to make the males of the species feel smarter.

So maybe this stupidity Jack exhibited extended to all men. Was it a flaw in their biological composition? Or was it an evolutionary mutation permitted to persist by the fact that women had looked after them for centuries, such that the need to think lapsed behind the need to procreate? It was a sound thesis—one she might have to explore in greater detail. If she could prove that right, then she could blame Jack and not herself.

Maybe he just didn't find her pretty or interesting. Maybe it wasn't him, but herself that was the problem.

Oh, but she wasn't ready to think on that. Right now, she planned to explore London in greater detail. Eventually, she planned to find her way to Griffin's door and ask if she might stay for a bit, at least until the rest fell into place, but not right away, because that was the first place Jack would look for her—not because he knew her so terribly well, but because King House was home to the only people she'd even begin to call her friends. It wasn't that Jack denied her the benefit of society, it was the fact that he had no friends himself. He had people he did business with, people he had a grudge against and people who wanted to use him, but no friends.

Except for her. Without her he'd be all alone again.

Mila paused in the middle of her packing and glanced toward the door. Maybe… No. Setting her jaw, she stuffed a pair of bloomers into the valise. Jack Dandy had managed to look after himself for years before prying open the lid to her crate. He'd do just fine when she was gone again. In fact, he'd probably be glad to be rid of her, and return to some semblance of normalcy. No more telling people she was his ward. No more hiding her, or explaining her presence to his "women friends." Once he'd told a girl wearing too much rouge and not enough dress that Mila was his cousin from Yorkshire. They looked absolutely nothing alike, but the girl had believed it. Jack was good at lying, but perhaps he'd enjoy a break from it with her gone. No doubt his repair bills would be a lot shorter and less expensive without her around to break things.

She couldn't take everything she owned with her—Jack had been generous with his gifts—but she packed the most important things—several changes of clothing, tooth powder, soap and her favorite book, *The Adventures of Pinocchio* by Carlo Collodi. She'd discovered it when she was with the automatons. Jack had given her a brand-new copy with beautiful illustrations when she moved in with him. He'd given her many books, in many languages, but this was the one she treasured most. She didn't need an extremely advanced logic engine in her head to understand why. It was only natural that she feel a connection with the puppet who wanted to be a real boy.

She wanted to be seen as a real girl, and the only way to achieve that was to go out and learn how to be one. Jack wasn't about to teach her. And she'd rather be just a machine again than go to Finley for help. Jack's precious "Treasure." Of course he'd want Mila to be more like her. She was strong and beautiful, and knew what words meant. Mila might be able to lift a steam carriage over her head, but that didn't make her unique, it just made her a freak.

Maybe she should find some other freaks. Maybe then she'd feel as though she belonged. Maybe they'd accept her just as she was. And maybe the ache in her chest that she felt every time Jack failed to understand her would go away. Or maybe it wouldn't. Either way, there was a world out there, and she'd never understand it, never be part of it, if she didn't go out into it and live.

Once she had packed everything she wanted to take, she opened the bottom drawer of the dresser and removed a small locked box. From it she withdrew a wad of pound notes. Jack gave her what he called pin money but since he bought her clothes, she'd never spent any of it. He fed her, let her read his books and made certain she had everything she needed—there was no need for money, so she'd put it aside. She had planned to buy him something with it one day.

Mila's resolve wavered. She was going to need the money now. She was going to have to look after herself. Surely she could do that. She had to do it. The only way not to be a pet or a doll, or a burden, was to go out and prove herself.

One thing Jack had taught her was that people liked money—and they'd do almost anything to get it. Stealing was a concept she understood—machines took what they needed to improve or enhance themselves without much thought to the consequences, unless the outcome lacked logic. Money was necessary, and people might very well try to steal hers. She hid part of the money in one of her boots, another bit in a secret pocket inside her corset, and the smallest amount in the little purse tucked inside her jacket. Then, she set a derby hat on her head, swung her valise over her shoulder and headed for the door. She didn't stop to look back at the room that had been her home for the past couple of months. If she looked back she wouldn't leave.

And she *had* to leave, otherwise Jack may as well set her on a shelf and let her collect dust. She wouldn't put it past him to pack her up like a doll. She'd been boxed up once, and the idea of having it done to her again was terrifying. So dark and close and lonely. There was a world out there and she wanted to see it. She needed to see it.

And she needed Jack to realize that he'd done the one thing he swore he'd never do—he'd hurt her. He had said that he'd always be there for her, and now she understood that he'd meant that like a father to a child, not as a man to a woman, or even a friend to a friend.

Downstairs she was intercepted by Mrs. Brooks. The older woman looked as though she'd just been taken out of a box, she was so neat and tidy. Mila hadn't looked that creaseless when she came out of *her* crate.

"Going somewhere, dear?" There was an edge of alarm in her voice. Of course she was surprised. Other than the odd outing with Jack, Mila had never left the house unaccompanied before.

Say no, whispered a voice in her head. *Ask for some cake and tea, and then go back upstairs where it's safe and familiar.* "I'm leaving."

The woman's eyes widened as color…*drained* from her face. "When should I tell Mr. Dandy you'll return?"

Mila forced a smile. "I don't expect to return, Mrs. Brooks. You may tell him that."

"But…I don't understand, child." The woman wrung her hands. "Has he been cruel to you? Has he done you ill?"

"He hasn't hurt me—not intentionally." How did she explain when she didn't quite understand herself? "He doesn't see me—not as I am."

Mrs. Brooks nodded as though she understood. In fact, a small smile curved her thin lips as her posture visibly relaxed. "Ah. And you hope your leaving will give him a little *perspective,* is that it?"

"Perspective," Mila repeated, impressed. "That's a very good word, Mrs. Brooks."

"Thank you, my dear. Is there anyplace I should send the mister if he gains perspective quickly?"

"I… No," she confessed. "I'm not sure where it is I'm going."

The woman with drew a pencil and paper from her apron and wrote upon it. "My sister owns a boarding-house for young ladies near Covent Garden. This is the direction. Can you read, child?"

"Yes." It came out a little defensive. And then, with a little too much pride she added, "Five different lan-guages." She didn't know how she knew them, she just did. Unfortunately, she only knew the words that she had already seen. It was as though she had a built-in translator engine, so that as soon as she learned a word in English, she learned it in her other languages.

"Plenty of jobs open to young ladies who know languages. You could become a governess." Mrs. Brooks offered her the paper with the address written on it. "There are also those who would take advantage. You will be careful, won't you?"

The concern in the housekeeper's face made Mila's throat tight. "I will, thank you." She tucked the paper into her pocket. "Please don't tell him where I've gone. Unless…unless he seems to miss me very terribly."

There was a name for the expression Mrs. Brooks wore. It was…*sympathy.* "Of course. You be a good girl and go straight to that address so I don't have to worry about you out there all alone, you hear?"

"Yes, ma'am."

"All right." Her tone held an edge of acceptance, as though she believed she could have stopped her if she wanted. Silly, sweet woman. "Take care of yourself. Keep your head up and your eyes open."

Maybe the woman was right to feel sorry for her, Mila thought as she walked out of the house, into the late-afternoon drizzle. She turned her collar up against the damp and cold and started walking in the direction of Covent Garden. Jack had taken her twice to the theater there, so she knew the way.

Mrs. Brooks obviously believed Jack would look for her. Would miss her. Maybe he would. Maybe he'd be glad to find her gone. Glad to wash his hands of her. It didn't matter. This wasn't about Jack. Jack wasn't her entire world, or rather he oughtn't be. No, it wasn't about Jack at all. It was about her. About finding out who she was, about being something more than a bit of metal wrapped in a flesh suit once intended to house a madman's brain.

It was about relying on herself rather than the charity of others. It was about being the girl she wanted to be.

And if Jack Dandy *didn't* miss her, then she was better off without him.

Death was not what Finley thought it would be.

First of all, there was a decided lack of angels, heavenly choirs and bright light. In fact, the Aether was fairly gray—as if everything wore a layer of ash. It wasn't depressing, but rather ethereal-looking. It was like walking through a dream, complete with mist swirling about her feet.

She'd never been here in a proper manner before. Always she'd been connected to Griffin somehow—even if it was simply being in the same room. Those times she'd been aware of the real world lurking beyond the veil, but not this time. No layers, just the Aether, and it was as real as the living world.

One moment she'd been in Em's lab, and now she was standing on a cobblestone path that wound through a forest dappled with silvery sunlight. Or maybe it was moonlight; it was difficult to tell. Regardless, it was beautiful and peaceful, so she wasn't the least bit afraid. Most people didn't get the opportunity to discover the secrets of this place while they were still alive. It was somewhat mollifying to realize that the realm of the dead was a welcoming place, rather than a frightening one.

But Garibaldi didn't know she was there yet. There'd be plenty of time for fear once he did, she reckoned. Griffin wasn't the only one he enjoyed hurting, and she had no doubt he'd love to play with her, as well. The knowledge of that did not deter her. Let The Machinist come. If he was after her then he couldn't be torturing Griffin, so she'd take him on anytime. Unfortunately, she needed to do more than think about the bounder in order to find him. She clenched her jaw and took a step forward. She had no idea how long it was going to take to find Griffin and no idea how much time the Tesla suit would give her.

The suit hadn't made the trip with her, which was

odd. A warm breeze drifted across her face as she walked. It was like a pleasant summer evening in the Aether, not at all cold as she'd thought it would be. She was perfectly comfortable in her boots, stockings, dress and corset. Death was supposed to be cold, wasn't it? Garibaldi deserved someplace cold and dark. Unforgiving and bleak.

As she walked, she caught glimpses through the trees—of what appeared to be little houses with lights on inside. People moved about in front of open windows, some dancing, some laughing or running. Some simply stared out at the forest. What were they looking at, or for? She couldn't tell—she couldn't see their eyes, or even much of their shadowed faces.

She came around a turn in the path. A lone bird sang mournfully from the forest. There were no houses visible here—just the narrow road surrounded by dense, lush trees. A girl in a long white dress sat on a low stone wall weeping, face in her hands. Her bare feet were dirty and rested on the nest of moss covering much of the wall.

"Are you all right?" Finley asked, then felt stupid. It was obvious the girl was not all right. She shouldn't have stopped to ask. She had to find Griffin.

The girl lifted her head at the exact second that Finley realized something wasn't right. Those weren't tears running through her fingers, it was blood—blood that leaked from the raw, gaping holes where her eyes had once been.

"Bugger me!" Finley cried, jerking back when bloody hands reached out to her.

"You don't belong here, Finley Jayne," the girl crooned. "Go back to the breathing world, little mouse, before the big bad wolf comes calling."

Finley scowled at her. She didn't like being frightened, and she liked the things that frightened her even less. "I'm not afraid of Garibaldi, and I'm not afraid of you."

Now it was the girl who frowned. Her dark brows pulled low over the glistening pits of her eye sockets. A trickle of blood dribbled by the corner of her mouth—there were stitches sticking out of her lips, like jagged little whips. "I don't know who Garibaldi is, but I know who the wolf is, and he wants you." She glanced over her shoulder. Could she actually see even though her eyes were gone? "He's coming. Run, mousey, run."

Her heart pounded in agitation, not fear. That was what Finley told herself. "Let him come." But she moved onward. She wasn't afraid to meet this "wolf," but she wasn't about to stand around and wait for him to show up, not when Griffin's life hung in the balance.

As she walked away, she heard the dead girl behind

her chanting, "Run. Run. Run. Run." It was so very tempting to do just that, but she'd rather be boiled alive than admit fear. Still, she quickened her step just a bit. Bit of a creeper, that girl. The memory of those missing eyes was going to haunt her sleep for a long time.

If she made it out of the Aether alive, that was.

The cobblestone path eventually led to a curved, moss-covered stone bridge that crossed a glossy river. Water as clear and bright as polished diamond danced over rocks that looked as though they were chunks of chiseled obsidian. Finley stepped onto the bridge and didn't pause to look over the side into the water. She didn't want to know what was in it.

She didn't even know if she was going in the right direction, but there was only the one path. How was she ever going to find Griffin in this place? How could she have been so foolish to think that it would be relatively easy? She hadn't expected to step in and find him right away, but she'd grossly underestimated the size of the place. It was the land of the dead after all—a place made of energy. There was no limit to its size, was there?

Her throat tightened, and her eyes burned. What if... what if she never found him? What if he was lost to them forever? There were so many things she wanted to tell him, so many things she wanted to hear him say to her. There were still so many things about his life that she didn't know—silly stories about his child-hood with Sam, or going away to school. She wanted to know more about his parents. She wanted to know what it was that he saw in her that made him want to be with her instead of any other girl in London.

A tear trickled down her cheek. Finley swiped at it angrily with the back of her hand and sniffed hard. Bawling wasn't going to solve anything, couldn't accomplish anything. Crying was a waste of time and the last refuge of a desperate girl.

Desperate as she might be, but she had not lost all hope. Not yet. She couldn't. Wouldn't.

"Run. Run. Run." The eerie whisper seemed to come from all sides—up above and down below, even from the trees themselves. At least a dozen voices urging her to run and run fast. A dozen girls hiding in the forest, watching her with raw-meat eyes. Who were they? *What* were they?

"Run."

Finley walked faster.

"Run."

Bloody hell, she was *not* going to run!

"Run."

She stopped in the middle of a sliver of that silver light. It had to be the moon. Shoulders back, arms

loose at her sides, she concentrated on her surroundings, opened up her instincts.

"Run."

"No." Her voice was quiet but firm. No need to
shout and call attention to herself—or more attention
to herself. "I'm not going to run."

"You'll be sorry."

"Sorry."

"A place with us."

"She'll be one of us."

"So very sorry."

"One of us." The gleeful tone of that last multivoiced
whisper made Finley's teeth grind together.

"Damnation," she whispered, and took off running as
fast as her legs would take her. She'd only gone round a
bend in the path when she saw a lavish house looming
above. Music played inside—the kind heard in dance
halls. She could smell cigar smoke on the air, and hear
the rumble of male laughter.

That laughter turned her bones to water. It was an
awful sound. A cruel sound. Was this The Machinist's
lair? Was she going to have to fight her way to him? She
had been wrong when she called it male laughter. Men
didn't make such an evil sound. No, it was something
else altogether that smoked and drank in that house.
Whatever it was, it wasn't human—not anymore.

She took a step back, but she couldn't go backward—even though she'd prefer those mad girls to this. She had to go forward. She had to know if this was where Griffin was being held. Tortured.

"I'll be damned," came a familiar voice from behind her.

A shiver slithered down Finley's spine. *It couldn't be.* Slowly, she turned around, her heart squeezing itself into her throat.

It was.

Not five feet away from her, on what had turned into a deserted street lined with theaters and entertainment parlors, was Lord Felix August-Raynes. He looked less angelic in this place, more like the devil he was. Tall, blond and blue-eyed, he wore a gray suit and carried a silver-topped walking stick that matched the small bar that bisected his eyebrow. The only thing he was missing from the last time she'd seen him was the imprint of her boot on his forehead.

He grinned at her as the eyeless girls crept up behind him, flanked him. They crouched about him, stroked his coattails as though they were so much less than he.

"Finley Jayne," he said, eyes glinting like flint. "The one that got away."

Before she could react, the girls rushed her. Lord Felix seemed to suddenly appear right in front of her—

so close she had to lean back to avoid touching him. The girls grabbed her arms and legs. She tried to fight them off, but there were too many. Lord Felix grabbed her by the chin, forcing her to meet his gaze. He grinned.

"I've got you now."

Chapter 6

Jack only came home to change. He wouldn't have done even that had it not been for the blood on his shirt cuffs and waistcoat. People tended to be alarmed by that sort of thing when one was out and about.

There had been trouble at one of his clubs. He owned two—one that was for gambling, drinking and any other sort of "manly" pastime. The other was a bit more sedate. He called it The Bastard Club and meant it in the literal sense of the word. Everyone who belonged to the club—male or female—was the illegitimate offspring of a member of the upper classes and peerage, such as Jack himself. His father was an earl and a top-notch wanker.

Not many people knew of the club. Jack had only approached those he was certain of when he first started it, and then let the members discreetly spread the word. It was the sort of place that the nobs might get all up in arms about and cause enough of a fuss to make running it difficult—wouldn't do for all their ignored, unwanted children to gather forces behind their backs.

At first, there were those who thought of the club as a place a body could go to rage about the unfairness of life, how they should have been the heir, and so forth. That wasn't the case, however. What happened within those thick walls was an exchange of information. They each had their own little group of people who were closely connected to the aristocracy. Most of the information came from servants who worked in the various households, and some came from the fringe of society with whom they spent most of their lives.

Servants often had the best information. They were broadly ignored by those who employed them, regarded as little more than furniture with limbs. By the same token, their masters often spoke freely in front of them, not even realizing they were there—or perhaps assuming they weren't bright enough to understand. And of all those underpaid and undervalued household staff, there was none better than a lady's maid. Not only did she overhear what the women of the house said to one another, but she would get news from other female staff, and—if she was comely enough—information from the male staff, as well. Plus, the lady's maid was often in the company of maids of the same position from other households when ladies visited one another or attended balls. A good lady's maid, possessed of wit and a degree of pleasantry, was one of the most informed people in all of London.

Jack had certainly befriended his share of lady's maids over the past few years. As a result, and thanks to his club, he knew more about the aristocracy and nobility of England than they knew of themselves, and he rarely hesitated to use it to his advantage if opportunity arose. A man armed with knowledge was richer than any king.

Today he had heard that he was going to be an uncle. His father's daughter—one of his wife's children—was with child herself. The news disturbed him. He would probably never know the child and was pissed at himself for regretting it. He didn't know his sister either, though he'd seen her several times. There was no denying their connection—even Jack saw the resemblance between them. She looked nice. Too nice to associate with her infamous bastard brother.

He had also heard that his father had taken a new mistress, a performer Jack knew quite well himself. That could certainly come in handy. The young woman would tell him everything she knew for the right amount of coin, and Jack didn't mind spending it.

But the best news—the absolute best—had been word that his father needed a rather large loan to cover his gambling debts. Jack owned all of the man's IOUs. Every debt. And now he planned to offer the man the money to pay them off, at an astounding rate of interest. Then, he planned to demand immediate repayment. He'd take silver, gold, whatever the lord had to give. He'd take the clothes right off the bastard's back. He'd take until the slimy lord had nothing else to give and was in complete ruin. Men had committed suicide over less, and Jack didn't care what path his father chose to take. He didn't care about the loss of his own money.

Just last week he'd ruined Lord Abernathy, the man who had hired him to transport the crate Mila had been kept in. Abernathy had a romantic interest in young men, and it had only taken a few words in a few well-connected ears for the bounder to get caught in the act at a certain brothel that catered to those tastes. Abernathy was no longer welcome in society, so Jack had heard. Seemed his lordship had fled to his country estate in disgrace.

The man had put Mila in a box. Treated her like something less than dirt. He had to pay for that.

The house was quiet as he walked up the stairs.

Mrs. Brooks would have departed for home already, as it was one of the days of the week when he cooked for himself and Mila. She liked to watch him in the kitchen and help him mix ingredients. It was a simple thing, but it was something he looked forward to every time. He wasn't a master chef by any stretch, but he could cook and do it well.

"Poppet?" he called as he loosened his cravat, walking toward his bedroom. "What do you fancy for supper?"

There was no answer.

Jack paused in the corridor, and turned his ear toward Mila's room, listening. "Poppet?"

Still nothing.

"Mila?"

Silence. She wasn't put out about earlier, was she? Sulking because he wouldn't treat her like something— someone—less than she was? Bloody hell, he wanted to kiss her—wanted to do lots of other things, as well. God knew he'd thought about it enough. She was his responsibility. He was supposed to protect her, not become one of the men he tried to protect her from. She deserved a good man—when she was ready for that. He wanted her to have the best of everything, and that hardly included him.

Mila didn't know how the world worked, didn't

know that it could be so completely cruel to a young woman, or so judgmental.

As he walked up to her door, he thought about one of his other meetings that afternoon. He had gone to an establishment that specialized in teaching deportment and other such skills about which he knew very little. Oh, he knew all about manners and society, but not everything expected of a young woman. He'd hired someone to come to the house and instruct Mila in all those things. When she was done, Griffin King was going to take over as her guardian, pass her off as a distant cousin, settle a large dowry on her and make sure she ended up with the sort of man she deserved.

Jack hoped King knew that he planned on being part of that process. His girl wasn't going to marry just any inbred lord. Jack would dig deep into the affairs of every prospect until he found the perfect one. Someone kind, with a good income. Someone with a decent family that would take her in. Someone strong to handle her stubbornness, but gentle enough not to hurt her emotionally. He wouldn't have to worry about her physical care, not really. She already knew to break the arm of anyone who tried to harm her.

There had to be at least one man out there who would see Mila for the gift that she was. Someone who could love her.

He knocked on her door. As he expected, only silence followed. He reached down, turned the knob and pushed the heavy slab of wood forward. "Mi—"

As soon as he crossed the threshold he knew something was wrong. Her bed was neatly made—something she rarely did even though he nagged her about it. The door to the armoire hung open, revealing a large, empty section. There were little items missing from her dressing table. Most importantly—and more disturbing—was that the copy of *The Adventures of Pinocchio* that he had given her was gone.

That meant Mila was gone.

Jack's chest tightened. And tightened. And tightened. He gasped for breath, pressing his fist against his heart because the damn thing felt as though it was trying to chew its way through his ribs. He staggered forward, his other hand coming down on the bedspread. His fingers curled around something small and cool. He gripped the unknown object and clung to it as he dragged deep breaths into his lungs, forcing the muscles of his chest to relax.

What the ruddy hell had that been all about? He'd been left before, had people run off on him when he'd served their purpose. It had started with his father, so why should it hurt so much now? She was just a girl. Not like she was Treasure or his mum.

No, Mila wasn't either of those women. Mila was something else entirely. Mila was strong like Finley, and full of the same wonder as his mother. Nothing had been able to diminish his mother's love of life, not even being treated like rubbish. But Mila was oddly smart and intuitive in ways that most people weren't. She made connections that most wouldn't make. She was so frank and so honest. Too much so, and more often than not, she was dangerously innocent and naive.

Where was she? It didn't matter that she could throw a grown man around like a rag doll. It didn't matter that her bones couldn't break. She could still bleed. She could feel pain, and there were people out there who would take advantage of her. He knew this because he used to be one of them. But he hadn't been *that* Jack since the day he decided he needed to save her. He wouldn't say he was necessarily a changed man, but he was certainly an altered one.

He straightened, the pain in his chest having subsided, and opened his hand. The object he'd found on the bed was a small brass cylinder—the kind used for capturing music or voice performances. It wasn't one that came with music already engraved because there was no stamp in the metal to identify it. It had to be one Mila had made herself.

With the brass clutched once more in his fist, Jack

went to his own room—"the cave" as he liked to think of it. It was decorated in white and black, with the odd splash of color. Normally, he found the austere colors soothing and peaceful, but nothing could calm him at that moment. He put the cylinder in the small Victrola and wound the clockwork mechanism tight. Then, he sat down in a chair near the small table and pressed the switch to begin playback.

Static crackled softly. "Hello, Jack." He smiled at the sound of her voice. "If you're listening to this, well, it's because I left. If you're not listening to this…well, I guess there's no point in saying much. I'm not terribly talented when it comes to words, but I'll try to say things properly. I just couldn't stay here any longer. You have been so good to me, and I…appreciate that. You've been a good friend, but I don't want to be your friend, Jack. I don't want to be your burden, your…responsibility. I want more. You already know this, and now I know that you don't want me the same way. I can't be your pet or your doll or whatever it is I am. I'm not a child, and I need to learn to take care of myself rather than let you or Griffin do it. You understand, don't you? I hope you're not upset with me, but most of all I hope you're not glad to be rid of me. Don't worry about me, Jack. But maybe…you could miss me just a little. I'll miss you." Her voice cracked on the last line, and Jack felt the lump that must have been in her throat erupt in his.

He swiped at his eyes with the back of his hand. He must have gotten something in them because they began to water. Mila was out there in the dark, alone. She was strong, but she was still vulnerable, and a pretty little thing like her was easy prey for a man like his father—or a man like him. God, why couldn't she understand that he wasn't good? Why did she insist on making him something he wasn't?

Miss her a little? God, was she daft? He was going to miss her more than a little.

No, he wasn't. He leaped to his feet and practically ran to the door. He wasn't going to miss her at all.

He was going to find her and bring her home.

When Griffin woke up, Garibaldi was blessedly gone, leaving him alone with his pain.

His eyes adjusted to the dim light—he had half expected the villain to leave him under searing lights to further torture him—as his ears opened to what sounds permeated the walls of his prison. He heard the in and out of his own breath, the soft whirls and clicks of the machines tethered to him, to this realm, preventing him from going home, and...music. It was Liszt if he

wasn't mistaken. Either his captor had an orchestra installed in his home or he had some superior recordings.

Music was good. He wouldn't be heard above it if
he screamed, but it meant that he wasn't alone, that
this was actually Garibaldi's main base. Homes were
more vulnerable than warehouses and prisons. Houses
had more nooks and crannies and places a body could
hide, even houses in the Aether. If he could get out of
this damn bed he could find some sort of advantage,
he just knew it.

He wished his parents were here, but the fact that
they weren't meant that they had either moved on to
some other realm, or Garibaldi had managed to con-
ceal him from them. There was no way they'd allow
him to remain in the clutches of the man responsible
for their deaths.

His limbs felt like lead, but instead of trying to move
his entire body, he concentrated on just his right hand.
It took almost all of his strength, but he managed to
flex his fingers and rotate his wrist. Bloody hell, just
that simple movement broke a sweat along his hairline.
He'd take it for what it was—a victory. Griffin took all
that strength and focused it on his left hand, putting it
through the same exercise. It left him exhausted, but
satisfied.

He could move. He wasn't entirely helpless. He drew

a deep breath and turned inside himself. In his mind he followed the path inside his body to the place where his power sat. It was all through him, but he felt it most in an area the size of a tea saucer, just between his navel and breastbone. It was into that sphere that he burrowed and breathed. He let the image of Finley fill his mind—his talisman, his reason.

His everything. She drove him to distraction, could make him laugh one second and throw his hands up in exasperation the next. She knew just how to tease him, how to engage his temper and his wit. She inspired the most tender of feelings as easily as the most passionate. Just the touch of her hand could make him tremble inside. That was the spot where he lingered now—the place where his power and Finley collided.

His soul.

Warmth filled him, cleansed him. Calm rolled down from his head to his toes, centering in that sphere in his chest until it began to swell, pushing outward against his ribs. There was nothing but Finley and a tiny spark of Aether that gave him more hope than it ought.

A little hope had been known to win more battles than the most fearsome of armies, and right now that hope was all he had.

"Do I know you?"

Griffin's eyes snapped open. At the foot of his bed

stood a man—one who looked strangely familiar. There was something about his eyes…

"I don't know," he replied. "Do you?"

The man frowned. He was in his late twenties or early thirties, and he was obviously a citizen of the Aether. Judging from the style of his clothes he'd been dead at least fifteen years or so. "I think I must. How else could I enter this place that I've never been able to enter before?"

This was interesting. "You've tried to infiltrate this house before?"

Looking around the room, the man nodded. "Ever since Garibaldi crossed the threshold to this place I've tried unsuccessfully to gain entrance. What are you doing here? It's obvious you're not of this realm."

"No, I am very much alive. For the time being, at any rate. Do you think you might be able to release me?"

His visitor moved toward him. He reached out for the shackle that bound Griffin's right foot, but the moment his fingers touched it, a flash like an exploding lightbulb filled the room, blinding the both of them. Griffin swore as color danced behind his eyelids.

"Reckon that answers that question," the man grumbled, shaking his injured hand. "Good lord, lad. What did you do to deserve his wrath?"

"Foiled too many of his plans," Griffin replied honestly. "And held him accountable for his crimes."

The man's eyes—a pale shade of brown—narrowed. "What's your name, son?"

For a second, he thought against telling the truth. This man could be friend or foe, but there was only one way to find out—to trust him.

"Griffin King."

"King?" The man reacted as though struck. "Greythorne's boy?"

At the use of his title, Griffin started. So, they weren't strangers, then. "Yes. And you are?"

"Thomas Sheppard. I was a friend of your father's."

Griffin stared at him, disbelief coursing through his veins. "You're Finley's father."

Finley woke screaming. The bruising pressure of the girls' fingers lingered on her skin. The smell of Lord Felix's breath was hot in her face, the gore from eyeless faces sticky on her fingers. She lashed out, flailing arms and legs, fingers like claws as she struggled to free herself. *Can't breathe. Can't see.*

"Finley!" Someone shouted. "Stop! Sam, I need you!"

Suddenly, a great weight settled on her, pinning her

limbs. There was a clicking sound and cool air rushed across her face.

"Be still," murmured a deep voice that rumbled through her ribs. "You're safe. Be still."

She knew that voice. More importantly, she trusted it. Sight and clarity returned. Sam loomed over her— held her down. Good lord he was heavy!

"Get off," she growled, lungs struggling beneath his weight.

She didn't have to make the demand twice. Sam jumped off her as though she were a hot coal. "Are you all right?" he asked, a flush of pink in his cheeks.

"I'm fine," she shot back. Normally she'd tease him for blushing just because he touched a girl that wasn't Emily, but she couldn't do it. Her nerves were raw, jumpy and pinging. She needed to punch something. She wanted to vomit. Fear tightened her body, refused to let go just yet. Lord Felix was going to be the subject of her nightmares again, the piece of dirt.

Sam held up one broad hand, palm out toward her. He didn't have to say a word—she knew what it was for. She pulled her fist back and then shot it forward, right into his open palm. She felt it all the way up to her shoulder, and it was good. The blow actually knocked him back a couple of feet. "Good shot." Then he offered her the same hand. She took it and let him help her into a sitting position.

Emily stood a few feet away, clutching the helmet of the suit to her chest. Her knuckles and face were white, tiny freckles stood out on her cheeks. Finley looked back at Sam. "Was it bad? Did I hurt anyone?"

He shook his head. "You didn't make a sound, not until Em woke you up."

"Then how...?" She turned her head and saw that they had company. Beside Jasper and Wildcat—who also looked alarmed—was Silverus Ipsley, the medium Griffin had befriended. The poor gingery fellow looked as though he might puke up his guts at any second.

"Miss Emily asked Ipsley to monitor you in the Aether, just in case you ran into any trouble," Jasper informed her. His green eyes were full of concern. "Which it appears you did."

"It was Lord Felix," she admitted with a shrug. She wasn't going to volunteer anything else.

"We know," Emily replied, voice hoarse. "He told us what he saw."

For a second, she was tempted to backhand the medium, but then she met his gaze and all anger—all humiliation—faded. He had only been trying to help, and he'd been shoved straight into a little bit of hell that should have been hers alone. "I'm sorry you had to see that."

He nodded, head wobbling as though his neck was made of Indian rubber. "I've never seen anything like it. Ever. I knew there could be bad things in the Aether, but that was…extreme. Did they hurt you?"

Finley shook her head. "No." That was all she intended to say on the subject. They could ask her questions later, and maybe she'd tell them what Ipsley hadn't revealed. Maybe she wouldn't tell them anything. The only thing she knew for certain was that she couldn't think about it right then. Couldn't think about it until they'd found and rescued Griffin, because the fear it had made her feel could cripple her if she allowed it to.

She turned to Emily. "Thanks for pulling me out, Em."

Her friend only nodded, as though she'd lost her voice, or couldn't trust herself to use it.

"All right, then, put me back in."

They all looked at her as though she'd lost her bloody mind. Maybe she had, but it hardly mattered.

"No," Emily said—in that tone of hers that she sometimes used with Sam and the other boys. It was the tone that meant "my word is law."

Their gazes locked. Finley thought she heard Sam

swear. She and Emily had never really butted heads before. "Yes."

The little redhead drew herself up to her full height, which still wasn't intimidating. Although, she did have a lot of dangerous-looking tools lying about. "He could have killed you."

"He didn't."

"Because we pulled you out."

"And you can pull me out again." She turned to Ipsley. "You fine with that?"

He didn't look fine at all, but he nodded. "If it will save His Grace, of course."

Finley didn't feel at all smug when she returned her attention to Emily. "Put me back in."

Two angry splotches of red appeared on Emily's cheeks. Her temper was up. That was fine—Finley's was on the rise, as well. "I'm not arguing, Em. You can put me back in, or I'll go slit my wrists. Either way, I'm going into the Aether." Of course, she wouldn't really slit her wrists, that would just be stupid. She probably wouldn't even find Griffin before she died, and if she was a ghost she might be able to reach him, but how would she get him back into the living world?

"Stubborn," Emily bit out. "Foolish, hardheaded…" The rest was lost because she'd launched into Irish—or what Finley assumed was her native Gaelic—and because the telephone on the near wall rang sharply twice, which was an indication that the call was coming from inside the house.

Jasper answered it. "'Lo? Mrs. D, darlin'. What can I do you for?…Uh-huh….Uh-huh….Send him on down." He thanked her and hung up. "Dandy's here. He's coming down."

Finley could have knocked him into the middle of next week. "We don't have time for visitors, Renn." She used his last name intentionally to let him know she was annoyed.

He wasn't the least bit cowed. "We have time for Jack."

Normally she'd agree with him. "Griffin is trapped in there—with The Machinist—and every damn second we spend doing nothing is another second he suffers!"

A heavy hand came down on her shoulder. It was Sam. "Em needs to make some repairs before you can go back in."

"Is that true?" she demanded of Emily.

Her friend nodded, looking much less aggravated. "The suit sustained some damage in the struggle when we pulled you out. Plus, I want to make certain we're not caught off guard like that again. It will only take about an hour."

"An hour here is nothing in the Aether," Sam reminded her.

Frowning, Finley nodded. She didn't like not getting her own way. She disliked it even more than she despised being wrong. Having both of these apply to a single situation was embarrassing. It was her fault the suit had been damaged, and now Griffin would pay the price of being in Garibaldi's clutches a little longer.

The lift engine whirred to life, driving the cage upward to collect its passenger. A few moments later, it came back down and Jack stepped out.

Finley stared at him. She'd never seen Jack looking any less than perfectly together, but his coat was buttoned wrong, and his long hair was a mess. He was without a hat and without his customary walking stick that concealed a razor-sharp sword.

He looked around the room and appeared disappointed. "Where's his lordship?"

Finley folded her arms over her chest to keep her heart from breaking. "Griffin's...gone." She frowned. Frowning prevented bawling.

Jack's dark gaze locked with hers. Was that suspicion she saw reflected back at her? "Seems to be goin' round as of late." He glanced at the others. "Don't suppose 'e 'ad poppet wiv 'im?"

"Mila?" Emily stepped forward. "No. What's happened, Jack?"

"I come 'ome and found 'er run off. Figured she'd find her way 'ere."

"She hasn't," Emily replied. "Did she give you any reason for leaving?"

He shrugged. "Said she wanted to see some of the world. Didn't want to be a bo'ver to the rest of us. To me."

To Finley's surprise, Emily smiled. She would have expected the little redhead to go off like a steaming kettle with worry. "She's growing up."

Jack looked at her as though she was mad. "What the devil 'as that got to do wiv it? Not very mature of 'er to just run off like that."

Emily arched a brow, hand on her hip. "What did you do to make her run off?"

Jack Dandy actually flushed. It was snowing in hell.

Sam stepped forward, fists clenched. "If you touched her…"

One touch on the arm from Emily stopped him. "He didn't hurt her, lad." Her bright gaze remained on Jack. "If I know our girl at all, I'm willing to bet she ran off to make him look at her as a person and not a child, or a machine."

Jack's flush turned to a scowl in a blink. "I know she's

not a child, and I know she's not a bloody machine. I know exactly what she is."

"She's obviously infatuated with you," Emily supplied. "She wants you to see her as a woman. The question I want to ask is, what are you going to do about it?"

His expression darkened. "I'm going to bring her home. The rest is none of your damn business."

Everyone but Jack seemed to notice that he had dropped his cockney accent.

"She may not want to go home. She obviously felt she needed to leave."

For a moment Finley wondered if Emily would also poke a bear with a stick. Provoking Jack had never struck her as a good idea.

"I want to make sure she's safe," Jack replied, his jaw tight. "I would like your help finding her."

"We can't," Finley blurted. Jack looked as though she had punched him. He was her friend, and he had been there for her every time she asked and even when she hadn't. "Jack, Griffin's been trapped in the Aether. By The Machinist."

Normally he would have sworn or made some sort of witty comment to break the tension, but he only nodded. A prickle of unease tingled at the base of Finley's spine. Was Jack in love with Mila? She was happy

for him, of course, especially if the girl felt the same
way but…

She was jealous. Since their first meeting she had
been Jack's favorite girl. His favorite person. She didn't
feel that way about him, but she loved him so dearly
as a friend. He was like her brother, her twin soul. She
didn't want to lose him.

Then she ought to be a better friend. "I can help
while Emily fixes the suit." She began climbing out of
it so her friend could get to work.

Jack shook his head. "No. You need to focus on your
duke." There was no judgment in his tone, but she felt
like dirt regardless. "I'll find her."

Jasper and Wildcat stepped forward. "We'll help
you," Jasper said. "We ain't much needed here, and
Cat's a right talented tracker."

Jack smiled, and Finley could have kissed the pair
of them.

"Take your telegraphs," Emily reminded them.
"Keep us updated and we'll do the same."

Finley handed the suit to Sam and moved to catch
up the three of them before they left. "Jack."

He stopped and turned. Jasper and Wildcat continued to the lift and waited there. Finley was grateful for
the privacy. "You know if it was anyone but Griffin
I'd help you."

He nodded. "And if it weren't for Mila I'd be help-ing you." His eyes glittered dangerously. "I'd like to have a go at The Machinist myself."

"I'll hit him especially hard a few times, just for you."

Their gazes locked, and even though they didn't speak, Finley felt as though they understood each other better than they ever had. This was the dividing line between love and friendship. She and Jack shared a deep bond, but they each had someone who would always come first, and both accepted that.

He leaned in and kissed her cheek. "I'll see you later, Fin."

She knew at that moment that he would never call her Treasure again. And oddly enough, it didn't make her the least bit sad.

Chapter 7

The boardinghouse was located in the area of Garrick and King Streets. Mila had absolutely no difficulty finding it at all, though it took her nearly three hours to get there. There was so much to do in London! So many amazing sights and delicious foods. She bought a rose from a flower seller and tucked it in her hair. One pub smelled so good she had to go in and order a meat pie—delicious. And she had ale for the first time. She wasn't mad for it, but it would do. Jack had brought her to this area before, but only to the theater, which she'd loved, but she enjoyed the everyday life even more.

Finally, with her belly full and spirits high, Mila set off in the direction of her destination. It was getting dark earlier and earlier these days, and she wasn't so naive that she wanted to be out wandering the streets at night. Nor was she terribly afraid of doing just that. She wasn't easily hurt, but she could be injured, and she knew that she was easily taken advantage of. She wasn't stupid, she was just new. Human subterfuge and deceit were lessons she was still in the process of learning.

She had good reason to be wary. Two men had been following her for the past hour. They tried to be sneaky, but they weren't that good at it. She didn't want trouble. All she wanted was to get to the boardinghouse, secure a room and maybe sleep for a few days. There were a few reasons she could think of as to why they were following her, and none of them were particularly good. Still, for those she thought of, there were probably at least a dozen more that she had not, and it didn't matter how strong she was if they took advantage of her naïveté.

And yet, she wasn't afraid. She was distracted, and annoyed. Was Jack thinking of her? Had he even noticed she was gone yet? Probably he had one of his doxies with him and he hadn't thought of her at all. The idea caused a burning sensation in her stomach. Was it rage or jealousy? Maybe both. Regardless, the nasty emotion did nothing for her...*disposition*—that was a brilliant word—and she practically itched to find a little trouble.

Which was exactly why, after turning a corner, she

pressed her back against a darkened shop front and waited. When the two men followed in her steps a few moments later, she grinned at them. They seemed surprised to see her.

"You fellows have been following me so long now I thought I'd give you the chance to catch up." And if she'd allowed them to follow her all the way to the boardinghouse, then they'd know where she was staying, and someone else might get hurt.

The first one—a lanky, skinny sort with spiky blond hair and icelike eyes grinned at her. He had two small metal bars through his left eyebrow, and six small hoops in his right ear. "Aren't you just the sweetest little bird."

"No. I'm a girl."

They seemed to find that very funny, but there was something in their laughter that made her spine tingle with unease.

"No denyin' that, ducks," the second one allowed. He was shorter than his friend and dark in skin, eyes and hair. He had what looked like metal studs coming out of his cheek and a small bar through his lower lip. Did these personal adornments serve any purpose? They appeared almost tribal in nature, and seemed out of place with their English clothing. "So, we've caught you, now what?"

Mila tilted her head. "You haven't caught me. I caught you."

The two of them shared a look—as though they thought themselves extremely lucky. "What are you goin' t'do with us, then?" The blond one smirked.

"First I'm going to tell you that it's not very polite of you to follow young ladies. It could be seen as… predatory."

The darker one whistled. "Predatory. Listen to that, would you, Len? What big words the little bird chirps."

She frowned at him. "I think you will begin to annoy me very quickly. The two of you don't seem very nice." In fact, the pair of them made her very uncomfortable. There was something…off.

"We're not very nice, poppet," the blond told her.

That name made her stiffen. Slowly, she moved her gaze to his. He was smiling. "Did you think we didn't know you? Dandy cut you loose? Makes you fair game for the rest of us."

Stillness settled over Mila. A cold certainty that if it came down to her or them, she'd leave them dead in the street. She didn't want to kill them—some part of her knew it would be wrong—but she would if she had to. For that reason, she wasn't afraid. The only weapons they had were a knife each. She could see the outline of the blades in their jackets—the fabric basically had

the imprint of the knives worn into it. Not very subtle, but effective. They didn't smell of gunpowder or
any other substance that would indicate they had more
dangerous items on their collective unwashed persons.

Now that they mentioned Jack she remembered seeing them at his house once. Their piercings should have
alerted her. Many of the young men that visited Jack
often sported similar decoration. They'd come to him
looking to get Jack involved in some scheme. He had
tossed them out with a warning never to come back. If
Jack didn't want anything to do with them they were
either very dumb or very evil.

Maybe a little of each, because they looked at her as
though they were going to hurt her—badly—and as
though they expected her to just let them do it. Not
just dumb—*imbecilic*. Another great word.

"You don't know me at all," she told them, softly.

The smaller one moved toward her, reached out his
hand to brush his dirty fingers across her cheek. "We'll
change that soon enough." His fingers slid down to grip
her jaw—hard. He liked pain.

Fair enough. She'd give him something to love, then.
Calmly, Mila dropped her valise, lifted her own hand
and wrapped her fingers around his wrist. Her gaze held
his glittering one as she applied just the right amount
of pressure in the right spots. How quickly his expres-

sion changed from triumph to realization to pain as she snapped the bones in his wrist with a flick of her fingers. So fragile, human bodies.

He yanked his hand back with a cry, leaving himself open for a punch to the face. His partner lunged for her, blade out. She grabbed his forearm and cracked it. He fell to the ground with a grunt, lashing out at her with his boot. She moved, but he still connected with her hip rather than her stomach.

Mila was not accustomed to violence for the most part. The kick didn't hurt badly, but it did hurt. Instinct made her grab that foot and give it a sharp twist. The blond screamed as a loud snapping noise filled the deepening darkness.

"Was that your knee?" she asked, dropping his foot and whirling around just in time to use her own boot to drive the darker bloke back to the ground. Her foot came down hard on his hand, smashing his fingers so he had no choice but to release the dagger altogether. His hand would never heal properly, she realized with a touch of shame, and even more confusion. Why did they come back for more when she had already hurt them so badly? Why not quit when they had to know she had them beat?

"I wish you hadn't made me hurt you," she told them. "Please don't ever do it again." Then, she picked up her bag and crossed the street to the boardinghouse. As she reached the steps, she looked up and saw an older woman with jet-black hair and violet eyes in the doorway. She wore a black gown made of feathers that made her appear otherworldly. There was something different about her, but Mila couldn't determine just what. Still, she was beautiful and nonthreatening. Somehow, she knew that if she let the woman hug her, everything would suddenly be right with the world.

"That was quite the show," the woman told her with a smile. "Are you hungry?"

Mila's stomach growled in response. "A bit, yes."

The woman stepped back and held the door open for her. "Then you'd better come in."

And Mila did.

Two months earlier...

"This is your room."

Mila walked through the open doorway. Her eyes widened at the sight before her.

"We can make it more to your liking if you want."

She whirled around to face her friend Jack. "I like it. You live in a palace!"

He chuckled at that. "Not quite, but I suppose anything's better than a subterranean cave."

Nodding in agreement, Mila moved about the room. She was almost afraid to touch anything, but she couldn't help herself. The wooden furniture gleamed and smelled of lemon and beeswax. The curtains were rich blue silk that matched the bedclothes. There was carpet on the floor, so soft her feet sank into it. Her feet also left dirty smudges on it.

Jack arched a brow at the marks. "I'm sorry," Mila said, sensing she'd done something bad.

"It's just a bit of dirt, poppet. It will clean, but we'd better get you clean first."

She cocked her head. "Clean. You mean to bathe?" Emily had done that in the cave. She'd wanted water to clean herself, and fresh clothing to put on. Mila's own clothing was dirty and smelled bad.

"Yes," Jack replied. "You'll feel much better once you've bathed. We'll get you into some clean clothes."

He sounded so sincere she just knew it would be a wonderful experience. She pulled the braces off her shoulders and let the baggy trousers she wore fall to the floor, and tore off the equally dirty shirt. When she was done—naked, it was called—she turned to Jack.

He was staring at her with wide eyes and an odd expression on his face. "Little warning before you disrobe in the future, pet." He shook his head. "You don't *look* like a child."

Mila frowned. "Why would I? I'm not a child."

"I know you're not, but you're new to the world, and that makes you like a child, doesn't it?"

She supposed it did. "I'm like Pinocchio. I wasn't real, but now I am."

His expression softened as he kept his gaze on hers. "Now you are." There was a little silence. She was starting to get cold. "Right, let's get that bath started. Finley sent over some clothes that should fit you."

He pulled the quilt from the bottom of the bed and wrapped it around her shoulders, then led her out of the room to another chamber down the hall. This one had odd-looking things in it—almost like the tank the master had been in, but thicker, and prettier.

"It's called a tub," Jack told her. "You fill it with water and sit in it."

"Why?"

He seemed to think that should be obvious. "To get clean. You really don't know anything about this, do you?"

She shook her head. "Not really. If you teach me, I'll learn."

He ran a hand through his long hair. "Teach you?" Jack looked around as though hoping someone else might appear and offer to do it instead. "I reckon it has to be me, doesn't it?"

Mila watched with great interest as he collected two fluffy lengths of cloth from a cupboard. Towels, he called them. He placed the towels on a strange little metal rack that he called a warmer, and then turned the handles inside the tub. Water began flowing into it at great speed. She gasped and, grasping her blanket more tightly around herself, peered into the porcelain vessel. "Astounding."

Jack chuckled. He seemed to find her amusing. "I suppose so. I'm afraid the only soap I have smells of clove. It will have to do for now, but I can get you some of your own if you don't like it." He offered her a brownish block.

She took it, and something made her raise it to her nose. It smelled strong, but wonderful. "I like it."

When the water reached a certain level, Jack stopped the flow and offered her his hand. "Climb in. Wait, give me the blanket first."

She pulled the quilt off and handed it to him. He took it with the hand not holding hers and set it aside. Mila swung her leg over the side and stepped into the water.

"Oh!" This was wonderful! "It's warm."

He grinned. He had a huge smile that showed off his straight white teeth. "Nice, what? Now, sit down. It's even better."

She did as he instructed, sighing as a shudder racked her body. *Delightful*. That was the only word she could think of to describe the experience—*delightful*.

Jack showed her how to lather a sponge with the soap and scrub herself clean. He also showed her how to wash her hair—his fingers massaging her scalp made her shiver. It was so lovely and felt so good that she thought it was only right of her to do it to him, as well.

She grabbed him by the lapels and pulled him over the side of the tub, into the water with her.

He came up sputtering, practically lying on top of her. "What the bloody hell was that for?" he demanded.

He was angry. Mila cringed. What had she done wrong? "I wanted to wash your hair. It's so nice I wanted to do it for you. Was I supposed to warn you first?"

For a moment, he glared at her, and then…then it disappeared. He shifted himself so that he was sitting up rather than reclining on her, and then he began to laugh. He laughed so wonderfully that she began to laugh, too, even though she had no idea why. Was this some part of human behavior she had yet to understand? Or was Jack Dandy just a very odd man?

"Yes," he said finally. "A little warning would have been nice." Then he dragged himself out of the tub, his sodden clothes dripping on the floor. "I'm going to disrobe, poppet. You might want to avert your eyes."

Why would she want to do that? Regardless, she sensed that was what he expected, so she pretended to take great interest in bathing herself while Jack undressed. She watched out of the corner of her eye. Oh. Males were certainly put together differently than females. She quite like the way Jack Dandy looked without his clothes on, but he'd probably get rather cold if he walked around naked all the time. Humans were very fragile that way. The less machine she became, the more she began to understand this.

Jack pulled a robe from the back of the door and pulled it on, tying it tightly at the waist. "I think you're clean," he announced. "Let's get you dried off."

The towels were warm around her head and body. He showed her how to rub the water from her skin, and then helped her into her new clothes. They fit so much better than the ones she'd been wearing, and the plaid trousers, white shirt and black corset were so much prettier. She ran her hands over them.

"We'll go shopping tomorrow," Jack promised. "Get you some new clothes. What's say I go get dressed and make us some supper? We'll stay home for the evening."

Mila's stomach growled in response, drawing another chuckle from him. She felt so…overwhelmed? No, that wasn't quite right. Lucky didn't quite describe it either. She felt…*good.*

She threw her arms around him and hugged him. Then, into his shoulder she said, "I don't know what home is."

Jack patted her on the back. "This is your home now, poppet. You'll know it soon enough."

"Is it ready?" Finley asked…again.

She expected Emily to tell her no, that it hadn't been ready when she asked five minutes ago, and it wasn't ready now. Instead, her friend looked up from the bench where she she'd been at work making adjustments to the suit's helmet for the past forty-three minutes and eighteen seconds. "Yes. Are you?"

She paused. "Is that a trick question? Of course I am."

"All right. You're so determined to do this, let's get it over with."

"Em, you can't be angry at me for wanting to save him."

"I'm not," came the snapped reply as Emily shoved her goggles up onto her forehead. "I'm bloody angry because Garibaldi is dead and still able to play with us. I'm angry because you're going to risk your life to save Griffin, and even if you succeed, we still might not be free of the bounder."

Finley hadn't thought of that. She hadn't thought of anything beyond saving Griffin, really. "How do you destroy a ghost?"

"You can't destroy energy, Finley. It's everything and everywhere."

She didn't believe that. "Birds have to rest. Lightbulbs burn out. Even fire will dwindle if there's nothing for it to consume, or if you snuff it out. We just have to figure out a way to extinguish him."

Wide eyes stared at her. The goggles had left indentations around her eyes and she looked like a little ginger raccoon. "I can't believe you thought of that and I didn't."

Finley's mouth quirked. "You can flog yourself later. Do you think you can figure out a way to drain him of his strength?" This was the first real hope she'd felt since Garibaldi's death. They'd known then that he might become powerful in the Aether. She'd been worried about Griffin ever since.

"If I can't, I know someone who can. Come on, then, into the suit."

"Oh, *now* you're eager." She walked toward the table. A bright but earnest gaze locked with hers. "Not really, but at least I'm not totally convinced that I'm going to end up having to bury both you and Griffin."

Fair enough. Finley hadn't thought of things that

way. It was still odd for her to think of herself as having a friend who would miss her if she died. She'd almost had a friend like that once, but they drifted apart. She didn't even consider how her mother would feel to hear such horrible news. She hadn't thought of anything beyond how painful it would be for her to lose Griffin.

She really was a terrible, selfish person. The realization didn't stop her from jumping into the suit once more.

The lift dinged just as she fastened the last latch and was about to let Emily place the helmet over her head. Sam and Ipsley walked out of the box. The medium looked so incredible fragile and lanky next to the much larger bloke. Ipsley's jacket was tailored to fit his lean frame perfectly, while Sam's shirt threatened to burst at the shoulder seams.

"Wait," Ipsley requested, coming toward them. "I need a personal item of Miss Jayne's."

"Why?" Finley asked.

The ginger smiled. "It will make it so much easier for me to find you in the Aether without physical contact."

Of course. He was going to shadow her in the Aether so that he could report to Emily and Sam on everything that happened. Normally Finley would protest such a plan—she would be afraid of Ipsley discovering her secrets, but she didn't care what he discovered about her if it helped save Griffin. If she was honest, she would have to admit that she rather liked the idea of having company on the journey, in case Lord Felix and his hellish girls decided to show up again.

She removed the earrings Griffin had given her a few weeks ago and placed the rubies into the medium's palm. As his hand closed around them, she wrapped her own fingers around his. "I didn't kill him," she said softly, trusting he would know what she meant.

Ipsley's gaze rose to hers. "I know. The father of a girl who committed suicide after being one of Lord Felix's victims had that pleasure. His lordship was a nasty bit of work, and well on his way to becoming even more of one."

Now that she understood a little better just what sort of monster Lord Felix had been—and had evolved into—she wished that she *had* been the one to end his miserable life. "You might have told me that the day we met," she said. Ipsley had made a point of mentioning the bastard, but had then left her in suspense, afraid to know the truth. She had thought she might have done the deed and not remembered—a pity. She'd also believed that Jack had done it. She was both relieved and a little peeved that he hadn't.

She truly was a horrible person sometimes.

The medium didn't look the least bit apologetic.

"You didn't need me to tell you a truth that in your heart you already knew." He pulled something from his pocket—it was one of Griffin's watches. "Hopefully this will help me guide you to him."

Why hadn't they done this originally? Finley wondered. Oh, yes—because she hadn't waited long enough. If she'd had patience Griffin might be home now, and Lord Felix wouldn't be waiting for her to enter the Aether once more. And he would be waiting for her; she was certain of that. Like he'd said, she was the one that got away. Not only that, but she'd taken him down and humiliated him. That was more than enough for him to want revenge. She could only imagine the pleasure he'd take in adding her to his little harem.

Once she saved Griffin, she was going to set those poor girls free.

Emily put the helmet over her head and secured the clamps, enclosing Finley in her little bubble. Instead of trying to listen to what everyone was saying, she focused on remaining calm. She would be lying if she said she wasn't a little nervous about going back into the Aether after her encounter with Lord Felix and his victims. How was he able to control them? Why didn't they turn on him for what he'd done to them? It made no sense, and it was unsettling. And they had been so strong. She wasn't accustomed to going up against more than a handful of people at one time. They would have ripped her apart had Emily not pulled her back out.

It made her all the more worried about Griffin. Not just worried, but terrified. She refused to let herself think about it, because her mind went immediately to the worst thing—and that was that Griffin was dead, or soon would be. Or even worse, that Garibaldi had totally destroyed Griffin's mind and soul, but left him alive.

For the first time since meeting him, Griffin wasn't there when she needed him. He was the one who gave her the strength and confidence to do half the mad things she did, even if he often gave her the very devil for doing some of them. She couldn't afford to second-guess herself, but that didn't stop her mind from doing it anyway. And she couldn't seem to stop herself from thinking those awful thoughts for much longer than a few moments.

What would she do without him? Who would challenge her? Who else would want to be with her even though she tested his patience on a daily basis? Who would test *her* patience on a daily basis? She pushed aside the useless wondering when tears began to burn her eyes. Time to pull herself together, if not for her own sake, then for Griffin's. If she couldn't stop these terrible thoughts, then she would at least endeavor to ignore them.

Emily knocked on the helmet, and Finley raised her gloved hand. Within seconds she heard the suit's system come to life. She began to breathe in the chloroform that would put her to sleep before the suit more or less killed her. Her eyelids grew heavier with every deep breath. And then, it was as though someone flicked a switch inside her, although she knew time had to have passed.

The dark that overtook her quickly faded to the familiar gray of the Aether as her eyes cleared. She stood on the side of a street lined with incredible mansions, beautiful grounds and ostentatious vehicles. It was truly an upper-class neighborhood—even more so than Mayfair, but in an overblown manner, she realized as she took a closer look. It was as though a satirist had designed the entire area—the incredibly tall homes, the perfect lawns that lacked character, and vehicles that were spotless, shiny and far more fancy than anything she'd ever seen. Everything was immaculate and pristine. She'd wager the cobblestones were all the exact same height—same for all the gates and walls and windows—and that the roads and drives were perfectly straight, any curves completely symmetrical.

It was the most god-awful place she'd ever seen. Completely lacking in personality or beauty.

"Heaven for the privileged," said a voice beside her.

Finley jumped, and turned to find Ipsley standing with her. Or rather, a shadow of Ipsley. He was almost completely transparent—she could just make out his features. It was unsettling because he looked like a ghost.

"Aetheric projection," he explained, seemingly reading her mind. "You can see me because I'm connected to you in our world, and I am able to travel the realm of the dead. This place is obviously the construct of someone who was very wealthy and very obnoxious in his or her life."

"His," Finley informed him. "Only a man could create this."

"How so?" His interest seemed genuine.

She shrugged. "If a woman had made it, there would be curtains in the windows and birds singing. The houses wouldn't be quite so austere. The gardens would be perfect. There's not a flower to be seen here— women care about flowers."

Ipsley nodded. "An interesting deduction. I hope to investigate it someday."

"I don't," she replied honestly. Then she turned from him and glanced down the street, as though her eyes were following an invisible finger. She felt a pull. "Down there." She pointed. "The house at the end."

The medium walked beside her. "Yes. I feel the same pull. His Grace is in that house."

Of course he was. It wasn't the biggest house, but it was the most obnoxious with finials and towers and flags flapping in the breeze. It was also a bloody fortress, complete with guards at the door. Only these guards were swirling black clouds—the things Griffin called Aether demons. They were Garibaldi's pets, and they were nasty. Finley had gone up against them before.

"You are stronger in this world as a ghost than I am as a projection," Ipsley told her. "You bring your strength from the living world with you when you die. You can become stronger, as well, by harnessing the energy around you. Garibaldi has had time to grow his strength, but Griffin is already strong. You are strong, and I will give you whatever strength I have."

"Thank you." How was she going to harness the energy around her? She had no bloody idea how to do that! But she did know how to hit, and these demons had fallen under her fists before.

"Surely you're not planning to go through the front door?"

She stopped and turned. Ipsley stood beside a perfectly boring hedge a few feet away. It was odd, seeing leaves where his eyes ought to be. "New to this world, remember."

"I sincerely doubt you're new to the concept of sneaking about? Subterfuge? Those are the same here as anywhere else."

Normally she'd be offended by his tone, but in this case he was right. "Won't he have prepared for such a thing?"

"Men who think of themselves as geniuses often make the biggest mistakes."

True. And no doubt Garibaldi believed that it would take them longer to get into the Aether—if he'd even entertained the notion of them having the technology. He probably thought he had plenty of time to torture Griffin. He probably didn't think they'd find this place at all if they could access the Aether.

Really, it would be quite stupid for him to underestimate any of them that way. He had to know Sam would do whatever it took to get Griffin back, and he had to know that Emily was just as smart, if not smarter than he was. And that Finley was slightly more mad.

The two of them slipped through the hedge, skirting around to the back of the mansion where two automatons that looked like rubbish bins were stationed.

"Pretty rudimentary," she remarked. "I expected better."

Ipsley glanced up at the tall walls of the house. "I would wager he's invested so much of his power into his demons, his fortress and imprisoning the duke that anything else is too much."

It made sense. Garibaldi had worked with machines all his life. These automatons would be easy for him to build and maintain—probably taking very little of his energy. "Does that mean he'll be easy to defeat?"

"While it would delight me to tell you that, I'm afraid I cannot. I suspect that he's installed several defenses and safeguards. I wouldn't put all your faith in his underestimation of you and your friends either."

"In other words, I should be overly cautious rather than overly cocky."

"Yes, exactly that."

All right, so no rushing in half-cocked and impulsive as she normally did. She had to be careful. She had to think. She had to be more like Griffin.

"Do you feel him?" she asked. "I feel like he's near."

Ipsley nodded. "I'm almost certain…there."

She followed his nearly invisible finger as it pointed at the third floor of the house. There, high above their heads, was a window with bars on it. From inside that room she saw a faint bluish glow, and her heart leaped for joy. She'd know that light anywhere—felt it reflected in her soul.

Griffin.

Chapter 8

As soon as the three of them arrived at Jack's house in Whitechapel, Wildcat removed the dark glasses she'd put on when they left Mayfair and turned those feline eyes of hers to Jack. It was deuce unsettling, that gaze of hers with the oval pupils and unflinching direct-ness. He couldn't help but feel like a very large mouse.

"Can I see her room?" the girl asked. "I need to get her scent in order to track her."

She smelled of oranges, Jack almost told her, but caught himself at the last second. "Follow me." He could have told her where Mila's room was, but he didn't care who they were, or how much Finley liked them, he wasn't going to trust them to wander about unwatched in his house. It went against every instinct he had, even though he was fairly certain the Americans couldn't care less about his business. Still, he hadn't gotten this far by being the trusting sort.

He led them upstairs to Mila's lonely room. She'd been gone a few hours but the house felt as though it had been empty for weeks. Jack felt her absence right down to his bones, the wrongness of it. She belonged here. With him. And this foreign girl walking about looking at everything with disinterestedness rubbed his nerves raw. Mila was not something to be rooted out or hunted. She mattered.

Wildcat picked up a pillow from the bed and looked at Jack. "Mind if I take the cover off?"

He shook his head, and watched as she carefully re-moved the fabric. She tossed the pillow back on the bed and lifted the case to her nose, inhaling deeply. When she lowered the fabric she sniffed the air once, then twice. The pillow case crumpled in her fist, she started for the door. She was honestly going to track Mila like a cat tracked prey. It felt all manner of wrong, but Jack didn't care if she hacked up a hair ball or ate a pigeon if it brought Mila home.

He and Jasper followed Wildcat down the stairs, through the hall and outside once more into the hustle and bustle of Whitechapel.

The afternoon had fallen to darkness, and the street lamps tried their best to illuminate the area. The girl paused on the walk, lifting her face to the chilly breeze. Her mouth opened slightly, as though she was tasting the night. When she lowered her chin and turned her head, her eyes caught the light and flashed like a cat's. Downright bizarre, that was—and oddly thrilling at the same time. What an extraordinary creature. He could have used her in his petty-theft days.

"This way."

When she began walking, Jack followed. He was going to suggest taking his motor carriage, but if Mila left on foot, then he wanted to proceed on foot, as well. Feet could go places wheels could not.

They walked to the Cheapside area, where the scent lingered around St. Paul's. Jack smiled. Of course his curious Mila would pause to explore and learn. She wanted to know everything, and he had indulged her as much as he could, taking her to museums and events. Now he wished he hadn't. Maybe she wouldn't have run off if she hadn't known there was so much world out there just waiting for her. It was a selfish thought, but honest.

Occasionally, Wildcat would stop and smell the pillowcase again, and then the air. No one seemed to notice the three of them trotting along despite the odd picture they had to present. Jasper was all cowboy, from his hat to his duster, right down to his worn boots.

Wildcat was exotic with a huge head of curls, and feline features. And then there was Jack, looking like a lanky undertaker—or a vampire, perhaps. Vampire certainly had a more romantic edge to it, and was better suited to the sinister image he'd worked so hard to cultivate.

In the past he'd been a bad man, and sometimes he still was. He imagined he would be bad in the future, as well. Yet, for all his connections and underworld associations—all the power he'd fought for and won— he had no real idea how to solve the problem that was Mila. He was a master of denial and subterfuge, but even he couldn't lie to himself that well. He would do everything in his power to give Mila the life she deserved, but he wanted her for himself, at least just for a little while. Maybe it was that rotten part of him that just wanted to ruin her innocence and goodness. Or maybe it was because he knew it was wrong to want her, but he wanted her in the worst possible way.

The trail led them onward to Covent Garden. He'd suspect she'd gone to a show, but the theater was closed this time of year—most of society was in the country at their grand houses, hunting and having lavish house parties. Mila knew there wouldn't be any plays for a few months because he'd explained it to her when she'd voiced her disappointment. So, why would she venture there?

They rounded a corner onto King Street and stopped. Wildcat sniffed and looked around. Then she turned and headed straight for a pub not far away. At this point Jack didn't care if Mila was sitting at the bar three sheets to the wind—he'd just be so happy to see her.

But Mila wasn't at the bar when they walked in. She wasn't at a table either.

"I don't see her," he said.

The American girl shook her magnificent head. "No, but I smell her. On them." She discreetly pointed at a table near the back.

Jack's eyes were nowhere as keen as hers, but as he peered through the smoke-hazed light, he spied two familiar faces at that table: The Twins. They weren't twins, of course, not even close. They weren't even related, but that was the big joke. Several times they'd tried to insinuate themselves into Jack's business, his circle. But they were more cruel than smart, and had a view of women Jack found deplorable, so he told them in no uncertain terms to bugger off or he'd make them very sorry.

The two of them had been to his house when Mila was there. In fact, the blond one had commented on her in front of Jack, making rude assumptions about just what sort of girl she was, and whether or not he might "have a go."

Jack hadn't killed him then because it had been broad daylight and there were witnesses. However, he didn't feel quite so particular this time.

Hands in his pockets, he adopted a lazy slouch and approached the table, Jasper and Wildcat close behind. As he neared them, he saw that one had crutches and his arm in a sling while the other had a splint over his wrist and hand. The tips of his fingers were purple and swollen. They looked as though they had been used very badly by someone who knew how to inflict damage.

He almost smiled. That was his girl.

"'Ello, boys," he greeted with a predatory grin as he joined them.

The blond looked warily to his darker companion. "Dandy," he said.

"You two look as though you 'ad a bit of an altercation wiv somefin nasty. Mind if I inquire as to what that was?"

"A gang," the smaller one said.

Jack kept his smile easy. "Lyin' to me ain't a good path to go down, mate."

Wildcat leaned in and smelled them both. "They reek of her."

The dark one shoved her. "Get off, bitch."

She laid open his cheek with one easy swipe of her claws—and claws was the only word to describe them.

The bloke swore and reached for a weapon, but then Jack blinked and Jasper was behind the table, a pistol pointed at each fellow's head. "I'd rethink any thoughts of violence you might be entertainin'," the American advised. "That's my lady you just insulted, and I'm a mite sensitive where she's concerned, so I'm sure you'll understand that I just might twitch and blow your useless heads off. Move and speak carefully now."

This was someone Jack could see himself working with in the future. Very useful indeed were his new American friends. He leaned down, placed both his palms on the scarred tabletop, ignoring that it was sticky beneath his fingers. "Let's give this anover go, shall we? Now, I know the two of you miscreants crossed paths with my girl. I know that she did the world a disservice by lettin' you walk away, but she's better than me in that respect." He looked at one and then the other, making eye contact until he felt them fall under his spell. "Where is she? Tell me quick and you'll walk out of 'ere with all your bits still attached."

The blond looked ill. "She went across the street. Brick place. Woman let her in."

"There, that wasn't so 'ard, was it?" Jack gave them both a small, cold smile. "Go near her again and I'll personally see to it that you spend the rest of your days pissin' out your eyes. 'Ave I made m'self understood?"

They both nodded.

"Excellent." He straightened and gestured at the darker fellow's bleeding cheek. "Might want to get that looked at." Then he turned and walked out—and he didn't care who watched.

"That was a lot easier than I expected," Jasper commented once they were outside. Both pistols were back in their holsters.

Jack shrugged. "People don't normally lie to me."

"And they give you what you want."

"Sometimes."

The American grinned crookedly. "Why, Mr. Dandy. You're a freak just like the rest of us."

Had he been wearing his hat Jack would have tipped it. "Don't let it go to your 'ead." He checked for a lull in traffic before running out into the street. His companions followed him up the steps to the pretty brick house. He rapped the knocker hard.

A gorgeous older woman with glossy black hair and intriguing eyes answered a few moments later. She looked at Jack and blinked, her smile slipping just a bit. He arched a brow—he was certain he'd never met the woman before.

"May I help you?" she inquired, her gaze not leaving his.

Jack inclined his head and put on his best posh, "Forgive us for calling unannounced, Madam, but I was told by two gentlemen that you may have seen a friend of mine."

"I seriously doubt that, my lord," she replied. "My girls are not of your class." Oh, she was good. Jack couldn't quite tell if that was an insult or not.

He smiled. "Her name is Emilia, or Mila. She's about this tall, uncommonly beautiful. A sweet girl. Have you seen her?"

The woman gave a little under his influence—he felt it. Then, she blinked again, and tore her gaze from his—purposefully avoiding contact. How in the devil did she know to do that?

"I'm afraid not, sir. Perhaps you should check with Mrs. Newberry down the street. I know she has at least one vacancy. We're filled up. Sorry I can't be of help. Good day."

Only Jack's well-placed and quick foot prevented the door from closing in his face. He took a silver case from his inside coat pocket and opened it. "Take my card. If you do see her, I would appreciate it if you let me know."

"Of course." Still, she didn't look at him. Instead, she took the card and yanked the door shut. Jack just managed to pull his foot free, otherwise she might have crushed it.

"So much for people not lying to you," Wildcat commented dryly as they walked down the steps.

"She did a poor job of it, too," Jasper added.

Jack nodded. "Indeed." But it was a lie told to protect Mila, and he appreciated it. She was with someone who would look after her.

Wildcat fell into step beside him. "Want me to talk to her?"

He shook his head. "No. Thank you. I would like you to keep an eye on this place, however. Mila's here and she obviously doesn't want to be found just yet. If she wants to prove a point by stretching her wings, I'll let her do just that." And maybe a little female guardianship would do her good. But it had taken every ounce of his strength not to barge into that house and find his girl.

"You want us to spy on her." There was a bit of an edge to Cat's voice.

Jack stopped on the walk and turned to her. "No. I want her kept safe."

"Did you see what she did to those two in the pub? She can take care of herself."

"Physically, yes. But Mila is good. Too good. I won't let anyone ruin that."

Catlike eyes narrowed. "Including you?"

Jack laughed humorlessly, and raised his arm to hail a hack cab. "My dear Cat, especially me."

"He knew I was lying."

Mila stirred honey into her tea. She sat at a small table in the comfortable kitchen in the back of the house that smelled of warm baked bread and freshly brewed tea. It was inviting and comforting. Safe. "Yes. Jack usually does know when people lie." It was an annoying trait because he was such a skilled liar himself.

Mrs. Brooks's sister, whose name was Delilah Rhodes, was very beautiful and not at all impressed. In fact, she looked rather...*peevish*. "You might have told me from whom it was you wished to hide, child."

She took a sip of tea. It needed more honey. "I thought you said you didn't know Jack Dandy."

"I don't." A strange expression crossed the woman's face. "But I know a relative of his, I think. Would you like a little tea with your honey?"

Unperturbed, Mila set the honey pot aside. "Jack doesn't have relatives."

"Everyone has relatives. Family."

"I don't."

The woman shot her a dubious look. "Are you an orphan, dear? There's no one with whom you share blood?"

Oh. Did Finley and Emily and Sam and Griffin and Jasper count? "I suppose maybe there is." She didn't want to discuss them. Mrs. Rhodes might wonder why she hadn't gone to them instead of going to her. "Does this mean you're not going to give me a room?"

The pucker between the woman's brows eased. "No. Of course not. You need a room and I have one for you." She watched Mila closely—enough that Mila reached up and touched her own face to make certain she hadn't dirt on it. "How did a girl like you come to be involved with someone like Jack Dandy? You hardly look his type."

Mila scowled. "I know. He likes girls with more..." She made a gesture around her chest. "He likes dark hair and painted faces. I'm surprised he didn't ask you to come home with him."

Mrs. Rhodes, who had said she was a widow, smiled. She didn't appear the least bit shocked or offended. "I think I'm too old for him."

Mila snorted. "Not bloody likely. He doesn't care about that. He doesn't care about anything."

"When I said you didn't look like his usual preference, I meant it as a compliment."

That did nothing to ease her scowl. "I know."

The chair across from her was pulled out from the

table and the other woman sat down in it. She poured herself a cup of tea. "You like him."

"Jack?" Mila took a sip. The tea was delicious—hot and thick with honey. "Of course. He's my friend. He can't help that he's stupid."

Was that a chuckle? "Men generally can't, darling. No, I mean you like him. You have romantic feelings for him."

"I…I don't know." She reached for one of the cucumber sandwiches on the plate in the middle of the table. "I'm not terribly familiar with romantic feelings."

Lavender eyes regarded her over the rim of a china cup. "You are a very odd girl."

"Yes. I suppose that's because I'm still fairly new to it."

The woman set her cup down and reached across the table to take Mila's hand in her own. She turned it over, studying every inch. "Not even a bruise. Those brutes didn't hurt you at all, did they?"

"I didn't want to give them the opportunity." She didn't pull away, but allowed Mrs. Rhodes to continue her inspection.

"You succeeded on that account."

Was that censure in her voice? Did she think Mila had been wrong to do what she'd done? "They wanted to hurt me."

"I know they did, dear," there was a wealth of re-assurance in her tone. "You did good, giving them a little of their own. How did you manage to hurt them so badly?"

Mila met her gaze. There was nothing in those pretty eyes that made her feel the least bit uneasy or threatened. Still, she wasn't stupid. She resisted the urge to blurt out everything. "I'm odd, you said so yourself."

"Yes, but how odd?"

"Does it matter?"

The woman released her hand and picked up her cup. "I'm curious. I know my sister referred you, but I wonder if I have reason to fear for my safety."

Mila cocked her head to one side. "No, you don't. You wonder if I might be of use to you."

Mrs. Rhodes chuckled again. "Mr. Dandy isn't the only one adept at knowing when a person is lying. Yes, I suppose I am wondering that. I'm also interested in you." She plucked a sandwich from the plate and took a bite. "As a girl I always wished I could be stronger than the boys."

Mila frowned. "Did someone hurt you?"

The other woman's expression became guarded. "It was a long time ago."

"Not that long. That's the same expression you had

on your face when you mentioned Jack having relatives."

There was a screeching sound as the woman shoved back her chair and jumped unsteadily to her feet. "Come, I'll show you to your room."

"I'm sorry for upsetting you."

"You didn't." Mrs. Rhodes rubbed the back of her neck with one hand. "I'm just reminded of things I'd rather not remember let alone discuss. Does that make sense to you?"

"Yes. I don't like to think of the time I spent in the crate."

Those unusual eyes widened. "The crate?"

People, Mila realized too late, did not normally spend time in crates. This was the sort of blurt-out she'd just patted herself on the back for avoiding. "That's what I called it. It was a very small space." Good thing Mrs. Rhodes didn't seem to be quite so talented at recognizing lies when she heard them. Of course, it wasn't that much of a lie.

"Oh, well, I hope you'll find your room much more to your liking."

Mila followed her down the narrow corridor to the polished oak staircase that led up to the next floor. Every other step her landlady took the tiniest bit stilted. She could hear the slight friction of oiled joints beneath

the rustle of skirts. Mrs. Rhodes obviously had a pros-
thetic leg—one of the modern, lightweight kinds that
were strong and made movement less of a chore for the
wearer. Mila wondered how she came about having
such a limb, but asking might be rude, and she didn't
want to offend.

She glanced around at her surroundings. The house
was old, but well cared for and very neat. The wood
gleamed with fresh polish and there was not a speck
of dust to be seen anywhere. Mila envied people who
could keep such a tidy house. Her dressing table at Jack's
was in desperate need of a good dusting.

"Where are the other girls?" she asked, finally realizing how odd it was not to have seen at least one
other lodger.

"At work. Most of my girls work with the Pick-a-
dilly Circus nearby."

"Oh, I love the circus! Jack took me there just last
week."

Mrs. Rhodes smiled over her shoulder as she led Mila
upstairs. "It's delightful, isn't it? It's one of the few en-
tertainments that stays open after the lords and ladies
have retired to the country to shoot poor defenseless
animals."

"Why would they do such an awful thing?" She
made a note to make certain Griffin never took part

in such behavior. She could always break his arms if he tried.

"Because they're rich and bored, and their parents are closely related."

Mila didn't understand, but she grinned because her companion was smiling and seemed to expect it.

At the top of the stairs they turned right and then continued to the second door down the corridor. Mrs. Rhodes withdrew a punch card from a pocket in her gown and inserted it in the slot beside the door. There followed a series of clicks as the lock disengaged. "This card will get you into the house, as well, so take care you don't lose it."

"I'll be very careful."

She opened the door and stepped inside, flicking a switch on the wall to turn on the new modern lights. Mila stepped in behind her, and gasped.

The room wasn't as ornate as the one she had at Jack's, but it suited her better. The walls were painted a soft sandy color, with creamy trim. The bed was large, the wood dark but simply carved as it reached upward to form a canopy high above the mattress. Gauzy lengths of fabric draped around it from a finial in the middle of the top frame. It was like something a princess would sleep in. There was a matching dresser, armoire and dressing table, as well.

"There's a water closet through that door," Mrs. Rhodes said with a gesture. "You'll share it with Henrietta and Millie, whose room is located on the other side of it."

"They share a room?"

The woman's expression changed ever so slightly— as though she wasn't certain what to say. "Yes. They're sisters, and very unique, as well. I'm sure you'll get on quite well with them. All my girls are extraordinary."

"I don't want to be extraordinary," she remarked, hoping she didn't sound whiny. "I just want to be like everyone else."

"Oh, my dear girl." Mrs. Rhodes' expression was caught between amusement and sympathy. "I don't believe that's possible."

Chapter 9

"How do you plan to get around the automatons?"

Finley glanced at Ipsley. They were hiding in some overblown shrubbery cut and shaped to resemble Garibaldi himself. It was ridiculous. He was easier for her to see now, her eyes accustomed to his shadowy form. "I don't," she replied.

"You…don't?"

She shook her head, turning her attention back to Garibaldi's ridiculously large house. "That's what he expects. It's why they're there. He's not stupid, but he thinks we are. He's too arrogant to put his safety and security completely in the hands of his creations—demon or machine. Their job is to preoccupy and deflect any attacks while he mounts his own defensive. A diversion so he can have the pleasure of doing the real damage."

"But how are we going to get inside?"

"Can't you just pop in?" That was part of the reason he was there, wasn't it? Because he could travel quicker than she could, and go places she couldn't?

"My connection with His Grace allows me to feel his presence, but transporting myself to him is almost impossible. I'm not sure what Garibaldi has done, but it's as though he's used some sort of Aetheric dampener. Trying to make contact is like trying to use a magnet to attract glass. I cannot get His Grace to acknowledge me."

Finley sighed. Why couldn't Garibaldi be less intelligent? Why did he have to be both evil and a genius? So much for avoiding the automatons altogether. Without the element of surprise they weren't going to get very far. She was definitely up for a fight, but not if it made things worse for Griffin.

"I'm going to climb up the side of the house to the room Griffin is in. Can you do that?"

"Perhaps. My current form has no mass in this realm, but that also means my tangibility is questionable."

"What if you popped up once I made it to the room? You can still get a fix on me, can't you?"

It wasn't often that Finley got to enjoy the look of someone who thought she was smart. It wasn't that she was dumb, but with Griffin and Emily around it

was next to impossible to look intelligent in compari-
son. Usually her smarts pointed in a different direction.
Granted, a more underhanded and violent direction, but
it was no less effective. She'd wager Emily didn't know
the exact amount of force it took for a punch to break
ribs without puncturing the lungs. Or how much stress
an arm could take before it snapped. It was a delicate
balance that changed with every opponent.

"Yes. The dampener seems to be focused exclusively
on the duke. I should be able to meet you when you
get to the room."

"Good. If the metal or ghosts start patrolling I'm
going to need you to create a diversion."

"Of course. I've got your back."

In the physical realm Finley had to admit that she
wouldn't feel exactly confident with Ipsley as her
backup. She doubted the dear boy even knew how to
throw a punch, but that didn't matter here. Here, Ipsley was more powerful than she could ever hope to be.

"Right, here I go, then." Crouched low, she darted
from the hedge where they had hidden and raced toward the mansion. It was a strange feeling, running
without feeling an increase in her heart rate, or the in
and out of her breath. She was dead, for all intents and
purposes, and the dead didn't breathe or have a pulse.
And yet, she had to climb the house because she had

no other idea of how to get to where Griffin was. She certainly couldn't just wish herself by his side the way Ipsley should have been able to do—her mind didn't allow for that sort of thing.

However, her mind knew full well her physical capabilities, and she capitalized on that confidence. Her foot came up on a lower windowsill and she vaulted up, catching hold of a low balcony. She easily pulled herself up and then hopped up onto the balustrade. From there she easily found another handhold in the brick. It was as easy as scaling King House.

Suspicion teased the edges of her mind. What if she was walking into a trap? Surely a man as smart as The Machinist would have made his fortress difficult to climb? What if Garibaldi was omnipotent in this realm and already knew what she was going to do before she did? What if she got to that room and Griffin wasn't there? Or worse, what if The Machinist had already destroyed him, leaving just enough of him for her to find?

She paused, and for a moment, entertained the thought of running back to Ipsley, but then she continued her climb. Fear was sometimes a good thing, but not in this case. She shoved it aside, tightened her grip on the stone and pulled. Garibaldi was smart in the same way that Griffin and Emily were smart. He could easily suppose what action people would take.

He was not, however, a physical being. He might expect someone like her or Sam to start a fight, to punch their way in, but he wouldn't expect someone to climb his house barehanded. He was probably prepared for a dirigible assault, but she'd wager the windows weren't even locked.

Eventually, she made it to the window. It took a bit of a shove to open it as it was—surprisingly—latched. That was the extent of the security. She didn't even see something to rouse an alarm if the window was opened.

So, maybe Garibaldi wasn't so smart after all, because Finley was pretty certain even she could come up with something better than an ordinary latch.

She slipped her legs over the windowsill and slipped into the room. It was austere—like a hospital ward only not as inviting. She wouldn't keep an animal in this place. There was one window, a bare lightbulb, and a huge machine near the bed from which wires and tubes ran. The engine hummed, vibrating through the floor so that she could feel it in the soles of her feet.

There was an old bed, and Griffin was strapped to it. She ran to him, falling hard on her knees beside the bed. She grabbed his hand—the manacle around his wrist had left bruises.

He looked awful. He looked as though he'd been gone days rather than hours. Stubble covered his jaw, and his thick hair was an unruly mess. There were dark circles beneath his eyes. Still, he was the finest thing Finley had ever seen. Tears burned her eyes and she didn't care to stop them from falling.

"Griffin," she whispered, before pressing her lips to his.

His eyelashes fluttered, then opened. His familiar gaze was cloudy and unfocused. That was when she noticed the wires connected to his head and chest. And there were runes etched into the irons that held him— runes much like those tattooed on his skin as well as her own. He'd used them—and ink made from Organites to help bind the two sides of her personality. Garibaldi used them now in some sort of incantation to imprison him, and probably drain him of power.

"Fin?"

Tears spilled down her cheeks as she set her cheek against his chest. "You're alive."

"For now," came the hoarse whisper. "Fin, you can't be here."

Her head jerked up, tears drying up. "Don't you dare start in on that nonsense. I'm here to save you, Griffin King, and I'm not leaving the Aether without you."

"He's locked me here. I can't escape. I can't even summon the Aether. He's won."

"Don't say that."

"As long as he has me, he won't bother you."

"You're an idiot," she informed him. "And I am so pissed at you for asking me to leave you. How dare you! Aside from that, Garibaldi will come for each of us before he's done with you, just to make you suffer a little bit longer."

"I know, but if you leave me it will give you more time to prepare, to figure out how to beat him."

"Bollocks. This ends now. I don't care how we have to do it, but I didn't die just to have you tell me to give up. Am I making myself perfectly clear?"

A faint smile tugged at the corners of his mouth. "I've missed you."

No more tears. They'd had their chance. "I miss you, too."

"How did you get here? You didn't really die, did you?"

It would be an absurd conversation under different circumstances. "Tesla suit—with some modifications. How do I get you out of these restraints?"

"He's using my own abilities against me. Remove the connections from my head and chest and the shackles should open themselves."

Finley reached up to remove the wires from his head. The first one came away with blood on it. "Griffin…" Her stomach rolled.

The connectors were *in* him.

"I know," he whispered. "Just do it, love."

Fingers trembling, she pulled another free—and saw him wince. "I can't do this."

"You can," he insisted. "If you want to free me you have to. It's not that bad. Keep going."

He was a horrible liar, but one thing he said was true—if she wanted to free him she had to do this. When she got a hold of Garibaldi she was going to kick his arse so hard he'd spend the rest of eternity spinning in circles. Gritting her teeth, she reached for another wire, and then another and another.

Finally, she had removed them all. Just as Griffin predicted the shackles clicked open. It was her turn to wince when she saw his battered ankles and wrists. Blood trickled down his naked chest and dripped down his face. She wiped at the sticky mess with the sheet from the bed.

"I want to kiss you but we have to leave," he said. "Now."

She stood and helped him off the bed. He was so weak he had to lean on her. She had carried him before and didn't mind doing so again, but the sight of him weakened cut deep into the meat of her. They made their way toward the window, where Ipsley suddenly appeared.

"Good to see you, Your Grace," he said. "Miss Jayne, I found someone—"

"Later," she cut him off. "Garibaldi has to know we're here by now." No sooner had the words left her mouth than the door to the room flew open and in walked the man himself.

In life Garibaldi had been a fairly attractive man of Italian descent with a metal hand and a mind ravaged by revenge and madness. In death he was perhaps even more handsome, but in a dark and sinister manner. He was dressed impeccably in a black frock coat, black trousers and black boots. Only his cravat had color and it was a dark, rich red.

"How wonderful," he said, his voice deeper and louder than she remembered. "Guests! I must admit, I had hoped you would come but doubted you would be able to make such hopes a reality. Miss O'Brien is one intelligent little girl."

Of course he would give all the credit to Emily. That was fine—Emily was brilliant. But didn't Finley deserve some praise for being the one reckless enough to hop into a death suit and cross over to save the bloke she loved?

Oh, God. She loved Griffin. While not a new thought, the depth of meaning behind it finally hit her. She loved him. As in loved him more than her own life. Loved him more than biscuits or hot chocolate. She loved him so much that she'd risked her life for him and hadn't even thought of how her own death might pain her mother and stepfather. She hadn't thought of anything but saving him.

This puffed up rooster was not going to have him.

"Ipsley," Finley said, not taking her eyes off Garibaldi. "Some help here."

Before the medium could even reply, Garibaldi raised his hand and sent a blast of energy spiraling at him, knocking him out the window.

"Finley, run," Griffin commanded, struggling to hold himself upright. His eyes began to glow faintly with blue power. It wasn't going to be enough. He wasn't strong enough to face The Machinist, and the villain had filled himself up on Griffin's power.

"No," she replied, standing at his side, letting him lean on her. "I'm not leaving without you."

"How touching!" Garibaldi grinned at them. "And you're right, Miss Jayne. You're not leaving. Ever." He tossed a bolt of energy at her. She barely managed to dodge in time and the heat of it brushed her hair. She could smell the burn.

Griffin fired back, but his aim was off and the bolt struck the wall by Garibaldi's head. He laughed. Finley had never wanted to kill anyone so much in her entire life—not even Lord Felix. She looked around for something to throw at him or use as a weapon or shield.

The light around Garibaldi's hands grew even hotter and brighter. If he hit her—and he most likely would—it was really going to hurt. She didn't fool herself that he'd kill her so quickly. She pulled Griffin toward the window. "We have to get out of here."

"Oh, I don't think so." Garibaldi fired again, and just as Finley braced herself for the blow, putting herself between him and Griffin, she was grabbed by a pair of strong hands and propelled closer to the window. A man held up an odd-looking shield that seemed to absorb Garibaldi's blast.

"Damn you, Thomas!" The Machinist shouted.

Thomas? Finley glanced at their savior as he shoved both her and Griffin out the window. Good God, it couldn't be... Then, he looked at her as they plummeted toward the ground, and she knew for certain who he was.

Her father.

Falling. It felt a lot like flying.

Garibaldi watched them from the window as they plummeted to the ground. He smiled at Griffin—even raised his hand in farewell. It wasn't over between them, not by any stretch of the imagination. It wouldn't be over until one of them was destroyed completely.

The fall seemed to take forever even though the wind tore through his hair, and The Machinist fell away. Griffin could still see his enemy so clearly, was aware of so much around him, as though time had slowed. Was this how it felt to be Jasper?

He should have told Finley about her father, but there hadn't been time. Should have prepared her. Thank God Thomas had come back when he did. When he'd disappeared Griffin had thought Garibaldi had something to do with it—that the villain was onto them. He was now.

He wasn't a violent person, but he'd like to kick Garibaldi's smug smile off his face. He couldn't even feel the Aether. Damn it, where was it? It was all around him, why couldn't he feel it?

"Let go," whispered a voice.

Griffin turned his head. Out of the corner of his eye he could see the ground rushing up to meet him, but somehow they were still miles above it. There, in the forefront of his vision was a beautiful young woman. He recognized her immediately—she was his mother. She smiled that serene smile he always associated with times he'd been naughty in a way that amused her.

"Just let go," she told him. "Let it all go."

He frowned. How could she tell him to do that when Garibaldi was such a threat? Or did she mean that he should let go of life and die? That would make sure Finley was protected, wouldn't it? No, but it would make it easier for him to fight Garibaldi.

God, he didn't want to let go. He didn't want to say goodbye to his friends, to Finley. He would, though, if he had to. Drawing a deep breath, Griffin closed his eyes and waited. He waited for death.

Then he hit the ground and there was nothing.

Finley had no memory of her father, but she had seen photographs of him. In an odd twist of fate, most of those photographs had been in Griffin's possession as Thomas had worked for the former duke as something of a chemist. It was that partnership that eventually led to her father inventing a potion that was supposed to bring out a man's full potential, but instead brought out an aggressive nature. Finley was conceived while her father tested the elixir on himself, and the mutation was passed on from father to daughter. Thomas was led to his death during one of his "episodes" by Leonardo Garibaldi. He was shot to death in the street by police who thought he was some sort of lunatic.

She'd only learned the truth about her birth and his death since taking up with Griffin. Prior to that she'd simply thought of herself as a freak, with a monstrous side to her nature that couldn't be controlled. When her mother revealed the reality of it to her, it had been something of a relief to know that it hadn't been her own fault that she was different. And then Griffin had helped her with the rest.

She looked a lot like her father, Finley realized. He was tall and lean and his eyes were the same amber color as hers. It was odd that he looked so much younger than her mother, but then he'd been dead for almost fourteen years.

There were so many things she wanted to ask him, not the least of which was how had they managed to escape Garibaldi. One second they were falling out a window and the next they were sitting in a comfortable drawing room with no windows. Griffin had lost consciousness and any questions vanished in the shadow of her concern for him. She sat on the sofa with his head in her lap, running her fingers through his hair as he slept, and looked around.

The room was comfortable, though a bit on the small side. The walls were dark green paper and oak panels, and the floors were highly polished slabs of wood covered with elegant carpets. Nothing fussy or the least bit feminine. There was a photograph of her on the mantel from when she was a baby, and another more recent one that she didn't remember having taken sat in a frame on the writing desk. Maybe the dead didn't need cameras or film. Maybe they could just capture a moment whenever they wanted. She turned to her father; he fidgeted under her gaze.

"I'd offer you tea," Thomas said, "but it's not as though there'd be any sustenance gained from it." He looked uncomfortable, as though he didn't know what to say, but couldn't stop staring at her. This probably wasn't how he'd intended for them to meet.

"What is that thing?" she asked, pointing at the shield he'd used against The Machinist.

"Absorption shield," he replied simply. "It does just what the name implies, takes and stores Aetheric energy."

"Did you make it?" Griffin inquired, his eyes still closed.

Finley started. She hadn't known he was awake. She tried to withdraw her fingers from his hair, but he reached up and touched her hand. She went back to combing.

"I did construct it, yes," Thomas admitted. "Come to think of it, why don't you sit up there, son. Let's see if we can redirect her and give your batteries a bit of a boost. You might want to move, Finley, my girl."

A peevish part of her wanted to inform him that she

wasn't his girl because he'd gone and gotten himself murdered before she even knew his face, but she kept her silence. Instead, she gently lifted Griffin's head so she could scoot out from under him and step aside. She stayed close, however, just in case he needed her.

Finley watched as her father lifted the shield, directed it at Griffin and then slid a lever on the back. A low buzzing sound came from the device, then it turned into a crackle as blue light danced along the polished surface. A bolt of pure, gorgeous energy shot from the shield straight into Griffin's chest. He jerked back on the sofa. She jumped toward him, but then she saw the bruises on his wrists begin to fade and the holes from the wires on his chest shrink a little. The darkness beneath his eyes faded some, as well.

"It's all right, Finley," Thomas said. "It will heal him."

"How?" she demanded. If he'd been wrong he could have killed Griffin. She didn't relish the idea of breaking her own father's face. "I thought absorbing too much Aether was dangerous for him."

"Having no place for it to go is what's dangerous, but taking it in? No, that just feeds his talent."

She sat down beside Griffin, and placed her hand on his arm. His shirt hung open, revealing his healing chest. She fastened the buttons to keep him warm.

It wasn't much, but it made her feel helpful. "How do you feel?"

"Better." He looked at her father. "I owe you a debt, sir."

Thomas waved a long hand. "You owe me nothing. You've been good to my daughter, and that's worth a fortune to me."

What was she supposed to say to that? The man obviously loved her, and she knew that on some level she loved him, as well, but they didn't know each other, not at all. And she wasn't certain how much they could trust him. Thus far, everything and everyone she'd encountered in the Aether had been malevolent.

"Why are we still here?" she asked. "We got you away from Garibaldi."

"Getting away from him isn't enough," Griffin explained. "If I leave now, he'll only come for me again, and he'd come for you, too."

She stared at him. "Don't tell me you plan to stay here?"

He wasn't the least bit intimidated by her, blast him. "I do intend to stay here, until I've destroyed Garibaldi once and for all. I could use your help, Mr. Sheppard."

"Of course, Your Grace. As soon as Finley returns to the living world I would be more than happy to assist in any way I can. Garibaldi is a monster that must be stopped. He thinks he's God now."

"He's more powerful that he ought to be," Griffin remarked. "Obviously he's been working toward this for some time."

"I'm not returning anywhere," Finley informed them both. "I'm staying right here and I'm helping in any way I can."

Griffin turned to her. She hated how tired he looked. How defeated. "Having you somewhere safe while all this is going on would give me peace of mind, Fin."

"But I'm not safe—you said that yourself. So long as Garibaldi exists in any plane, he'll hunt for us. I'm not going to sit around and wait for him to come for me. I'm fighting him—with you." She looked at her father. "With you, as well. Shame on you for thinking you could just show up and dismiss me."

Thomas shook his head, but there was a smile on his face. "I suppose I'd hoped you were more like your mother than me in regards to this sort of thing."

"Garibaldi took you from me." Her voice shook with anger. "He's trying to take Griffin. I take both of those things very seriously. Personally." Not to mention that all the fantasies she'd ever had about what she'd say if she somehow met her father had played out completely differently than this. She couldn't even enjoy it.

Couldn't ask him all the things she wanted to know, because of bloody Garibaldi. God, she didn't even completely believe he was good! Part of her wanting to stay was so she could protect Griffin from him if necessary.

"All right," her father capitulated. "You have as much right to take part in this as we do."

"But not him," she pointed at Ipsley, who had been quiet all along. "You need to tell Sam and Emily not to bring me out unless it's absolutely necessary. And then you need to stay out of Garibaldi's way. This isn't your fight."

"Perhaps not," the medium agreed, "but I'm in it, regardless."

Finley's opinion of the young man rose several notches.

"Silverus, do you think you could organize a séance at my house?" Griffin asked. "Use our friends and a couple of yours who are the most sensitive to the Aether?"

"I'm sure I could, even on short notice. What do you have in mind?"

"If you could summon Garibaldi to a séance, he would be less of this realm and perhaps easier to defeat."

"But we also run the risk of him possessing one of those summoning him."

Griffin made a face. "He has too much power in this

realm. He won't give that up for a human suit, but he can't resist the urge to brag."

"It could work," Thomas agreed. "Weaken him just enough to give us a power advantage."

"You've been here longer than him," Finley said. "Why aren't you as strong?" It wasn't an insult, just curiosity.

Her father smiled. "Most of my strength has gone into anchoring myself to this realm rather than moving on as Edward and Helena have done."

She turned sharply to Griffin. "Your parents aren't here anymore?"

He shook his head, old sadness reflected in his eyes. "After the last time Garibaldi tried to use them, we agreed it would be better if they passed over." He turned away and Finley's eyes narrowed. What wasn't he telling her? He was usually honest to a fault, so the fact that he was keeping secrets irked her.

"Why are you still here if your friends are gone?" Finley asked of her father. "Why not go to heaven or, wherever?" She certainly hoped he wasn't bound for hell!

The three men looked at her as though she should know the answer.

"To watch over you, Fin," Griffin said, voice strangely gentle.

"Oh." She didn't know what else to say. Fourteen years was a long time to drift around in limbo—purgatory—especially for a man who was insatiably curious about the secrets of the universe and how everything worked. "Thank you."

"You don't thank a father for doing his job, my dear," her father informed her with a smile. "Now, we have work to do. Griffin, I'm going to get started on rebuilding your strength. Mr. Ipsley, you have a séance to plan, and Finley—you and I have something that needs to be taken care of before we can engage Garibaldi."

Finley frowned. "What's that?"

Her father's face took on a darkly grim expression. "Felix August-Raynes."

Chapter 10

Mila met the rest of Mrs. Rhodes's boarders the following morning. All of the girls were Pick-a-dilly performers, some of whom she had actually seen perform when she attended the circus with Jack. There was Sasha, the tightrope walker, Marissa and Gina, who flew high above the audience on the trapeze, Lizzie, who did dangerous and amazing things with fire, and Millie and Henrietta—the twins.

The twins were perhaps the most amazing to Mila. They were pretty girls, both with dark hair and eyes, but they were literally joined at the hip. The circus called them the Gemini Sisters and they did things like juggling and playing instruments where the entire act depended on their cooperation and timing.

"Our entire lives have been about learning to work

together," Henrietta told her as she helped herself to another scone, and took one for her sister, as well. "It's not really all that difficult to do what we do."

"We know each other so well, it's fairly simple to predict our behavior and actions," Millie added as she slathered strawberry jam on the scones she sliced into halves. She set two halves on her sister's plate.

"I think it's wonderful," Mila replied, and she meant it. She smiled at the table full of girls. "I'm so envious of each of you for having such exciting employment."

Gina, a gorgeous girl with large blue eyes and tanned skin, made a scoffing noise as she poured herself a cup of coffee from the silver pot on the table. "Yes, it's so exciting to risk our lives for the enjoyment of others."

Helping herself to some eggs, Mila looked at her. "Is there something else you'd rather do?"

The girl seemed surprised by the question. "Of course not."

That drew laughter from the rest of the table. Mila smiled, not quite certain she understood the joke.

"What do you do, Mila?" Lizzie asked as she slathered a thick coating of soft butter on a piece of toast.

"I don't know," she replied honestly. "I suppose that's why I'm here. To find out what I'm good at."

Marissa, a short but strong blonde, raised a brow. "But how do you pay the rent?"

Gina elbowed her. "That's none of your business."

"I have a little money," Mila replied. She didn't know exactly why, but she knew it was important not to say how much she actually had. It had been given to her for nothing, and these girls worked hard for every penny. Plus, then she'd have to explain about Jack, and she didn't want to talk about him. Didn't even want to think about him. It was bad enough that she'd dreamed of him the entire night.

"Excuse Sissy, Mila," Lizzie said. "She likes to know everything about every person she meets."

Marissa looked chagrined. "I'm sorry. I didn't mean to pry."

Mila smiled at the girl and accepted Henrietta's offer of more coffee. She tried not to stare as Henrietta managed the coffee pot while her attached sister added cream and sugar. They managed to avoid collision despite how close their hands and arms often came. They were more impressively graceful and exact than many machines, a fact she found utterly fascinating.

"His Lordship came for Gracie last night," Gina informed them all in a dramatically low voice. This announcement seemed to mean something to the other girls. Something important.

"She'll be set for a while, won't she?" Marissa asked no one in particular. "And it's not as though he's ugly."

"He's old!" That was from Sasha—tall and willowy and very pale with sable hair. She didn't say much, but then she wasn't given much of an opportunity.

"He's handsome," Henrietta allowed with a shrug, "but it could have been worse."

"How?" Gina demanded. "She doesn't love him."

Henrietta looked around the table, her gaze settling on her sister's face. "He could have chosen one of us."

"Chosen you for what?" Mila inquired, glancing around. "And who is he?" She took a drink of her coffee.

"Lord Blackhurst," Marissa told her when no one else spoke. Her expression was stoic—tight. "He likes circus girls."

"So?" Mila liked pie, but she'd never been as grave about it as these girls were.

Henrietta reached over and patted her on the leg. "He likes to set them up as his mistresses, sweetie. Buys their clothes, pays their rent and in return expects them to share their bed with him."

"Oh." And then her brain caught up. *"Oh."* He made the girl his doxies. Only Jack never paid anyone's rent—not that she knew of. In fact, she hadn't seen him pay any of the girls anything. His girls seemed to like him well enough. Perhaps they shared his bed for free.

She disliked them even more now. And she wasn't quite certain how the idea made her feel about Jack.

"Such things are hardly suitable breakfast conversation," came Mrs. Rhodes's voice from the doorway.

The girls jumped. "Yes, missus," Sasha said, and they all went back to eating rather than gossiping. Though a meaningful glance went around the table, and Mila understood it loud and clear—they would continue the conversation as soon as they could.

Later, as the other girls were getting ready to leave for the circus to practice their acts for the evening performance, Gina suggested that Mila come by and watch the show.

"I would like that," Mila agreed with a grin. She had learned about friendship from Emily, and delighted in feeling the sort of warmth that came along with making a connection with another person. Plus, it would be boring hanging about the house all day. She could go out, but Jack was out there, and he just might follow her. If he was watching, she wanted him to see her with the girls, as part of the group and not by herself. She wanted him to believe that she was fine without him.

The girls all smiled at her as they filed out of the house. As the door closed there was a sudden and violent crash from the street. Shouts rose up and people screamed.

Mila pulled the door open. The girls were still on the steps and front walk, staring in horror at the sight just across the cobblestones. It looked as though a giant hand had reached down, grabbed up a couple of vehicles and gave them a good crumple before tossing them on the ground.

"He swerved to avoid a cart and the carriage went over," Sasha informed her, eyes wide and face pale.

A steam carriage had indeed tipped and crashed, trapping its driver beneath it.

"The exhaust will burn him alive!" Gina exclaimed in horror, pressing her hand to the front of her corset.

The man was terribly close to the brass pipe that expelled the hot vapors from the engine. He cried out in pain as a puff of steam rolled out, burning and dampening his flesh.

Mila didn't think, she simply reacted. People cried out, but no one moved. A bell clanged, summoning help, but the man would be horribly burned before anyone arrived. She jumped from the top step to the sidewalk and sprinted across the street. People jumped back when they saw her coming. Too fast. She knew she moved faster than a regular person and she didn't care. She ran to the wreck, crouched beside the man and grasped the edge of the carriage with both hands—avoiding the discharging steam.

"What are you doing?" the driver demanded. "Get away, you'll hurt yourself."

The right half of his face was bright red, already burned.

"I'm going to lift this off of you. As soon as you can, you crawl out."

"You're mad! You can't lift—"

She could, and she did. She squatted and gripped the edge of the frame, her fingers finding purchase on a thin lip of trim. The man's jaw gaped as she pushed with her legs, lifting the heavy vehicle from his pinned body. She glanced down at him. "More? Or are you good?"

"G-good," he replied, scurrying out from beneath the vehicle. Once he was clear, she lowered the carriage back to the street. The gathered crowd chattered around her, gasped and applauded. She heard the click of a camera and turned her head—a photographer had set up not ten feet away. He could stop to take photographs but not to help? What sort of man was he?

"I don't suppose you could help us out, could you?" asked a voice above her head.

Mila looked up. A man's head poked up through the door of the overturned carriage. He offered her a shaky smile. "We can't quite climb out."

"Oh, of course." Bracing her palms on the carriage, she hefted herself up, opened the door and offered her hand to the man and young boy inside. She hauled the boy out first, then his father, and assisted them both to the street. She hopped down with the boy in her arms.

By then, the authorities had arrived. Mila gave the boy to his father, and slipped into the crowd. She was followed by a few people, including the photographer.

"Miss!" he called. "Miss, a word, please?"

She whirled on him. "Leave me alone. You didn't even try to help."

He looked at her as though she were mad. "Why would I?"

What a disgusting waste of humanity. An embarrassment to his kind. She turned her back on him and rejoined the girls at the boardinghouse. People watched her, but no one else approached. The girls stared at her.

"Well," said Marissa with a grin. "I think we've found what you're good at."

From the number of poor people in London, Mila had thought getting a job was a difficult endeavor. Even Jack didn't have a *job*. It turned out, however, to be quite simple to gain employment. All she had to do was walk into the office of Mr. Anders, the manager of Pick-a-dilly Circus, and pick up his desk.

With him and all the girls from Mrs. Rhodes's sitting on it.

"I'll be jiggered!" the man exclaimed from his perch, little round glasses sliding down his thin nose. "You start tonight! Go talk to Elsie about arranging the act."

Mila peered up at from beneath their feet. She had lifted the desk almost completely above her head. "Should I put you down first?"

"A sound notion," her new employer replied with a chuckle. He looked like a baby sparrow.

The girls giggled in glee as they escorted her to the main performance area where a petite, voluptuous woman with impossibly red hair piled on top of her head was arguing with a man easily twice her height.

"That's Georges," Millie whispered, leaning across her sister to do so. "He's from France and just over ten feet tall!"

"Millie thinks he's cute," Henrietta added.

Her sister flushed. "Well, you like Elsie."

Henrietta blushed, as well, and Mila stared at them both for just a second before looking at the man and woman about whom the twins spoke. The world was much more complex and incredible than she'd first thought. People came in all shapes and sizes, and apparently love didn't care if the object of your affection was the same sex as you or not—though she'd read text that tried to make her believe otherwise.

And how extraordinary were Millie and Henrietta?

On the way there someone had called them freaks. Mila wanted to punch the woman, but Millie just smiled and said, "Yes, and it's contagious." Then she pretended to sneeze on the woman and her companion, who scurried away, making all sorts of disgusted and fearful noises. All the girls had laughed, linked arms and continued on their way.

The moment Gina's arm looped through hers, and Henrietta took her other, Mila knew what it was to have friends. To belong. She would do anything to protect these girls and that feeling.

"I wish I knew what they were saying," Marissa whispered. "They sound angry."

Mila glanced at her. "She's saying that he has no romance in his soul, that he's an embarrassment to Frenchmen everywhere and ought to be ashamed of himself for that abysmal performance."

The girls all stared at her. "You understand French?"

Right, that wasn't normal either. But these girls didn't know she had begun life as a highly complex machine with a enhanced logic engine capable of infinite learning. "Yes," she said. "And he just told her that she's heartless because his routines are nothing but a study in passion."

Beside her the twins sighed. Gina snorted. It was that rude noise that interrupted the fierce exchange going on just a few feet away. Elsie turned around and stared at them. "Oy, what do you lot want?"

Mila's brows shot up. It was hard to believe that such flawless French could be followed by such a typical cockney accent. Then again, Jack could speak Latin. He would do that sometimes around the house. He said it was to keep both of their minds sharp.

"This is Mila, Elsie," Gina said. "Mr. Anders just hired her."

"To be wot?"

"The World's Strongest Girl," said Millie.

"Woman," corrected her sister.

Elsie ignored them. "'Ow strong are ya?"

"Strong," Mila replied with a shrug. She had no idea if there was a limit to her strength—it had never been tested.

Georges picked up a large pair of iron manacles and tossed them at her. She caught them easily—which seemed to surprise the giant. "What do you want me to do with these?"

"Put 'em on," Elsie instructed. "Then try to break free."

"That seems like a waste of time." Mila grabbed the thick links of chain in either hand and pulled until the iron snapped apart. Easy. She tossed the ruined restraints back to Georges. "A ruin of good chain, too. Anything else?"

"*Mon Dieu,*" said Georges. "*Elle est fantastique!*" He then brought her a large steel bar—solid—and made a motion that she should try to bend it.

Mila bent the bar in half. She liked the way it felt in her hands, all that metal helpless against her will.

Georges grabbed her head in his huge hands and kissed her soundly on either cheek, laughing and praising her in his native tongue. He called her magnificent, beautiful—a gift from God even.

"Now, that's wot I'm talkin' about!" Elsie enthused and clapped Georges on the hip—she only came up to just above his waist. "Give this girl an act, Georgie boy! Meanwhile, come wiv me, girlie. We've got to get you outfitted. You start tonight."

Her friends cheered and hugged Mila, who grinned happily and allowed herself to be pulled into the wardrobe area to try on costumes.

Jack had said the world could be dangerous. He never said just how wonderful it could be, as well!

Finley watched Griffin as he slept. There was little else for her to do.

That was wrong. She could hunt down Lord Felix, but he wasn't worth leaving Griffin's side. Wasn't worth leaving her father, even though he'd tried to talk her into doing just that. Truth be told, she was a little afraid of facing Felix and his girls again. There wasn't much in the world that frightened her, but those girls did. She didn't want to end up one of them.

She glanced at the stranger with the familiar face. Her father. She didn't know what to call him—Papa seemed to personal. She didn't even know how to talk to him. She loved him by virtue of who he was, but he was a total stranger. He didn't seem to know what to do with her either.

"How much longer do you have before you're forced to wake up?" he asked.

"No idea," she replied honestly. "Soon, probably." She wasn't worried. Emily would make certain she did what she was supposed to. She was just going to sit here and guard Griffin while he regained his strength.

"He means a lot to you."

She didn't look up. "Yes."

"His father was a good man. I was honored to call him a friend." He stretched out his legs from the chair where he sat, across from her own. Griffin was between them on a settee. "You know, it's odd that you and Griffin found one another again. You played together as children."

That made her look up. Her astonished gaze met his twinkling one. "We did?"

He nodded. "The former duke and duchess, God rest their souls, used to invite your mother and me over from time to time. They didn't care one wit that we weren't of the same social circles. They believed in playing with children, and spending time with them. They would ask us to bring you with us so that Griffin could play with another child. Sometimes his steward would bring his son, as well."

Good lord, she and Griffin *and* Sam used to play together? She would have been very young—three at the most. "I wish I could remember it." And then, before she lost her nerve, "I wish I could remember you."

"Yes, well…" He rubbed the back of his neck. He looked so young. Far too young to be the father of a girl almost seventeen, but then, he was frozen for all eternity as the father of a toddler. A man who probably intended to have more children. A man who should have been given the chance to have more children— normal children.

"It's all right," she said when he didn't seem to know what to say.

"Finley Jayne Sheppard, had I known I had passed my affliction onto you, I would have tried harder to be a better man and a better father. But I…I thought you and your mother would be better off without me, so I fell for Garibaldi's trickery and died when I should have fought. I should have fought for you. I should have killed Leonardo when I had the chance. Instead, I gave up and I am so very sorry for that."

What could she say to that? She couldn't say it didn't matter because it did. She couldn't say it was all right, because it wasn't. "I wish you had been around to teach me how to handle my other self."

"Yes. I wish that, as well."

"But he taught me." She gestured at Griffin. "He helped me when I thought no one could. He believed in me when I couldn't believe in myself."

Her father smiled. "You love him."

"Yes." There was no shame in admitting it. No fear. "I do. What am I supposed to do?"

"Help him when no one else can. Believe in him when he doesn't believe in himself."

She scowled. It was callous to throw those words back at her in such a blasé tone. "Don't mock me."

"I'd never mock you." In fact, he seemed offended by the accusation. "Griffin King is quite possibly the most powerful Aethermancer on the planet. If he cannot defeat Garibaldi, no one can. What he needs from you is strength and support."

"I don't know how." If she cried she was going to slam her head into the wall for being such a sissy.

Her father reached across the tea table and took her hand. "My dear girl, you braved death itself for him. You already know how."

Yes, she supposed she did. She closed her fingers around his. Helplessness wasn't an emotion she experienced very often, but it almost always attached itself to a situation that involved people she loved. Her feelings for Griffin made this time even worse. "Thank you."

He smiled, amber eyes crinkling at the corners. "I am so very proud of you, and so thankful for the opportunity to tell you."

Oh, damn. There came the tears. Her father rose out of his chair and came around to kneel before her, gathering her into his arms. Finley wrapped her own arms around his neck and hung on for all she was worth. She was hugging her father. Her real father. Silas Crane, her stepfather, was a good and wonderful man, but this man was part of her. This man, flawed as he was, was the one who set her on the path that brought her to the best friends she'd ever had. To Griffin, who had helped her realize her potential and start becoming the person she wanted to be.

This man had died because he thought it would make

the world better for her. If that wasn't love, she didn't know what was.

He held her until her tears dried—it didn't take that long. Then he ran a hand over her hair, kissed her forehead, stood up and left the room. Finley watched him go until she realized why he had left.

Griffin was awake.

Finley went to him and placed her hands on either side of his face, feeling the stubble on his jaw scratch her palms. His eyes were brighter now, the kind of blue that a summer sky sometimes aspired to.

"I dreamed about you," he murmured with a slow smile.

She pressed her lips to his, kissing him as though she hadn't kissed him in weeks, as though the fate of the world depended upon a thorough kissing. He didn't seem to mind. He kissed her back, fingers curving over the back of her neck as though he was afraid she might try to break the kiss before he was ready. Silly boy.

Eventually, they had to breathe, and they had to speak.

"You have to wake up," he told her. "I don't want you to hurt yourself."

"I will."

"I mean it, Fin. I can't lose you."

Her heart swelled—not just because of his words, but

because she knew he intended to make it through this. He intended to make it back to the world of the living, and whatever Griffin set his mind to he achieved.

"Emily will no doubt pull me out very soon. My father's going to keep you here while I'm gone so you can get your strength back."

"And then we take on Garibaldi."

"Yes. Hopefully for the last time." But first, she was going to have to take on Felix. She couldn't risk him coming for her when she was trying to focus on Garibaldi, and she couldn't let those poor girls go on as they were any longer. It didn't matter that he had made them monsters—they hadn't started out that way.

His fingers brushed against her cheek. "You are the most beautiful, bravest girl I've ever known."

She blushed. "You don't get out much."

Griffin chuckled. "I get out plenty. One of those times I happened to hit a girl with my velocycle."

"That's one way to get her attention."

He grinned. "Do you reckon it was a bit much?"

"It might have been a little excessive, yes." She returned the smile. "Though some girls need a good cosh on the head to make them realize a good thing when they see it."

"Well, I am pretty impressive."

Finley laughed and rubbed her cheek against his hand. "Indeed."

"How are the others?"

"Fine last time I saw them. Emily and Sam are fretting over you—both of us. Jasper and Wildcat are helping Jack."

"With what?"

"Apparently Mila ran off."

"What?" He struggled to sit up. "What did that lunatic do to her?"

"Griffin!" A hand on his chest kept him from exerting himself too much. "Be nice."

He sighed, reclining against the cushions. "What did that lovely bloke Jack do to instigate her departure?"

A little smile curved her lips. Griff always wanted to think the worst of Jack. This was one of the times his jealousy was adorable rather than vexing. "I'm thinking it might have been something he didn't do instead."

His expression went from annoyed confusion to horror. "Don't tell me she's in love with him. Oh, the poor creature."

"She's a girl, not a creature."

"I know. She's a dear girl. Too sweet for Dandy."

"Or maybe just sweet enough to be exactly what Jack needs."

He eyed her rather closely. She knew exactly what he was looking for. "You're not jealous?"

Oddly enough, she didn't have to think about it, because sitting there with him, feeling how happy she was just to see Griffin's face, she didn't begrudge Jack the opportunity to feel the same happiness. "Not at all." She leaned in to kiss him again, but was stopped by a tug in her stomach.

"Are you all right?" Griffin asked, his hands clasping her shoulders.

"I don't know." Another tug. She pressed a hand to her stomach. "I feel odd."

"Emily's pulling you out."

She met his gaze. "How do you know?" Another tug. Much more of this and she was going to vomit.

"You're fading," he explained.

She reached for him, not ready to leave him just yet, but her fingers passed right through him. "I don't want to leave you!" She didn't know if he heard her because one last tug pulled her free of that world and sent her crashing back into the world of the living.

Finley never thought she'd see a day when she'd be annoyed to be alive.

Chapter 11

"Have you seen this?" Jasper tossed the afternoon newspaper on the desk in front of Jack, who had no choice but to look at it, because it landed directly on the ledger he'd been balancing.

The headline read Mysterious Heroine Lifts Carriage with Bare Hands! Heroic Girl Saves Driver And Passengers.

Jack swore. The photograph was grainy and shot in profile, but he'd know Mila anywhere. Just the sight of her made his heart skip a beat—even if she had done something so foolish as to call attention to herself. Look at her, rescuing people. Risking her own safety but revealing her abilities because someone needed help. Noble, but the bloody foolish chit was going to end up poked and prodded by the Royal Society if she wasn't careful. They called themselves scientists, but anyone who'd slice open a body just to see how it worked was not to be trusted.

Damnation, but it was good to see her. The relief he felt at knowing that she was all right was a tangible thing, spinning happily in his gut.

He took another look at the photograph, at everything that wasn't his girl. "That's the house we visited yesterday."

"Yup." The cowboy sat on the edge of the desk. "Seems you were right—that pretty lady knew more than she wanted to share. You see those girls there in the background? They're not right clear, but Cat says those Siamese twins are Pick-a-dilly Circus performers."

"Interesting." Jack leaned back in his chair. He was slightly giddy all of a sudden. "Why do you suppose they're called Siamese twins?"

"No idea whatsoever."

"They don't look like they're from Siam."

"Dandy, what are you jabberin' on about?"

Jack tossed the paper aside with a disgusted sigh. He was being an idiot, avoiding what was really bothering him. "I should have pushed that woman yesterday. I should have used my powers of persuasion on her."

"You said yourself it wouldn't have done any good. Mila isn't ready to be found just yet."

No, but he was ready to find her. Damn this letting her spread her wings and see something of the world. She belonged there with him, not gadding about rescuing people left, right and center. She was his special girl, and he wasn't about to share her with all of bloody London. Wasn't going to allow her to be a freak on display.

"Cat also says that the circus is lookin' for a new performer. She reckons the girls will take Mila to meet the owner if she's keen on joining up. That sound about right to you?"

There weren't enough curse words to aptly describe his mood at that moment. "Oh, yes. It certainly does." Mila had no concept of what sort of people there were in the world who would love to manipulate a girl like her. She'd see only kindness and adventure. The moment she stepped into that ring she'd be a target for any and all who would prey upon her. He understood that she needed to do this, that it was his own fault she'd run off, but he'd be damned if she'd suffer for it.

"Would Cat be inclined to talk to her sister? If Mila sees you, me or Wildcat, she's likely to bolt." Maybe not, but he doubted she'd jump into his arms and beg to come home either. He wanted to let her come back on her own, not push her further away.

"She's already gone off to pay her a visit." There was a pause—an expectant one. "Can I ask you a question?"

Jack leaned back in his chair. "I suppose."

"Why don't you just go talk to the girl?" He tossed a paperweight into the air and caught it. "Tell her you were wrong and ask her to come home. Simple."

"Nothing's ever simple where women are concerned, Renn. A fellow your age ought to have learned that lesson by now."

The cowboy arched a brow, but didn't take the bait. "Will you look at that. Jack Dandy's afraid of a little girl."

Jack folded his hands over his stomach. "That little girl could snap you like a twig, and I am not afraid of her."

"Huh." Renn obviously wasn't convinced. However, Jack wasn't going to swing at his bait either.

"Any word on how Finley's doing getting her duke back?"

"Apparently there's going to be a séance or something. You mind if Cat and I go?"

It was a testament to what a bizarre world he lived in that Jack didn't even blink at the word *séance*. "You're not my employees. You can do as you wish."

Arms folded over his chest, the cowboy watched him—studied him. He must be one hell of a card player, because there wasn't even the smallest hint of an expression on his face. If only Jack had gotten to him before King had, because he could use such a fellow from time to time.

"What is it, Renn?"

"You're an interesting man, Mr. Dandy." His tone was perfectly blank, as well.

"I try."

"I don't trust interesting men."

"A wise choice. We are very often untrustworthy."

A pause. Then, Renn said, "Your daddy's a lord ain't he?"

Fortunately, Jack was a bloody good card player, as well. "What makes you think that?"

"The way you hold yourself and the way you talk. It reminds me of Griffin."

"I'm *nothing* like the Duke of Greythorne." Griffin King was an honorable prig who wouldn't say "shite" if he had a mouthful of it. He was all morally upstanding and all that muck. He wasn't even remotely interesting.

"All right." The American stood. "You want me to go have a chat with the photographer who took her picture?"

No need to say her name. "No, leave him to me."

"Right, those powers of persuasion you have?"

Jack smiled. "Something like that." As Renn turned

to walk away, Jack called after him, "You said I should just talk to her. If it was Wildcat, what would you say?"

"That I was sorry and that I wanted her to come back home."

"I have to say, that's disappointing. Aren't you American's all about grand gestures?"

The cowboy grinned. "It ain't what you say, Dandy. It's why you're sayin' it. Women don't want a bunch of fancy words, they want emotion—action."

His assessment irked Jack. It made sense, damn it. "Have a lot of experience with the ladies, do you?"

"Depends on your idea of experience. Notice I'm not the one of us who spends most of my nights alone."

"I can have company whenever I want, Renn. Don't think I can't."

The cowboy paused at the door. "You could have five women in your bed and you'd still be alone, Jack." He didn't wait for Jack's reply, just opened the door and walked out, leaving Jack staring after him. Bloody American didn't know what he was talking about.

Unfortunately, he was also right.

The costume Elsie had found for her fit Mila like a glove. It was flesh colored beneath black lace, sleeveless and with very short, snug trousers. Elsie had explained that leaving her arms and legs bare allowed people to better see her muscles, and see that there was no trickery involved. Mila twisted this way and that, admiring herself in the dressing-room mirror. A lace mask covered the upper half of her face, as well—to "preserve the mystery" according to Elsie. Her hair was pinned up on top of her head and her lips had been painted a dark red.

She looked like a stranger to herself. Why, she could almost pass for one of Jack's doxies! The thought made her incredibly happy. The thought of Jack, however, did not. So much for being independent and strong. She missed him. Missed him terribly, and she hadn't even been gone a full twenty-four hours! Here she was having a brilliant adventure and the one person she wanted to share it with wasn't there. Maybe she'd invite him to a performance. But what if he didn't come? No, that was foolish. Jack was not the sort of man who let emotion rule him. That was part of the problem, wasn't it?

She was glad she left. Jack had become her whole world, and now her world was so much bigger. It wasn't nearly as frightening as she'd thought it would be. People were lovely! She was doing exactly what she wanted to do, without anyone trying to tell her what she ought to think or how to behave. It was liberating.

"You're up next, love," Elsie told her as she stuck her head through the open doorway. She made a clucking sound with her tongue. "You look gorgeous."

"Thanks." Up next? Her stomach fluttered. She was going to go out there, in front of all those people, and show them what she could do. Since her creation she'd been told to hide what she was, to protect it. And now, at least to an extent, she could embrace it and let it be a part of who she was. Not what, but *who*. If she wanted people to treat her like a person—a real, genuine person—she had to think of herself that way, as well.

She left the dressing room and went to take her place backstage until it was her turn. Not even five minutes later, the ringmaster—a man by the name of Maxwell—introduced her. "And now, ladies and gents, The Circus Pick-a-dilly is proud to present a new performer for your entertainment. She may appear delicate. She may look like any other sweet girl, but do not allow your minds to deceive you! She is not like any other girl you have ever known! The one! The only! The World's Strongest Woman!"

Applause followed, pushing Mila's heart rate up another notch. She couldn't do this! Her palms were sweaty and her stomach was in knots. She turned to run away.

The girls stood there, blocking the way. Each one of them wore a huge grin. They were excited for her. They were there to watch her. Support her. They were simply there for her. That was what turned her around and sent her out into the spotlight. There were some whistles and suggestive calls from the faceless crowd, but the response was mostly positive. It wasn't a packed house, and that was all right. She wasn't doing this for the audience.

Her first task was to bend an iron bar that Georges had a man in the audience try to bend first—to show that it wasn't a trick. The man pushed and strained until his face flushed and sweat broke out along his hairline.

"That eez enough, monsieur," Georges said gently, taking the bar away. "You will give yourself the seizure, no?"

Then, Georges gave the bar to Mila. As he had instructed earlier, she made a show out of trying to bend it. Making it look too easy was anticlimactic—and would make the man in the audience feel puny and weak. You had to give the audience tension and suspense—what they paid for. The bar gave easily under her strength, but she made it look like a strain. It was so much more fun than she thought it would be! She grinned in triumph at the audience as they cheered.

During the afternoon with Georges, she had learned that she could juggle. There were some distinct advantages to having a mind that used to be a logic engine, and a body that had been built to do whatever was asked of it. No one else could do what she could do. Before that had made her feel alone, but now…well, now she was somewhat proud of it. The audience certainly seemed to enjoy watching her juggle cannon balls! Each one was just a little smaller that her head. Any bigger and they'd be too big for her to hold in one hand. Up into the air she threw them—the height depending on what she had to do before she caught them again. She did a cartwheel over Georges and then caught the balls, keeping them in the air.

She performed for ten minutes total and left the ring to enthusiastic applause. Backstage she was greeted by her friends who hugged her and squealed. They jumped up and down and chattered over top of one another until Elsie came along and shushed them. She also gave Mila a hug. "Good show, luvvie. Knew you'd be a nat'ral."

Henrietta and Millie had to leave to go perform, but the other girls accompanied Mila back to the dressing room.

"You were so good!" Marissa trilled. "How did it feel?"

"Extraordinary," Mila replied. Her stomach was still quivering. "I enjoyed it so much more than I thought I would. I was so nervous!"

Gina waved a dismissive hand. "No need to be nervous when you know what you're doing."

"I just wish—" She stopped herself.

"Wish what?" Gina asked. The rest of the girls pressed in with wide, curious gazes. For a moment they reminded her of the automatons that had kept her underground not long ago. Her heart gave a tremendous thump. These were not automatons. They were her friends.

Mila looked down at her hands. "Nothing. I just wish a friend could have seen me do all that."

"Ohh," they all chorused knowingly, making her blush.

"What's his name?" Marissa demanded. "Tell us or we'll vex you incessantly until you are forced to confess!"

"Jack." She smiled just a little at the thought of him, the scoundrel. "And I wish he was here right now." Not so much because she missed him—she did, and she wanted him to see her perform—but because this sort of behavior was not what he wanted for her, and he'd likely have a fit if he saw.

"I think you're about to make a new friend," Sasha whispered, her gaze directed at the doorway.

They all looked. Standing there with Elsie was a very handsome older man with graying black hair and steely eyes. He was tall and lean, with a warm and charming smile. He was familiar to Mila in some way, but she couldn't quite put her finger on it. It was as if she knew him—or rather that she ought to know him.

"Girls, you have someplace else to be," Elsie said in a stern tone—no trace of the cockney. "Not you, Mila. You have a visitor."

She didn't understand the tightness around Elsie's eyes, but the little woman looked displeased, and as her friends filed out of the room, each girl shot her a sympathetic glance.

What the devil was going on?

"Mila, this is Lord Blackhurst."

Oh. He was the man who liked circus girls. Didn't someone say he had just picked a new girl? Why would he be there to see her? And why was he looking at her as if he thought she'd be good on toast?

She offered him her hand because that was what Jack told her ladies did when introduced to a gentleman. "Hello, my lord."

He took her hand and raised it to his lips, pressing a warm kiss on the back of her knuckles. Mila didn't like the feel of his lips on her skin and pulled her hand away. She thought she saw Elsie smile.

"I'll leave the two of you alone. Mila, I'll be in the office." A subtle warning that she wouldn't be far away if needed. Then she exited the room, as well, leaving Mila alone with the stranger.

"You put on quite a show, Miss Mila."

She regarded him warily. "Thank you, my lord."

Blackhurst smiled at her. "There's no need to look at me as though I was the big bad wolf, my dear. I'm not going to eat you." Mila added a silent *yet*. This man was not what he seemed. Oh, he was charming, but there was something dark inside him.

"I don't think you're a wolf, sir. But I do think that perhaps you are a predator of some sort."

Blackhurst's eyes brightened. "Do you feel hunted?" He moved closer.

Mila didn't budge. She could snap him like a twig, and if they tried to hang her for it, her metal neck wouldn't break. So, even though every instinct told her to run, she stood her ground and let him come right up to her.

"You're very pretty," he told her, reaching out to touch her cheek. He thought he could have her simply because of who he was. She knew this, but didn't know how she knew it. She also knew that he expected her to be grateful for it.

Mila grabbed his hand. "I'm not going to be your doxy." Suddenly, the true meaning of that word was very clear. A doxy was a woman whose charms were for sale—who men thought they could own for money.

He looked surprised. "My dear—"

"No," she said firmly. "I won't be anyone's doxy." She didn't even want to be Jack's. No, she wanted to be someone's love, not their toy. Not someone they held the door open for the next morning, or walked out on when they were done. This man wanted someone to wipe his boots on and thank him for the dirt.

Blackhurst's expression tightened. "How much do you want?"

"I beg your pardon?"

"Money, woman. I will give you whatever you want. Name your price."

She frowned. He couldn't give her what she wanted. "I don't have one."

"Everyone has one."

"No, they don't." Mila shook her head. "How sad that you think that. Please leave, my lord."

The man's face was dark with anger. He wasn't so handsome anymore. "No one says no to me."

He sounded like something out of a badly acted melodrama. Jack had taken her to one of those a few weeks ago, and the lead actor had been almost this sinister and overbearing. "Then this is going to be a disappointment for you. Now, you can leave, or I can carry you out and dump you in the street."

"You'll regret this." He pivoted on his heel and strode toward the door. "You'll crawl to me before this is over."

"It never began, my lord," she said, but he was already gone.

One week earlier...

"What is this place?" Mila asked as they climbed the steps to the old, but tidy brick building in Whitechapel. It was a cool day, but the rain in the morning had given way to sunshine, and the stink that sometimes festered in this part of London had yet to return to full potency.

Jack turned to her, an odd expression on his face. Was he nervous? He seemed uneasy. "This is a place where I spent a lot of time as a child."

She glanced up at the shutters in need of painting. "What is it?"

"It's a place where women and children can come for food or clothing—some kind of assistance."

Oh. "Did you need assistance?"

He shrugged as he reached for the bell. "Sometimes. Other times my father would have given my mother money and she'd come here to share it with others. She was good like that."

Mila slipped her fingers through his. When he squeezed back her heart gave a little thump. "Why did you bring me here?"

"I'm not sure." The shy smile that curved his lips seemed so out of place on his face. "I just wanted to show it to you."

Her heart was in her throat now. She swallowed hard. "Then I want to see it."

The door was answered by a thin older woman with gray hair and eyes that were almost as faded. Her dress and apron had barely any color to them, as well, though at one time they had probably been blue. Her lined face lit up when she looked up. "Jack!"

Grinning, he bent down and picked the woman clean off her feet. She squealed in delight. At first, Mila thought it wasn't any big feat—she could do the same thing to both of them at the same time—but then she realized that this woman had known Jack since he was a child, and seeing him as a man delighted her. The passing from child to adult was very important to people, as she was continuously learning. She felt as though she had crossed that threshold into adulthood herself for the most part, but there were times, like this one, when she was aware of the fact that she wasn't quite grown just yet.

And maybe humans never stopped.

"Annie, this is my friend, Mila. Mila, this is Annie."

Mila hesitated—as shocked as she would have been if he'd suddenly announced he was from the moon. He'd never introduced her to anyone as his friend before.

She offered her hand to the older woman. "Pleased to meet you."

"And I you, darlin'," Annie replied with a gap-toothed grin. "Any friend of Jackie's is a friend of this 'ouse. Come in, come in."

The house was full of women and children of all ages, and they all seemed to be either arguing or taking care of one another. Mila watched it all with wide eyes as Jack was passed around like some sort of rare gem. They all knew him—even the children. And they all seemed to love him.

This did not fit with the dastardly reputation he had worked so hard to cultivate. But then, she had already learned that the real Jack was nothing like the one he presented to the world. She didn't know why he hid himself, when there was this wonderful side to him, but she supposed one couldn't be a criminal lord and look like a nice person, as well.

Though, when was the last time he'd actually committed a crime? What did she know? He never talked to her about his business. For all she knew he could have robbed a bank that morning. But then she looked at him. No, Jack wouldn't do something that would harm anyone innocent. He saved all his cunning and thievery for those who deserved it. She believed that, and no one would tell her otherwise.

He approached her with an infant in his arms—a little girl. "You've never held a baby have you?"

Mila shook her head.

"It's about time you did. Take her."

It didn't occur to her to refuse him. She simply held out her arms and allowed him to place the child in them. It felt awkward.

"You're holding her like a wet cat," Jack remarked with a chuckle. "Here." He adjusted her arms so that it felt more natural to hold a baby in them. Mila looked down at the sweet, round face.

"She's lovely, isn't she?"

Mila nodded, but didn't speak. Her throat was so very, very tight. This was how humans were supposed to begin. They started out small and helpless and fleshy. They didn't begin with metal frames and logic engines. It didn't matter that she had a heart that pumped blood, lungs that breathed and a stomach that growled. It didn't matter that she was biologically capable of producing an infant of her own—she hadn't been born. She'd been constructed. She would never fit in. Never belong.

A sob caught in her throat and she shoved the baby

back at Jack before escaping out the kitchen door. Jack called her name, but she didn't stop. Several of the women exclaimed over her departure, but she didn't care. Let them think she was an idiot or lunatic. It didn't matter.

She stopped at the rickety fence that enclosed the back garden. They must grow vegetables here. Had Jack helped with that as a child? How much did he help now? She wouldn't be surprised if he was the reason the place still existed. He probably gave them money every month. For some reason, that only made the tears streaming down her face pour harder.

Bloody hell, she hated crying. Hated this silly weakness inside her.

"Poppet?"

Mila sniffed. "Don't call me that. Poppet is for children, and I was never a child."

Jack's hand came down on her shoulder. "Is that what's got you in such a state? The fact that you were never a baby? You just skipped a very messy step on the evolutionary ladder, I reckon."

How could he make it sound so inconsequential? "I'm not human, Jack. I'll never be human." Fresh tears erupted at this dramatic announcement.

"Oh, Pop…sweetheart." He turned her around and

wrapped his arms around her. "Wearing nappies doesn't make you human. I've known people that have always been flesh and bone who are less human than you are."

"That makes no sense," she sobbed.

He chuckled. Somehow, she always amused him, but she never felt as though he was laughing at her. "Did starting out a puppet make Pinocchio any less a real boy in the end?"

Mila pulled back, swiping at her eyes. They were hot and scratchy. "Pinocchio doesn't really exist. He's just a story."

"But you're not." His warm hand settled over her left breast beneath her coat. Mila jumped at the contact. What the…? "I can feel your heart beat. Machines don't have hearts. Only people have hearts."

"And animals," she muttered.

Another chuckle. "Only living things have hearts." Both of his hands cupped her shoulders, and he bent his knees so he could look at her even though she'd ducked her head. "You know Sam—Griffin's friend? His heart is actually mechanical. Would you say he wasn't human?"

She shook her head. "Of course not."

"No, because humanity is something you carry inside, and you have it in spades, my sweet girl. I'll slap the snot out of anyone who says otherwise."

The thought made her laugh despite herself. When he hugged her again she didn't fight. She liked his hugs.

"Are you sure I'm human now?" she whispered, hating that she was so needy. "Like Pinocchio?"

"You're more than human," he said against her hair. "Magic, Mila. You're magic."

Chapter 12

What the hell sort of costume was she wearing? Jack sat in the back of the dim performance area for a few stunned moments after Mila left the center ring. Every instinct he had told him to get up, go after her and wrap her in a blanket before tossing her over his shoulder and taking her the bloody hell home!

The problem was, he was too stunned to move. He sat there as the audience applauded and cheered her, and watched with every other lech as she ran from the ring, the muscles in her legs flexing. Hips swaying.

He swallowed. He had seen her in various states of undress around the house—even seen her naked—but for the most part never really noticed until recently. He'd been adamant about modesty from the beginning, but seeing her in that outfit…well. Getting her into King's care was the best plan, and the sooner the better. Every bloke in that house had a bird of his own so they'd keep their hands to themselves.

More than the costume, however, was the look on Mila's face when she'd finished her act. Her smile lit up the entire building. It was obvious that she had loved every minute of it. Who was Jack to deny her this adventure? Why shouldn't she be allowed to have a little fun before he handed her over to the duke? She certainly wouldn't be able to do this sort of thing once she found a gentleman to marry. No decent man would let his wife carry on in such a fashion.

He would, though. But that was beside the point. He was not the sort of man Mila deserved. And she was much better than he deserved. The irony of that was that he was perhaps the only man in the world who realized just how lucky he'd be to have her.

But that smile…Jack couldn't help it, he smiled, as well, at the thought of it. So much joy in her pretty face. The mask hadn't hidden her identity from him at all. She could have come out with a bedsheet over her head and he still would have known her.

He glanced toward the ring exit where she had gone; his gaze fell upon an older man rising from his seat. Damnation. Jack knew exactly where the man was going and whom he was hoping to find. Without hesitation, Jack stood and followed after, keeping a discreet distance between them. He slipped into the shadows backstage, concealing himself from view. He watched the girls leave Mila, eavesdropped on the conversation that followed. When Mila said that she wouldn't be a doxy he almost cheered in relief. But Jack saw the expression on his lordship's face, and he knew the man wasn't about to accept a simple no.

Jack emerged from the shadows and slipped out a side door into the night. It took a few minutes to find the vehicle he sought in the crowd of waiting carriages. It was a shiny black steam carriage with a tall brass pipe and a soft leather seat for the driver—a chap who was talking to another driver a few vehicles down the line. Jack took advantage of his absence, and when Lord Blackhurst returned to his carriage, Jack was sitting there, waiting.

"Damnation!" The older man swore when he caught sight of him. "What the hell are you doing here? Get out or I'll have you horsewhipped!" He reached for the door.

Jack braced his foot across the door and smiled. It was not a friendly smile. "Shut up, or I'll break your nose."

The man sneered at him, but he didn't speak. He did, however, lean back against his seat. And he didn't yell out for his driver.

Jack crossed his legs and toyed with his walking stick. It was so tempting to pull the sword free and stick it in the man's gut. "I'll make this quick. The girl you visited tonight. Stay away from her."

Blackhurst scowled. "I've no idea what you're talking about."

"The redhead. Leave her alone."

"Why?" His expression quickly changed from anger to interest. "Is she yours?"

Yes, she was! "Just stay away from her."

His lordship snorted. "Or what?"

"I'll make certain you regret it." And he'd make certain very slowly.

"I'm not afraid of you, boy."

"You should be very afraid of me, my lord."

"Oh?" Amusement danced in his companion's eyes. Mockery. "Enlighten me."

Gladly. Jack set his cane across his lap. "You owe me twenty-thousand pounds." It was a staggering sum, but one Jack could easily afford. Crime had paid him very well in the beginning, and the investments he'd made with that money had multiplied like mad over the past couple of years.

"I owe you nothing!"

This was when it got good, Jack realized. "You lost ten thousand to Lord Aberley, three thousand to Lord

Dunnebrook, two to Lord Redbury and five to a Mrs. Birch. I paid your IOUs. You owe that money to me now."

"You lie!" It was all bluster.

Now Jack was the one to smirk. "I assure you, my lord, when it comes to money I do not lie."

"You paid out such a sum just to have me in your debt?"

"I did."

"You dishonorable cad!" Blackhurst looked as though he might have a stroke. "What do you want from me?"

"I told you—stay away from the girl."

"I want my IOU's in exchange."

Jack shook his head. "Not going to happen. I didn't engineer having you right where I want you to give it up so easily."

"She can't mean that much to you, then. Besides, she seemed very agreeable to the idea of becoming better acquainted with me."

Before he could stop himself, Jack's hand lashed out. He grabbed the older man by the throat and pinned him to the velvet seat cushions. "You listen to me, you piece of filth. I can ruin you, and I'd enjoy doing it, but if you go near her again—if you're even in the same room with her—I will end you. Do you understand?" He pushed every ounce of his talent into making certain the sincerity of his words was reflected in his eyes. "I'll kill you, and I'll do it slowly. So slowly, that you'll beg me for death and I'll still…take…my…time."

Blackhurst's gaze widened. Jack took a lot of pleasure in the fear he saw there. He wasn't proud of the pleasure, but he enjoyed it all the same. He enjoyed it so very much. "You understand me now, don't you?"

The man nodded. Slowly, Jack released his hold on his neck and then reached for the door handle. "We'll talk another time about your debts."

"You bastard," Blackhurst rasped as Jack stepped out of the steam carriage. "You'll pay for this. You and your little whore. You'll pay."

Jack, standing on the sidewalk, said loud enough for passersby to hear, "It was lovely seeing you again, as well." His gaze locked Blackhurst's and he smiled— a cold smile, full of promise. There was their resemblance.

"Good night, Father."

Emily wouldn't let Finley go back in—not right away.

"It's dangerous!" she insisted. "Dying and coming back takes a heavy toll on the body, Finley. You need to recover."

"I need to be with Griffin." And she needed to deal with Felix, although she had no idea how to do that.

Her friend sighed, and Finley was tempted to cuff her upside the head. If it were Sam in there, Emily wouldn't be concerned about the possible ramifications either.

"Look," Emily said in a gently annoyed tone, "I know you want him back. We all do. I know you're thinking that if the situation was reversed I'd be hell-bent on going back for Sam, and you're right. I would. But you would be the voice of reason, and you'd stop me from hurting myself."

"Em, he's in there—"

"With your father." Emily obviously wasn't in the mood to entertain her anxiety. "In a veritable fortress. He's safe and he's recovering. Ipsley is checking in on him every hour. If he needs us he'll let us know. Meanwhile, you need to rest and reserve your strength for the séance. Bringing Griffin back to this realm is not going to be easy."

"If he had his strength back he could leave on his own."

"Is that what he told you?"

There was enough of an edge in Emily's voice that Finley looked askance at her. "No. I just assumed he could."

"You shouldn't make assumptions like that."

The tension between them was too much. Finley slapped her hand hard against the laboratory wall. "Are you having your monthly, or did I do something to upset you, because we haven't had a conversation in which you haven't been pissy with me in days!"

"Both," her friend replied. "I have a headache and I'm terrified that I'm going to lose both Griffin and you, and you just keep harping on me that things aren't good enough or fast enough, and you don't seem to care that if I don't do my job properly you could die! I don't want to be the person who kills you. Can you wrap that great thick head of yours around that?"

Finley didn't know what to say, so she grabbed her and hugged her instead. Emily hugged her back. "I'm sorry."

Finley squeezed her tighter. "So am I."

"You're cuttin' off me air, lass."

"Oh!" Finley released her. "Sorry."

Emily looked at her and grinned. She grinned back. Then, the grinning turned to chuckles. God, it felt good.

A few moments later she asked, "Em, what did you mean about me not making assumptions?"

Emily sighed, and fiddled with one of the ropes of her hair. "If he had the strength—if he were able to

break free, he would do that. Ipsley told me that something felt off about Griffin's aura."

"Off how?"

"Did he look tired to you? A little different?"

"Yes. He's been tortured and held prisoner."

"He's fading, Finley. At least, that's what Ipsley says.
He thinks Garibaldi has drained so much of Griffin's
Aetheric energy that Griffin is bound to him. That's
why he didn't bother to chase you when you escaped.
He knows Griffin's not going anywhere, and I'd wager
the scoundrel figures he'll get you, too, and your da, if
he waits long enough. He's got plenty of time after all."

Bloody hell. Finley braced her hand against the cool
wall, bracing herself so she didn't crumple to the floor.
Just when she thought things were heading in their
direction. Just when she thought this nightmare with
Garibaldi might soon be over...

"Is he certain?"

Emily nodded, her expression a study in sympathy.
"As much as he can be— Not like the lad's had a lot of
experience with this, but he said that Griffin seemed
like a true ghost to him, unlike you who had a glow
about you."

"So how do we fix it?"

"No idea. It's like Griffin's lost a piece of himself.
His soul."

Finley clenched her jaw. Bloody hell, this was awful. Terrible. She wasn't terribly smart, but even she could figure out that trying to bring Griffin back in that sort of state could end in tragedy. She would not cry. "Garibaldi's not going to make it easy for us. He'll use it against us." She rubbed a hand over her face. She was so bloody tired. Dying was exhausting.

"Do you think Griffin knows?" Emily asked.

"Of course he does. Garibaldi probably told him exactly what he was doing as he did it." And of course, he wouldn't tell her, because he wouldn't want to worry her. Oh! She could just slap him silly! He was going to hear about this the next time she saw him.

"I'm sorry, Fin. I didn't want to upset you, but I couldn't not tell you."

"I know, and I appreciate that. I'm going to go polish up some fighting techniques and gather information about the Aether with your fellow. Let me know when I can go back in."

"Just before the séance. We'll be able to direct energy at Griffin using your father's apparatus."

"All that mucking about in the Aether is going to attract Garibaldi."

Emily nodded. "Ipsley thinks forcing Garibaldi to come to us is our best chance of beating him and getting Griffin's Aetheric aura back."

"Let's hope he's right." Finley walked toward the lift. With every step she said a little prayer—and she wasn't much for God and such. She prayed for strength and she prayed for Griffin. She prayed for hope, and she prayed that it would be enough, but in her heart she was terrified of the truth.

They didn't have a prayer at all.

The girls convened in Mila's room when they all arrived home much later that night. Each and every one of them was wide-awake and anxious to discuss the evening's events, especially those involving Mila.

"You were so good!" Marissa enthused. "No one would ever know you were new."

"You're one of us now," Gina commented, patting Mila on the back as she offered her the bottle of wine they'd been passing around.

Mila shook her head at the bottle. "The last time I imbibed, I punched a hole in the ceiling."

Gina passed the bottle onto Millie. "While the place could use some renovation, I'm certain the missus would appreciate your restraint."

"I can't believe you turned down Lord Blackhurst," Henrietta blurted.

From the rapt attention of the others, Mila figured this was a topic they'd all been wanting to bring up.

"It wasn't very difficult," she answered. "He's not a nice man."

Henrietta waggled her brows. "Who wants nice?"

That got a few chuckles, and even Mila smiled. "I'm serious. He's not someone a girl should trust."

"No one's ever turned him down." Millie's eyes were huge in her pale face. "Mila, you're the first to refuse him."

Mila frowned. "I find that hard to believe. Why would any girl take up with him?" Then she remembered that they had a friend who went with Lord Blackhurst just a short time ago. "No offense."

Gina waved a dismissive hand. She was on her stomach on the bed, feet crossed above her backside, head propped on her hand. "You haven't offended anyone, ducky. Chits don't refuse him because he could make our lives very difficult if we did. Plus, he is handsome and he's rich. I've heard he pays the girls he takes quite well, and settles a large amount on them when he's done."

"That's not all he leaves them with," Marissa commented. "I've heard horrible stories."

"And I've heard ones that turned out all right," Gina interrupted, giving the other girl a warning glance. "Money can fix all that other stuff."

"Not the scars," the other girl challenged. "You can't ever fix those."

The two of them stared at one another, and Mila wondered what it was all about. It was none of her business, though, so she didn't ask. It was fairly obvious anyway that Marissa, and quite probably Gina, had been ill-treated by a man in the past, and had opposing views on how to carry on.

Mila had heard of "pleasure automatons" that were available for humans to use for their pleasure. It had to be awful to not have any choice in the matter. She just as easily could have ended up one of those poor machines, forced to give herself over to whoever owned her. Instead, she'd ended up with Jack, who didn't want her at all.

Henrietta cleared her throat. "Girls, what if Lord Blackhurst comes back for Mila?"

"If he comes back I'm going to break his bloody arm," Mila informed them. "It's a crude, but effective plan."

Her new friends chuckled. Only Henrietta remained quiet. "He's dangerous, Mila. Be careful."

The girls sobered a little—enough to make Mila reconsider. "I'll be careful, Hen. I promise."

"Speaking of dangerous men," Marissa piped up,

clearly wanting to change the subject. "Did any of you notice who else was at tonight's performance?"

They shook their heads. "Who?" Gina asked.

The other girl smiled coyly. "Jack Dandy."

Mila's heart stopped. For a split second she thought she might have to punch herself in the chest to get it going again. Jack had been there?

"Ohh," Gina pursed her lips as though she was about to kiss someone. "He's entirely too delectable. I'd like to have him for dinner. And breakfast."

The other girls laughed. Mila did not. "What do you mean?"

Their laughter trailed off. Gina shrugged. "I'd like to have a go at him, that's all."

Mila stared at her. Gina had become her friend, but at that moment she could have cheerfully broken the girl's nose.

Instead, she said, "I can introduce you if you like."

The girls all sat upright. Millie pointed the wine bottle at her. "You know Jack Dandy?"

Mila nodded. "He's a friend."

"You've been holding out on us!" Henrietta cried.

Gina scooted closer to her on the bed. "What's he like?"

Mila opened her mouth and hesitated—just for a second. "Brooding."

The girls giggled. "What else?" Marissa demanded, leaning in.

"Violent. I once saw him take out three men at once and receive barely a scratch for the trouble."

More giggles. This time it was Henrietta who demanded more. Mila gave it to them. Some of what she said was true, but most of it exaggeration. The truth—the real Jack—she kept to herself. She wasn't about to share the man who read to her, who took her to shows and played cards with her, even though he mostly taught her to cheat. That Jack was *her* Jack, and he wasn't up for public enjoyment. She saw a side of him he didn't show other people, and that was a gift. She wasn't going to dishonor that gift by treating it as if it had no value.

Besides, these girls wanted to think of Jack as a dark and gothic hero, and he was that. He was also so much more.

And he'd been in the audience. He'd seen her performance. Had he recognized her? Of course he had. Jack didn't miss anything—except the fact that she was a girl, apparently. Maybe he had finally seen her differently. No, she would be foolish to even entertain the idea. He probably had wanted to wrap a blanket around her shoulders and protect her, but he hadn't wanted her like Blackhurst did. And even if he did, Jack Dandy had too much honor to act on it. For a man who prided himself on being a rake and a rogue, he did a piss-poor job of it.

"I can't believe you know Jack Dandy," Marissa remarked.

"I just gave you ample proof," Mila responded. While she understood the concept of lying, it was not something she'd found use for thus far in her existence, and she resented the implication that she might not be truthful. Truth was important. Truth meant something.

Henrietta touched her arm. "She means she's surprised, love, not that she doubts you."

"Oh. All right."

Millie was watching her. "You're so odd." It was delivered with about as much judgment as "your eyes can see things," so Mila decided to take no offense.

"I'm bored," Henrietta bemoaned dramatically. "Let's go out."

Mila's head whipped around. "But it's late."

The girls laughed. "That's the point, silly!" Marissa informed her. "We want to go have some fun. It's not as if anyone's going to punish us for it."

"That's right," Gina joined in, jumping to her feet. "We don't answer to anyone. If we want to go out, we can go out."

"Provided we don't disturb the missus," Millie reminded them all. "She's done all right by us, so we ought to show her the appropriate respect."

It occurred to Mila at that moment that the girls were a little tipsy from the wine, which explained their somewhat uninhibited behavior. She didn't particularly feel like going out, but who was going to look after them if she didn't? They were all capable girls, but there were dangerous things that skulked about London after dark, and Mila was the only one of them capable of handling just about anything.

As quietly as they were able—which wasn't very— they collected their coats and belongings and made their way downstairs in a flurry of petticoats and loud giggly whispers.

Mrs. Rhodes was in the parlor in her dressing gown, reclining on the sofa reading a book while enjoying a cup of tea. She looked up as the girls filed past.

"Going out?" she inquired.

Mila stopped in the doorway. "Yes, ma'am."

The older woman smiled. "You're allowed to come and go as you please, Mila. Do you have a key?"

She nodded.

"Have fun, then." The lady went back to her book.

Mila couldn't believe it! Jack would not be impressed that she was out so late. But then, Jack seemed to assume that everyone she met was out to hurt her in some way.

As they left the house a steam carriage rumbled up to the curb and stopped, its engine running and chugging steam into the darkness. The driver tipped his hat to them. "Is there a Mila amongst you?"

"I'm Mila," she said warily, stepping forward. She didn't know this man.

The man offered her a slight smile. "For you, miss." He leaned down, offering her an envelope.

Mila took it. "Thank you."

"Good evening," the driver said and pulled away.

"Ohh, Mila got a letter from an admirer," Gina cooed.

"Open it! Open it!" The girls all chanted. Two doors down a woman opened her window. "Shut up out there!"

The girls giggled. Mila frowned and opened her letter. It read:

I know who you are It is imperative to the well-being of our mutual friend Mr. Dandy that you come to my house. Now. Use the servants' entrance.

It was signed with a simple B. Blackhurst. Under any other circumstances Mila would assume he meant that Jack was in danger, but having met the man, she knew that any danger to Jack would be at the hand of his lordship himself if she didn't do as instructed.

"I have to go," she said, crumpling the note in her hand.

Her friends were confused. Henrietta blinked. "What...?" But Mila was already gone, moving faster than she ought toward Mayfair—moving faster than humanly possible.

If Blackhurst hurt Jack, she'd break every bone in his body—one at a time.

Chapter 13

How did she fight a ghost in its own element? This was the question that plagued Finley as she lay in the Tesla suit waiting for death to claim her. In the living world Lord Felix wouldn't be much of an opponent at all. The one time they'd tangled, she hadn't even had confidence in her strength or fighting abilities, and she'd still kicked his arse—hard. But in the Aether he was much, much stronger than her, and had every advantage—including an army of murderous girls.

The odds were very much in favor of her getting ripped limb from limb. At least Ipsley would be there to help her, and to let Em know if she needed to be yanked out in a hurry.

If she was nervous about facing Felix she was even more aggravated by it. This detour took up time she could have spent with Griffin. Time that could have been used in getting him out of the Aether and back where he belonged. Time that then gave Garibaldi opportunity to plot against them. He'd already drained so much of Griffin that he obviously wasn't worried about anything they might do in retaliation. He didn't believe they were the least threat, and that was the real pisser.

If only he had a physical body—she'd make him pay. But Garibaldi was something she couldn't pound into a bloody pulp, and had to be dealt with in other ways.

Her eyelids began to droop. A chill crept over her flesh, covering her with a shiver. Dying wasn't so bad, but she could use a blanket. As her life faded away— surely dying this many times in such a short period had to be hazardous—the colors of the world gave way to that now familiar misty gray. She found herself standing on that spooky road where she'd first seen the girl on the wall.

That was intriguing. She'd managed to bring herself to this place, whereas before she'd not had the ability to choose where she entered the Aether.

"You're gaining some degree of power here," Ipsley commented, as though reading her thoughts.

"Is that good or bad?" Finley asked. He seemed clearer to her, as well—sharper.

"I'm not entirely sure." But he was *somewhat* sure,

she suspected, judging from his tone. She had a feeling that this newfound ease in the Aether was one of those hazards she'd wondered about. Would she enter the Aether one of these times and not be able to find her way out? Would she die for good?

Not before she saved Griffin she wouldn't.

She walked on a distance before coming to a halt. "This is where I encountered Lord Felix before."

The medium glanced about. "There's nothing here to indicate this is a regular haunt for him."

Finley smiled at his unintentional pun. "No, but he'll be here."

"How can you be certain?"

She met his gaze. He obviously didn't have a mean bone in his body if he couldn't guess the answer to that. It was so obvious. "Because I'm here, and he wants to kill me."

"Oh. Yes. Well…" He frowned. In any other situation it would have been humorous to watch him pull himself together. "So we just wait, then?"

A cool breeze lifted Finley's hair. She heard giggling. "Yes, but not for long."

Tempting as it was to run, she held her ground. This had to end, and she was going to be the one to end it, regardless of how it went. Lord Felix had been in her life for far too long, and had been something to be feared for the entire time. Even after he was killed she lived in fear of having been the one to end his miserable existence. Funny that now she relished the thought of sending his sorry self straight to hell.

The giggling grew louder. Tendrils of mist came together a few feet down the road—wisps of smoke flying into one another, twirling and undulating until they formed girl-like shapes. Those shapes turned to shadows and then into Felix's ghost girls. One. Two. Three… six. Six of them coming toward her with smiles pulling at their stitched lips.

"Playtime," one whispered through black thread. What had been the point of sewing their mouths shut if they could still talk? Or was it only Finley who could hear them? She didn't have time to contemplate it as their master had materialized behind them and was sauntering toward her swinging his walking stick. He smirked as he drew closer. And for the first time Finley noticed that he had a small mesh pouch hanging from a chain at his waist. The pouch was filled with eyeballs.

"Good God," Ipsley rasped.

Finley's eyes narrowed. She didn't quite share the medium's horror as her mind had suddenly seized upon an idea. It was risky, and stood a better chance of ending with her entrails scattered all over the gray ground, but it was the only idea she had.

"Ipsley, can I conjure things here? Like in a dream? Just think of something and have it appear?"

He glanced at her. "You can do that in your dreams? By Jove, Miss Jayne, that's extraordinary."

And Felix was almost upon them. "Can I?"

He nodded. "By all rights, yes. You should be able to do just that."

"Back so soon?" Lord Felix cooed as he drew closer. The bars through his eyebrow glinted. "Couldn't stay away from me, what?"

She arched a brow. "Indeed." Her mind, however, was centered on something else—turning the single thought of *dagger* into a real thing that she could feel in her hand.

"I knew you'd come back," the blond ghost was saying. "You're just one of those girls who likes a little pain."

She was going to like inflicting some pain on him. In her mind she saw the same sort of wisps that formed the girls swirling around her hand. She looked down and there they were, and as she watched a wickedly sharp, double-edged dagger took shape, until it was solid and real. Brilliant.

Felix hesitated when he saw the blade. "Little bird's learned a trick or two since her last visit." He held out his own hand and suddenly he had a dagger, as well. "What splendid fun."

"Fun," his girls echoed, clapping their hands excitedly as they slowly surrounded her. *"Splendid fun."*

Finley changed her stance. She kept her attention centered on Felix, even as the girls began to close in. They were shadows in her peripheral vision. Then, when one got close enough, she whipped to the side, grabbed the girl by the front of her diaphanous gown and pulled her close. She lifted the dagger and slashed with concentrated intent—slicing through the stitches that pierced her bluish lips. The girl gasped and Finley shoved her away.

"Oy," Felix snarled. "Don't touch my girls."

Finley smiled at his reaction. "What? Your mama never taught you about sharing?"

"Nine o'clock!" Ipsley shouted. She lunged to the left, grabbed another girl and repeated the action on her, again severing the blackened threads. Felix lurched at her, making a vicious swipe with his blade that she just barely avoided. The tip of the dagger tore her sleeve. She pivoted on her heel and drew her arm back so that the blade pointed behind her, then she followed through, bringing her weapon up so that it kissed her adversary's cheek, leaving a thin line of blood in its wake.

"Five o'clock!" Dear Ipsley again.

She whirled around and slashed another of the girls, and then a fourth. Only two more to go. The first of them had started to moan in a manner that was almost like singing, only more mournful than any song she'd ever heard before.

Felix growled—a wretched, hollow sound that shriveled her soul. His face distorted for a split second— became a skeletal mask that would have stopped her heart were she not already on the threshold of death. This time when he attacked she wasn't fast enough, and his blade dug a trench along her side. It was deep and it hurt. A lot. In the living world it would have dropped her to her knees as she fought to hold her insides where they belonged, but she wasn't ready to die just yet, and she certainly wasn't going to let Felix August-Raynes be the one to send her on to her maker. This wasn't the living world and the same rules didn't apply. It was going to take a lot more than that to kill her.

"Finley!" Ipsley cried. She ignored him, and instead freed the mouth of the fifth girl. This time she drew blood. The girl raised her hand to her mouth, and stared at her bloody fingers in wonder before raising her eyeless gaze to Finley.

"Sorry," Finley said. Why the devil was she apologizing when these creatures had tried to tear her apart?

"Kill her," Felix commanded. Somehow he'd gotten a second blade and he wielded them both as if he'd been born holding them. "But I want her alive when I cut out her eyes."

The girls closed in at the same time Felix did. Finley tensed, and tried to block out Ipsley's shouting. He drove in and around the girls, but he was ineffectual in his current form, and no more help than a shadow.

Felix struck. His blades sliced her arms, her chest, her throat, her face, and Finley struggled to ignore the pain. It wasn't real. She was just a ghost. If she believed in the injuries it would make them worse—make them reality. True death was not an option.

Blood ran down her arm, slicking her fingers, making it difficult to keep a grip on her own blade. She ducked as Felix took another swipe, and stumbled. As much as she fought it, there was a part of her mind on the verge of hysteria over her injuries, and it was strong enough that she wasn't at her best. She only barely managed to avoid another attack, but this time she dodged toward her attacker, rather than away from him. She grasped the top of the pouch tied at his waist and pulled him close, slicing through the cord with her dagger. Then, she lifted one foot and drove her boot into his chest, shoving him backward before he could make another strike.

It took all of her strength to move, but she wasn't

fast enough to avoid the girls. They grabbed her with talonlike hands as they closed in on her like vultures on a corpse. Their fingers tore at her clothes and her skin, dug into the wounds their master had made. Finley screamed, but she didn't stop. She shoved the pouch into the hands of the final girl—the one she'd found on the wall and who had told her to run. Then, she cut the stitches that sealed the girl's mouth.

"You're free," she told her. "He doesn't have any power over you anymore."

The girl froze, and one by one the others followed. Finley's knees began to buckle, and it was only those cruel hands that kept her upright. She watched, stomach rolling and vision blurring as the girl reached into the pouch and withdrew two of the eyes. She lifted them to the gaping sockets in her face and set one then the other in place.

"No!" Felix screamed.

The girl turned her head and looked at him as she thrust the pouch at one of her sisters. Felix ran toward them—ran toward Finley. As the girls each retrieved their eyes, they released their hold on her, and her legs refused to hold out any longer. She was bleeding badly—to the point where the pain had begun to recede into peaceful nothingness.

"I'm getting you out of here!" Ipsley shouted.

"Not yet!" Finley cried, but he was already gone. She sank to her hands and knees. Felix's boots appeared in her line of vision. She couldn't even tense to prepare for the kick he was surely going to deliver to her head.

But no kick came, and Finley lifted her head.

The girls—all with their eyes returned and bloodied lips free—surrounded him.

"Kill her," he commanded, pointing at Finley. "You kill her now."

The girls cocked their heads in unison—a disturbing sight. Then, they snapped upright, hissing with teeth bared and eyes wide. She didn't know which one attacked first, but they lunged at him like dogs at a bone, snarling and snapping. A cry of pain echoed in the fog. And as the world dropped away, the last thing Finley saw was Lord Felix screaming for mercy as he was devoured by his former victims.

Five weeks and four days earlier...

"Where are we going?" Mila asked as she sat beside Jack in his sleek steam carriage. They were racing through the streets of London—well, perhaps racing wasn't the best word. They raced from time to time, and then other times they were held up in the chaotic throng that seemed to be normal traffic. Mila didn't understand how people could get so jammed up, and she didn't want to understand it.

"I told you, it's a surprise." Jack shot her a small smile. "Think of it as a belated birthday present."

"Birthday present?" she echoed.

To his credit, he didn't look at her as though this was something she should know, or common knowledge among "real" people. "It's a custom that on the anniversary of someone's birth you give them a present."

"But I wasn't born."

He made a face as he steered the carriage between two carts, a swearing farmer and an angry man shouting in Chinese. Something about a cow... "Of course you were. Maybe not in the conventional sense, but you had a day when you were awake and became aware of yourself as a being and not a machine."

Yes, he had a point. "That was weeks ago."

"That's why this is a belated present."

She shrugged. "All right." This didn't really make a lot of sense to her, but it was nice to be out of the house. She liked it when Jack took her out exploring. He took her to interesting places like museums where she could learn about things. She enjoyed learning.

She stared out the window at the passing city and all it's strange wonder. There were so many things to see.

It was a clear morning, and a dirigible was flying high above them. *L'air France* was written in script on its side.

"What's it like to fly?" she asked.

"Like flying," Jack answered.

Mila frowned. "I don't understand."

His lips tilted on one side. "It's something you have to experience for yourself. No one can tell you what it's like."

"Oh." She peered up at the ship again. "I would like to find out someday."

"I'll see that you do."

She believed him.

They pulled up in front of a large brick building with white columns. It wasn't fancy, but it was lovely. Jack shut down the engine and got out of the carriage, coming around to open her door for her. He was adamant about opening her door—another thing she didn't understand. Her limbs worked just as well as his, and she understood the procedure of turning a handle. Still, it wasn't that important a detail, so she didn't push it.

She turned her head to look at the sign in front of the building, but her gaze went instead to what appeared to be a pile of rubbish beside the steps. Her heart skipped a beat. Was that what she thought it was? She moved closer. It was.

It was an automaton that had had its logic engine

ripped out. There was what looked like dried blood on its tarnished brass face. Its mouth was slightly open—it was a humanoid machine—and she could see what appeared to be two humanlike teeth.

"Damnation," Jack swore. "Come away, poppet."

"Why would someone do this?" she asked, horrified. It had been murdered.

He led her away, up the steps to the building. "Someone probably got scared. Some people are afraid of the automatons that have become sentient."

"Why would they be afraid?"

His gaze locked with hers. "Because machines are smarter and stronger than we are, and that's terrifying."

And that was the moment that Mila realized she could never tell anyone who didn't already know what she really was. It was going to have to be a secret, and a closely guarded one. She didn't want people to be afraid of her.

"I'm sorry you had to see that," he said. "Let's go inside."

She followed him into the building. It smelled of dust and paper and ink, and when he led her into the main room her jaw literally dropped. Thank goodness it was bolted to her skull.

Books. Wall after wall, row after impossibly long row of beautiful books.

"What is this place?" Was that breathy sound in her voice?

Jack was grinning. "It's a lending library. You can borrow whatever books you want, take them home and read them. Then we bring them back and you can get more. Do you like it?"

"Oh, Jack!" It was all she could say. She didn't know the right words to correctly articulate just how wonderful it was.

"Go," he instructed. "Find ten books. I'll wait."

"Only ten?"

His smile turned patient. "We can come back tomorrow."

She ran into the first row.

Half an hour later they left with an armload of books that Jack insisted on carrying. Mila wore a huge smile on her face—until they stepped outside and she saw the discarded automaton again.

Jack put the books into the boot of the carriage before joining her. "You want to take it, don't you?"

"I wouldn't know what to do with it," she replied. Then she turned to him. "Jack, what would you do for a real person?"

He shrugged. "Bury him—or her."

"Then…can we bury him or her?"

Jack didn't say anything, he just went and picked up

the automaton. It was heavy, and his back bowed with the strain. Mila could have done it, but she sensed that he would not have liked it if she had. He put the remains in the boot with the books.

They drove to a cemetery not far from Jack's house. It was a little shabby, he explained, but it would suit their purpose. This time, he let Mila carry the automaton, as he carried a shovel and an old fence post he found near the entrance.

Mila found a nice little spot, out of the way, beneath a tree. It was a pretty spot—the sort where one might like to sit and read a book on a summer day. She'd never done that, but she'd like to.

Jack dug a hole just big enough for the discarded pieces. He was sweating when he finished, but he still hadn't said one word of complaint. Mila was more grateful for his silence than she could ever say—and somewhat unsettled by it. She put the machine into the dirt, arranging it carefully before standing back so Jack could bury it. When he was done, he stuck the fence post into the ground beside it.

"A grave should have a marker," he explained.

A grave. People had graves. Humans.

Hot wetness filled Mila's eyes. She blinked it away.

Jack held her hand as they walked back to the carriage. He opened her door for her and she climbed in.

She didn't know what to say. This feeling—like someone was sitting on her chest—was new and unpleasant.

"That was a good thing you did," Jack told her when they were almost home. "A very good thing. I'm humbled by your compassion—honestly."

The wetness burned her eyes again, and this time she let it come, let it run down her cheeks before finally wiping it away.

She didn't say anything until they were back at Jack's. She carried her books into the house and made to take them up to her room. Jack said he had work to do.

"Jack," she said, partway up the stairs.

He looked up from hanging his coat. "Yes, poppet?"

Poppet. She liked it when he called her that. It was his special name for her. "Do you think it would be all right if today was my birthday?"

His stared at her for a moment, then he smiled. "I think that would be grand. Happy Birthday, Mila."

She almost giggled in relief. Hugging her books to her, she ran the rest of the way upstairs to her room.

Finley. Griffin's eyes snapped open as he jerked upright on the sofa. His chest felt as though someone was pounding on it with a sledgehammer—from the inside—and sweat dampened his hairline. Damnation, he was shaking.

"Your Grace?" Looking up from the book on his desk, Thomas Sheppard's eyes were very much like his daughter's, so much so that Griffin had a hard time meeting his gaze. "Is everything quite all right?"

Was it? The sense of panic that had forced him awake abated. Had it been real or had he dreamed it? "Was Finley here?" he asked, wiping his forehead with his sleeve. He shivered. Was it cold in the parlor or was it just him? He could barely feel the heat from the fire.

Sheppard shook his head. "No."

"Must have been a dream, then." He forced a smile as another shudder ran down his spine. He drew the quilt from the back of the sofa around his shoulders.

The older man didn't look convinced. "She was in the Aether, though. I felt her when she came in."

Griffin's heart thumped hard. For future reference he would have to remember that Finley's father was very literal. "Here" was obviously their immediate surroundings. "Do you feel her presence still?"

"No. She's gone."

He pulled the quilt tighter around him. Finally, he began to feel warm again. "She was going to confront August-Raynes, wasn't she?"

"Yes." Finley's father returned to his book. "I do hope she was successful."

Griffin almost laughed at the absurdity. "If she

weren't I rather think she'd be with us right now—as a ghost."

"Unless August-Raynes imprisoned her like those poor souls he's attached to his will."

Staring at the man, Griffin felt his jaw slacken. "Mr. Sheppard, you're not easing any anxiety I might be feeling." Did the man not realize what he was saying? Or had he been in the Aether so long that he'd forgotten what it was to be alive? To want to live?

Sheppard glanced up once more. At least this time he appeared somewhat contrite. "Forgive me, Your Grace, for not explaining. I'm sure I must seem quite callous and uncaring in my lack of concern for my daughter's well-being. Since Finley is of my blood, I would have felt her death in the Aether. She is alive. Hurt, but alive. My apologies for adding to your worries."

He was ill-tempered and he knew it, so Griffin said only, "Thank you." Adding to his mood was the fact that this man—who barely knew her—had a bond with Finley that he did not. A foolish thing to be jealous of—a girl's father—but he was. No matter where she went or what she did, Thomas Sheppard would always be a part of her. She could leave Griffin tomorrow and never think of him again.

Finley wasn't about to leave him, he knew that. She'd take on August-Raynes and Garibaldi himself if she had to. The foolish girl would get herself killed, and while eternity with her was a pleasant thought, it was *not* Finley's time to die.

His head swam, heat creeping through his skull. Pinpricks of discomfort trailed up his arms and neck.

"Your Grace?" Sheppard steadied him with a firm hand. Good thing he was already sitting.

"I'm weak." An unnecessary announcement, but he made it all the same. "I've never stayed in the Aether this long, and Garibaldi drained all my strength. I am little more than an invalid, and it feels like days since I've had anything to eat or drink, which only makes me weaker."

"I've had some success with manifesting in the living world," the older man shared. "I could see about getting something for you."

Griffin shook his head. A cough scratched his throat. "If you leave I'll be a sitting duck for Garibaldi." God, he despised weakness.

"Your Grace, I don't know what to do for you."

He met Sheppard's gaze. "That makes two of us, my good man."

That didn't seem to appease the older man at all. "But I am a man of science. In life I prided myself on being able to find a solution for any problem I encountered." He laughed humorlessly. "Some of those solutions were to my own detriment, but I saw every new possibility as a success. Other than gathering up Aetheric energy and giving you another blast, I have no idea whatsoever of how to treat your current condition."

Griffin smiled—it took a lot of energy. He wasn't so peevish anymore. "Whatever happens to me, sir, Finley won't blame you."

Sheppard looked away. Were they in the living realm he probably would have flushed with embarrassment of being so transparent. "I would rather help you and reap the pleasure of seeing her happy."

"The chance to meet you has made her very happy, I know it has." Griffin withdrew his left hand from under the quilt and placed it on the other man's arm. He coughed again. "And I appreciate all you have risked on my behalf—and hers."

A proud smile brightened Sheppard's face, making him look his age. It was odd to see this man—who ought to be in his late thirties—looking not even a decade older than himself. But when he glanced at Griffin's hand, the smile slowly melted away. "Your Grace…"

Griffin followed his gaze. His breath caught on a sharp pain in his chest.

His hand was the same lifeless color as Sheppard's face. He pulled out his right hand to compare the two.

The right still had a pinkish hue and blue-veined vitality running through it. He pulled up his sleeve—the gray continued almost to his elbow before giving way to normal flesh tone.

"Perhaps when you touched me…"

"Sheppard," Griffin interjected with a pointed look. "As you said, you're a man of science. We are both learned men, so I am very well aware that you know what's happening just surely as I do."

His companion shook his head. "There is a wealth of possibilities to consider."

"No. There isn't." Griffin pulled both arms back into the welcoming warmth of his quilt cocoon. The time for pretending and hoping for a miracle had passed. "When Finley returns you won't say a word about this to her."

Sheppard protested. "But, Your Grace—"

"Promise me." Griffin fixed him with an unyielding stare. "Finley cannot know that I'm dying.

"I'm dying."

Chapter 14

Mila used the servants' entrance right enough, but she didn't knock. She very calmly turned the knob so hard it snapped and pushed the door open. She crossed the threshold much to the shock of two maids who were in the kitchen having a cup of tea at the table. They must have been waiting for her, or aware of her impending arrival because they each simply pointed at another doorway, indicating that was her desired route.

"Thanks," she said, and crossed the spotless wooden floor, through the doorway and into a small corridor. A footman in the act of removing his livery jacket froze when he spied her.

"I'm here for Blackhurst," she informed him.

"Up the stairs and to the right, miss," he replied.

Somewhere in the house a bell rang. Someone had

just been alerted to her presence. Mila smiled a grim smile. This would go so much more smoothly if she didn't have to hunt the bastard down.

The servants' stairs were slightly bowed in the middle of each worn step. The wood creaked under her weight. She wasn't a big girl by any stretch, but a metal skeleton tended to add a few extra pounds. It didn't matter if she made noise, if Blackhurst heard her approach.

She reached the top, opened the door and turned right. The house was incredible, of course. Almost as fancy as King House, but a little shabbier—as though Blackhurst couldn't be bothered to fix things up. Or maybe he hadn't the money. Jack had told her that many aristocrats had no idea of how to manage their fortunes.

Mila paused and focused on her hearing. She could hear Blackhurst's voice—it was slightly muffled—but he was talking to a servant or someone. He told them to ready his bedchamber.

Blood rushed to her cheeks, but it was anger more than shame. Is that what this was all about? He would threaten Jack's life for that?

As she approached the room from where she heard his voice, a door to her left opened and a young woman peeked out. When she spied Mila she froze, a look of sheer terror taking over her pretty, but bruised face. The bruises were oddly shaped—four perfect hexagons.

"Who are you?" Mila asked. When the girl hesitated, Mila took a wild guess. "Gracie?" That was the name of the girl Gina said Blackhurst had come for at the circus.

The girl's blue eyes widened. "Yes," she whispered. "Who are you?"

"Mila. I'm not going to hurt you."

"Mila?" The girl lost some of her frightened rabbit look. She slipped out of the room and closed the door. When she spoke again, it was a whisper. "Did Jack send you?"

A frown pulled at her brows. "Jack? No. Are you a friend of his?"

Gracie hesitated once more. What had happened to her to make her so afraid? "Yes. I have information for him, but I haven't been able to leave to take it to him."

That was when Mila noticed the marks on the girl's wrists. She'd been bound.

Rage took root deep in her stomach. "You can leave now."

The girl shook her head. "He won't let me. He has people watching me. Even his wife won't help me."

Mila took her hand and pulled her back toward the hall where she'd come upstairs. Instead of going the servants' route, she hauled the protesting girl straight to the front door. When a footman approached them with a stern look, Gracie gasped in fear. Mila punched the man in the face and he crumpled to the floor like a doll.

Gracie fell silent, tripping along behind Mila, staring at the fallen man.

Reaching the door, Mila pulled it open. Another footman stood on the steps. She punched him, too.

"You're amazing," Gracie whispered.

"That's what got me into this mess," Mila muttered. Suddenly, Jack's overprotectiveness made sense. The world was a mad, dangerous place for a girl who didn't quite understand it all. And now that she did understand—all too well—she was in well over her head. She ought to have been smarter, but she foolishly thought that her strength made her impervious to pain. What had Jack told her? That there were people who could hurt her in ways that weren't physical.

She pulled some coins from her pocket and pressed them into Gracie's hands. Then she took off her coat and put it around the girl's shoulders. "When you get to the street you hail a cab. You take it straight to Jack, yeah? He'll protect you. You do *not* tell him you saw me. Understand?"

The girl nodded. "What are you going to do?"

Mila glanced through the open doorway. "I have a meeting to attend. Go. Now."

The girl didn't need any extra encouragement. She

ran quick as a little mouse down the steps to the drive, and straight to the gate. She pushed it open and slipped out into the night. Mila watched her wave down a cab and climb in. Only then did she relax a little. Only then did she turn on her heel and go back inside. She nudged the footman on the steps out of the way with her foot so she could close the door, and stepped over the one lying sprawled on the foyer floor. She continued on to the room where she knew Blackhurst waited and opened the door without knocking.

Blackhurst stood in front of the fireplace in his trousers, shirt and waistcoat. His dark hair glinted in the flickering flames—which were the main source of light in the room, other than a lamp. It was then that she noticed he wore a metal brace on his right arm. It started at the shoulder and continued all the way down to his knuckles. Reticulated to move with him, it was intricately etched and attached by leather straps. The part that fit over his fist was almost like a glove, and had hexagon bolts—brass knuckles. That explained the bruises on Gracie's face.

"Mila," he greeted with a smile. "I knew you'd come."

"You should know I don't bruise easily," she informed him.

For reasons she couldn't fathom, that seemed to please him. "No. I don't imagine you do."

As he walked toward her—like a big cat after a mouse—Mila was once again struck by that sense of familiarity. Then the light struck him just the right way as he tilted his head and looked down at her. And smiled.

Shock hit her hard in the chest. She could almost feel a dent in her breastbone. "You're Jack's father."

Blackhurst stopped, a frown knitting his arched dark brows. Oh, yes, there was no denying the resemblance now that she'd finally seen it. Damnation. Of all the things she'd seen, heard and experienced, this had to be one of the worst on an emotional level.

"You threatened your own son."

His handsome face—so much an older version of Jack's—twisted with hatred. "That boy is *not* my son. He's been nothing but trouble since his birth. He has made it his mission to ruin my life and destroy me in every way possible."

If that was true—if Jack had put that much effort into this man—then there had to be a good reason for it. "What do you want from me?"

That charming smile returned in a blink. "You, of course. You're a strong girl, Mila. So very strong. I think you and I could have a satisfying relationship for quite some time. Most of my companions wear out so quickly."

She stared at him. "You're a monster." Jack had to know that.

"Like is attracted to like," he murmured, reaching out to touch her face with his hand. Before she could react, he'd drawn back the metal covered one and punched her hard in the face. She felt the cartilage in her nose break as her head snapped back.

Mila shook her head. Blood dripped on her boots and on the carpet, ran down her face. She reached up and set her nose back where it should be. "My turn." She hit him in the mouth, but held back. This was not a fight she wanted to end quickly.

Blackhurst spat blood on the floor and smiled, flashing red-stained teeth. "Brilliant."

She did not understand this man, not at all. And she hoped she never would. "I'm not going to stay with you," she informed him. "Using Jack against me was a mistake."

He wiped his mouth with the back of his sleeve. "I realized that after I sent the note. I was a bit hasty, agreed. But you see, Jack Dandy threatened me, and I needed to find a little leverage against him. I don't think the boy realized how he tipped his hand when he told me to stay away from you."

Jack had done that? "Well, it won't work. Jack isn't afraid of you and neither am I. Stay away from both of us." She turned to leave the room.

"I'm afraid you don't understand."

Something in his voice made her turn. A door on the other side of the room opened and in walked another footman, but this one had an Aether pistol in his hand and it was pressed against the head of a frightened Mrs. Rhodes. Mila froze.

"This isn't about you, my dear. It's about that miscreant daring to interfere in my affairs." Blackhurst's face was hard and cruel in a way Jack's could never be. "It's about teaching him a lesson, teaching him how to acknowledge his betters."

"Let her go," Mila commanded, but her voice shook. She was beginning to understand fear now. Sometimes it didn't matter if you were the fastest or the strongest, there would always be something that could hurt you. Blackhurst couldn't do anything to her physically that she couldn't recover from, but he could hurt Jack.

"Oh, no. Our dear landlady is the only leverage I have against you. You see, I will have Victor blow a hole the size of an apple in her head if you don't do exactly what I say. You and I are going to spend some time together, and when I'm done you and Mrs. Rhodes will be allowed to leave."

Mila's jaw tightened. She ran the odds of escape in her head. If she charged Blackhurst, Mrs. Rhodes would die. If she charged the footman, Mrs. Rhodes would still die. If Jasper were there he might be able to move fast enough, but she couldn't. And there was nothing within reach that she could use as a weapon. She couldn't risk Mrs. Rhodes's life. She just couldn't. Blackhurst knew that. This was the person who had taught Jack that there was more than physical hurt in the world.

"You expect me to believe that you'll just let us leave?"

"Oh, I'm a man of my word, my dear." His lips twisted into a mocking smile. "Otherwise how can you crawl back to Dandy and tell him all about what I did to you and had you do to me?"

Still, she didn't understand. Why were humans so complicated? God, she hoped she was never completely human if this was what it meant—being capable of such terrible evil. And this was evil, there was no doubt.

"Let me speak plainly so your feeble mind will comprehend." His tone dripped with derision. "Dandy cares about you in a way that he's cared about no one else. He cares about you more than he cares about himself. Ruining you will hurt him more than any physical wound ever would. So, yes. I will let you leave, because I want you to tell him what happened here, and I want him to know that nothing he does to me will ever change it."

Finley was awake when the door to the room she shared with Griffin opened. She hadn't slept much in the past couple of days, but then, who needed sleep when she was technically dead at times? She had been listening to a recorded cylinder of Beethoven in the hopes that it might help her sleep, but it only made her all the more restless. Smelling Griffin on the pillow beside hers didn't help either. What if she never got to wake up beside him again?

"Em?" she asked, sitting up. She reached for the lamp and winced. Her insides felt as if someone had used her organs in a cricket match, but other than that she was unhurt. The injuries she sustained in the Aether hadn't come back with her physically—only mentally and spiritually. Apparently those were just as dangerous as the former. Emily had explained it but Finley hadn't absorbed too much of it; she was still reeling over the fact that she had defeated Lord Felix.

"It's me," Emily replied as the lamp lit the room.

"And me," said Wildcat.

Finley managed a smile as they closed the door behind them. They were exactly the distraction she needed. "You brought me things."

"I brought you dinner," Emily said. "You need to keep your strength up."

"Mmm. Dying takes a lot out of a girl," she agreed, in a weak attempt at humor.

Wildcat held up a large paper sack and a bottle. "I brought chocolate, cake and cider."

"I love you," Finley told her.

"Dinner first." Emily shoved the tray in front of her. On it was a plate of cold cuts, bread and cheese—her favorites.

"I love you, too, Em."

The redhead preened. "I know." Then she went to the cylindrograph and switched the key to the off position. "Für Elise" ground to a halt. "How are you feeling?"

Finley shrugged as she placed cheese and meat between two pieces of bread. "Better than I ought, I reckon. That Organite bath you drew for me helped."

"Good. You should be healed in time for the séance tomorrow."

The irony of healing just in time to get beaten again—to die again—was not lost on her. She took a bite of her food, chewed and swallowed. "At least we'll have my father in our corner. He's been in the Aether longer than Garibaldi."

"That must be strange," Wildcat remarked, opening the bottle of cider. "Seeing your dead daddy."

"It was." Finley smiled when Emily placed a hand on her arm. "It's all right, Em, I can talk about it. I'm not sad. How many people get the chance to meet their deceased parent while they themselves are still alive? Not many, I'd wager."

"I'd settle for knowin' who my daddy was," Cat tossed in. She handed Finley the bottle. "Forgot cups. Sorry."

She raised the cider to her lips. It smelled sharp and sweet. "So long as you don't have the plague I reckon I'll survive."

"No plague," the darker girl assured her as she drank. "I do have this odd rash, though."

Finley choked, almost spraying cider all over herself and the two of them. Cat just grinned. "Sorry."

"Well done," Emily praised dryly. "Next time wait until she's taken a bite, maybe then you can get her to choke to death and we won't have to use the suit anymore."

Finley dragged the back of her hand across her mouth. "Is it broken? The suit?"

Her friend waved a hand in her direction as she plopped down in a nearby chair. "It's fine. Sam washed out all the vomit."

Oh, right. She cringed. That hadn't been one of her shiniest moments, but all that dying and waking up, and almost getting killed had taken a toll on her. If a girl couldn't cast up the contents of her stomach after coming back from the dead, when could she? "I will have to thank him for that."

Emily's full lips curved. "Oh, I imagine he'll see that you do, never you worry."

For a second her heart was light and Finley chuckled. But then she remembered why Sam had to clean up that vomit and her good humor faded.

"Don't you dare push that plate away." Emily had a fierce expression on her freckled face. "I don't care how terrible you feel—you eat."

She ate. It did make her feel stronger—perhaps a little more confident and strong. Mostly it gave her something to do while the other girls sat with her. When Wildcat offered her cake she took it.

"I had to sneak it past Jasper," the American explained with a knowing smile. "Sometimes I think that boy has a nose like a bloodhound."

"He's still growing," Emily told her. "It will calm some in his early twenties, but his abilities will always give him a larger appetite than most. Sam's the same."

"I've seen Griffin eat an entire batch of biscuits all

by himself." Finley grinned at the memory. "I sat on a kitchen stool and watched him do it."

Emily lifted a dubious brow. "He ate the *whole* batch?"

Warmth filled her cheeks. "Maybe I helped a little."

"I've eaten an entire pie in one sitting." Wildcat took a bite of cake. "And then turned around and had griddle cakes."

One of Emily's pale hands came up. She had dirt under her nails from working in her lab. "I don't want to hear about it. Talking to machines doesn't expend much energy. If I ate like the two of you I'd weigh twenty stone."

"It's not all that fun having to eat a lot." Finley finished off her cake. "Sometimes it's a pain in the arse."

Cat grinned. "But mostly it's just fun."

Emily threw a cushion at her, but Cat snatched it out of the air with agile ease.

A knock on the door ended the lighthearted moment. "Come in," Finley called.

The door swung open to reveal Jasper. "Sorry to intrude gals, but I just saw something that y'all might be able to help me suss out."

He looked completely confounded—it was a new look for him, Finley thought. "What is it, Jas?"

Sam appeared behind him, wiping his hands on a towel. "Whatever it was you ate for lunch, Jayne."

Even Finley had to laugh at his quick wit, but Jasper shot him a brief scowl. "I was comin' back from fetching those parts you wanted, Miss Emmy, when I saw Mila standing on the front steps of the big house on the corner—the one with the lions on the gates."

This time it was Sam who scowled—no real surprise there, Sam always scowled. "Blackhurst's house?"

Jasper glanced at him. "Is that who lives there? Huh. Anyway, Mila was there. Is that cake?"

"What would Mila want with an earl?" Emily wondered aloud. Finley shrugged, and offered Jasper some of the cake Cat had brought. He took a huge piece.

"Seriously?" Sam seemed genuinely perplexed, but that didn't stop him from taking some cake either when Jasper offered it to him. "Don't any of you know who Blackhurst is?"

"He's an earl?" Wildcat smiled lamely.

Sam's frown deepened, but he directed it at Finley— as though she ought to know better. "He's Dandy's father."

"What?" they all chorused.

The big lad shook his head at them, his inky hair glinting blue in the light. "It's obvious if you've ever seen the man. Dandy looks just like him."

"I don't recall ever seeing him," Finley remarked—a little defensively. She looked at Emily for backup, but her friend looked just as dumbstruck as she felt.

Sam shrugged. "I thought Dandy probably told you."

"No." She wouldn't have expected him to, but it needled her just a little. She was the closest thing Jack had to a real friend. He knew about her father. "Maybe he doesn't know."

"He started a club for bastards," Sam informed her with his usual blunt delivery. "I think he knows. More importantly, why would Mila go to the house of a man Dandy obviously despises?"

"I wonder if Jack knows?" Finley thought out loud. She turned to Jasper. "Last time you saw him had he spoken to Mila?"

The cowboy shook his shaggy head. "No, he had not."

"Oh, my God." Cat stood up with a hand pressed to her mouth. She looked at each of them before settling her gaze on Finley. "My sister works at Pick-a-dilly. She told me that there was a rich fella who came sniffing around some of the performers. He likes young, pretty girls. Agile girls. *Strong girls*. She said his name was Blackhurst."

Oh, no. "Mila would be awfully appealing to such a man." Finley's lips thinned. She was getting heartily sick of men who liked to take advantage of young women. "But would she go along with it?" This she asked Emily, who knew the girl better than any of them.

Emily shook her head. Her aqua eyes flashed with anger. "She's a little naive, but she's not stupid. Plus, she's got a terrible crush on Jack. If she's at Blackhurst's house, he's either coerced her or she thinks he's a threat."

Finley paused, her brain sticking on the remark that Mila had a crush on Jack. "How much of a crush?"

"Jealous?" Sam inquired sweetly.

She glared at him. "What would you do for the person you loved, Sam? Would you pound the snot out of, oh, the father who abandoned them and treated them like rubbish?"

"Good point," he agreed. "If Mila hurts an earl, she could hang for it."

"The drop wouldn't break her neck," Emily remarked—rather needlessly, Finley thought.

"It would still hurt," Jasper commented. "And they'd keep trying till they found something that took."

Emily fidgeted, folded her arms over her chest. "This is all just speculation."

Finley glanced at her. "We should check on her just to make certain. I don't want to be the one to tell Griffin or Jack that we let Mila get herself into trouble—and Blackhurst is trouble regardless."

"Let's go, then," Sam said, already crossing the threshold. One by one, they followed out after him. Finley took another piece of cake with her. She had a feeling she was going to need it.

Chapter 15

When the bell rang, Jack's first thought was that it was Mila, even though he knew in his heart that it wasn't. She would never use the bell. Still, it was a surprise to find Gracie Adams standing on his step, and a less pleasant one to see the state she was in.

Blackhurst was a monster. If there was some way to remove his father's taint from his blood Jack would do it in an instant. Every awful thing he had ever done was because of that man—either to spite him or because he'd had little other choice given the relative poverty he and his mother had been left to. His father had paid for him to be educated, but that didn't put food on the table when you were stuck in Whitechapel.

"Hello, Jack." The young woman peered inside his house. "Can I come in?"

"Of course, pet." He stood back to allow her entry. As soon as she crossed the threshold his attention was drawn to the coat draped over her shoulders. It was a dark teal with shiny brass buttons, and he'd know it anywhere. After all, he had bought it when Mila insisted that she had to have it, even though it was one of those ready-made items he despised.

"Gracie? Where'd you get that coat, love?"

Wide eyes turned to his. Poor thing looked a fright. Looked as if she thought he might hurt her—him of all people. She knew him. Knew he wasn't like that. "Mila." Her voice was frail.

He was going to kill Blackhurst, and after that he would do all he could to make this up to her. God, he felt responsible. "Where did you see Mila?"

"At Blackhurst's," she whispered. "Jack, I think she's in trouble. She helped me escape, and Blackhurst isn't going to like that she laid out his footmen."

No, he wouldn't, even though Jack could hug her for it. This was his fault, as well. If he hadn't threatened Blackhurst over Mila, the bastard might have forgotten about her, or at least lost interest eventually, but now that he knew she was important to Jack, she was that much more attractive to the lech. He'd be that much meaner to Mila knowing that Jack cared about her.

The thought of that man touching her... He ground

his teeth as he strode stiffly to the cabinet where he kept his Aether pistols. "Stay here." Gone was all pretense of cockney. He yanked the door to the cabinet open and removed both pistols, checking to make sure both were fully charged. "If I'm not back in an hour call the authorities."

"The authorities?" Obviously that distressed her more than the sight of the weapons. "Jack, what do you mean to do?"

"I'm going to make certain Blackhurst doesn't hurt another woman ever again." He fastened the holsters for the pistols around his hips and cinched the belt snugly. "You'll be safe here."

"Jack, I got something from his safe you need to see." He grabbed his coat. "Later."

"No, Jack." Gone was that waifish tone, replaced by one of sheer determination. "You need to see this *now*."

Jack stopped at the door, and turned his head toward her. Bruised and disheveled, she faced him with a grim countenance as she held out a folded piece of yellowed paper. He snatched it from her fingers and opened it. His gaze skimmed over words that his brain struggled to make sense of, even though he was fully capable of comprehending them.

Blood drained from his face and dropped to his feet. For a moment he thought he might do something embarrassingly foolish like pass out. "Where did you get this?" His voice was a hoarse rasp.

Gracie's eyes were full of sympathy, perhaps even pity. "Blackhurst's safe. That is your mother's name on the paper, isn't it?"

Jack nodded, his fingers holding the page so tight they crumpled the edges. "You don't tell anyone about this, Gracie. Do you understand? No one can ever know."

She frowned, clearly not understanding at all. "But, Jack—"

"No one. *Ever.* Give me your word." He pushed a little persuasion behind the words, let his will shine in his eyes. In a second, Gracie took on that slightly dazed look of someone open to whatever suggestion he had to make.

"I swear to tell no one. On my honor."

Jack didn't like using his abilities on people he liked, and using them on Gracie after all she'd been through seemed a tad callous, but it was necessary. "That's a good girl. Now, go on upstairs and run yourself a bath. Use my tub. What are you going to do if I'm not back in an hour?"

She was still a little dazed. "Send for the authorities."

He kissed her forehead. "Off with you now." He only spared a moment to make certain she was off to do as he instructed before yanking open the door and stepping out into the dwindling night. Blood pumped wildly through his veins as he fought to control his emotions. He couldn't lose himself. He had to remain focused and calm, but damn his eyes if it wasn't almost impossible at that moment.

Behind his house was a somewhat run-down-looking shed. In actuality it was a rather sturdy structure that concealed an even larger one where he kept his vehicles. Everyone in Whitechapel knew that stealing from him would be a mistake they'd only make once, but Jack didn't see the point in flaunting how well his business paid, nor was he an enthusiastic tempter of fate.

He chose his glinting black-and-brass velocycle—a sleek two-wheeled machine that could easily maneuver through traffic and navigate narrow alleyways and tight spaces. It was going to be necessary for him to do just that. He swung a leg over the seat and started the machine's engine—it came to life with a powerful roar. Gripping the steering bars, Jack took his feet off the ground and leaped forward.

The velocycle hugged the cobblestones as it sped through the streets of Whitechapel. Jack wove in and out of traffic—and pedestrians. He narrowly avoided an old drunk who shouted obscenities at him as he whipped past. People screamed and jumped out of his way as he steered the machine down the steep steps of the Aldgate East underground entrance. He sped down the platform, rose up on the footrests, out of the seat and pulled the steering bars up. The velocycle leaped from the platform onto the dark track, its headlamp illuminating the long stretch ahead. Rats scattered as the wheels spun up debris as they grasped for purchase.

Jack knew every inch of London. He'd made it his business to know the city like the back of his own hand. He drove west to Moorgate, then swerved to the left toward the Bank stop. From there he continued west, rushing headlong into another long tunnel—an almost straight line to Oxford Circus. He pushed the velocycle as fast it could go. The goggles he wore prevented his eyes from watering as he bent low over the bars, but the wind tore at his hair and tried to tear his coat right off.

A lucky bit of debris—some old crates tossed over the side of the track—at his desired station formed a makeshift ramp that made it easier to jump the machine up onto the platform at Oxford Circus. People shouted when he emerged from the station—driving straight up the stairs as if he were escaping from hell with the devil hot on his heels. He swerved to miss a carriage and almost toppled over, his leg scraped the street before he managed to get upright once more.

From there it was a short drive into Mayfair to where

Blackhurst lived—not far from King House. He drove over the mechanism to open the gate and sped straight up the drive to the front steps. He steadied the velo-cycle, disengaged the engine and jumped off. He ran up the steps and tried to open the door. Locked. Jack stepped back and threw himself at the heavy oak, but he bounced off it like a child's ball.

He swore—profusely.

"Move."

Jack glanced over his shoulder at the familiar voice. It was Sam Morgan—and the rest of the Duke of Grey-thorne's little family, minus the duke, of course. Even Finley was in attendance. "What are you lot doing here?"

"Same as you," Finley answered. "We heard a friend might be in trouble. Your trying to break down an earl's door proves it. Step aside, Jack. Sam's been dying to break something."

The big lad grinned, and Jack immediately stepped out of his way. "Be quick about it."

Morgan walked up the steps, lifted one foot and kicked. The door flew into the house, through the foyer, across the front hall and partway up the stairs. A footman yelped in surprise.

"Nice," Jack praised, stepping in front of the young man to cross the threshold. He pushed the footman aside when he tried to engage them. Finley or Morgan punched the man in his already-bruised face and knocked him out. Jack didn't feel the least bit sorry for the fellow, as he was obviously one of the ones who had tangled with Mila.

"Where is she?" Jack asked, going still. It was a big house. He turned to Wildcat, who was already sniffing the air.

"Upstairs," the girl said, and took the lead. It was little disconcerting to see her drop to all fours and bound up the staircase like a human-cat creature. Jack ran after her, the rest giving chase. At the top of the stairs she'd barely paused to sniff again before leaping to the left. She stopped at a door almost at the end, poised in a crouch, her mouth slightly open as though tasting the air. Her fangs gleamed.

"In there," she murmured, pointing. "But it smells like trouble."

There was an odd mechanical lock on the door—the kind that required a punch card and a numerical code. If the wrong sequence was entered, or if someone tried to break the lock, it was rigged to spray acid outward in a wide arc. There were nozzles along the top of the door, as well, so that the spray was guaranteed to strike its target.

"Get back," Morgan instructed. "I'll heal."

The tiny little Irish girl stepped up. "Or, you could let me do it."

Immediately the tall fellow moved back, but he didn't stray far from her. Jack knew if something went wrong, Morgan would throw himself on her to prevent her from getting sprayed. That was loyalty. That was love.

Kind of like risking hanging for murder to save a girl. It wasn't something he wanted to think about. "Just open the bloody door."

The fact that no one had opened it—or that no staff had come to see what was going on was unsettling enough, but then his father was the sort of master whose wrath was to be avoided. He needed to find Mila and get her out of there. Now.

The redhead placed her palms against the wide metal plating of the lock and closed her eyes. Within seconds Jack heard clicks and groans as the mechanism inside did as she bid. He arched a brow. She was a handy little girl to have around. There was one final click and she dropped her hands. "Go ahead."

Jack turned the knob and pushed. The door swung open and he ran inside. He skidded to an immediate halt. The room was obviously a bedroom, but it had a small fighting ring in one corner. In that ring were Blackhurst and Mila. His father wore only his trousers and Mila was in her corset and shift. They were sparring, and there was no doubt that Mila held back because Blackhurst was still standing. Not far from the ring a footman stood with his arm around the neck of the woman from the boardinghouse, a pistol to her head.

"What the tarnation…?" Jasper Renn asked.

Jack reached for one of his own pistols, but the footman jerked the woman toward them. "Don't."

The sparring stopped. Mila looked at Jack as though she couldn't believe it was him. When she tried to leave the ring Blackhurst stopped her.

Jack growled.

"This is an interesting party," Blackhurst said. "I'll have you all arrested if you don't leave immediately."

Jack took a step forward.

"I'll kill her, boy," his father said. "Both of them."

It was then that Jack noticed the strange shackle around Mila's ankle.

"Electrical charge," Irish explained. She was so much smarter than she ought to be. "One flick of the switch on his wrist and it will send enough current through her to stop her heart."

Even Mila couldn't survive that. Could she? Jack's own heart jumped into his throat. Just as he was about to offer Blackhurst whatever he wanted something flickered in the corner of his vision.

THE GIRL WITH THE WINDUP HEART

Renn—the cowboy. One second he was standing at Jack's shoulder and the next he was in the ring holding not only the switch for Mila's shackle, but a pistol, which he trained on the footman. Blackhurst stood there, stunned. Jack knew how he felt.

"Drop it," Renn advised the footman. "I'm a lot faster than you, friend. A much better shot, too."

The footman dropped the pistol and the woman ran to them. Finley intercepted her, wrapping her in a hug. "I've got you. You're safe now."

Suddenly Renn was with Jack again. He gave him the wrist-strap switch, which Jack then offered to Emily. "Would you?"

She touched it. It grew warm in Jack's hand and he smelled hot metal. "Done."

Mila ran to Jack and threw her arms around him. There were so many things he wanted to say and do, but he couldn't do them just yet, not with this cold rage running through his veins. Gently, he pushed her toward Finley and the others. "Would you all excuse us, please? I need to have a word with Lord Blackhurst."

"Jack…" Finley's voice carried a wealth of meaning, all of which he ignored.

He looked at each of them, making eye contact. "Go."

And they did. The area behind his right eye throbbed

from the effort of imposing his will on them, but it was worth being saved the inevitable argument that would have ensued. They filed out of the room like obedient children—even the footman went with them.

Jack turned to his father.

Blackhurst smirked at him. "Well played, boy."

Jack punched him in the face—hard. The impact jarred all the way up his arm but it felt bloody good. The older man's head snapped back. Blood spurted from his nose. Jack hit him again. "You like violence?" he challenged. "I'll give you violence, you son of a bitch!" He hit him again. His father struck back, but Jack struck again and again, until his hand throbbed and bled.

Blackhurst was slumped against a dresser, his face bloody. And still there was that mocking grin. "Apple didn't fall far, did it? Half an hour later and she would have been mine, Dandy. She might still, someday."

"You stay away from Mila." God, he'd never wanted to kill someone so much in his life.

"Or what?" the earl challenged. "You'll call in my markers? Go right ahead. I'm already rebuilding my fortune. What can a piece of trash like you possibly do to someone like me? Kill me? You can try."

"I have this." Jack shoved the paper Gracie had given him in Blackhurst's face, and had the satisfaction of watching the earl blink blood out of his eye, and his face go pale beneath the crimson. "Where did you get that?"

"Where do you think?" When Blackhurst tried to grab the paper, Jack yanked it back just in time, and shoved his father back with his other hand. "You actually married her, you rotten bastard. I can't believe you were stupid enough to keep the evidence."

The earl stared at him in horror. Jack might have enjoyed this power if he weren't so damn angry. "You stay away from Mila. Stay away from me and anyone who knows me. Do whatever the hell you want with your money—I don't want it. But if you come near her again, I'll let the entire world know that I'm your legitimate heir. I'll make your life miserable. Your wife and your children will be social outcasts. Everyone will know the truth, and when you die you'll be on your death-bed knowing that I will inherit everything that was yours. Maybe I'll let your granddaughter work here as a chambermaid." It was a lie, of course, he'd never harm a child, but it was effective against his father. He didn't even have to use his talent to drive the threat home.

Blackhurst didn't insult him by challenging him with a "you wouldn't" sort of thing. He knew better. The apple, as it were, had not fallen that far. "You have my word," his father rasped. "Now get out."

There was no satisfaction in this victory. Jack folded

the paper and stuffed it inside his jacket as he left the room. It did nothing to change the fact that he and his father hated each other. It didn't change that his mother had died in relative poverty when she'd in fact been a countess. Jack's life should have been completely different.

And yet…he wouldn't change who or what he was. He would rather be the person he'd made himself into than whatever Blackhurst would have made of him. He could ruin the man. He could take everything from him, but he didn't want it. All he wanted was to go home with Mila and watch the sun come up.

They were all waiting for him when he stepped outside. Mila, her pretty face already healing from the blows she'd taken in the ring, turned to watch his approach, her amber eyes wide. "Jack?"

He hesitated. Oh, to hell with it. He walked right up to her, cupped her face in his hands and kissed her—a proper kiss. It was the sort of kiss he had been wanting to give her for quite some time but had been afraid of. All that rubbish about wanting her to have a better life and a good man had left the same second he realized he wasn't going to ruin his father. Things had become suddenly clear at that moment—all the important things—and the rest didn't matter anymore.

Mila wrapped her arms around his waist and kissed

him back with enthusiasm. Things might have gotten a little heated if Jack hadn't started laughing. It felt good.

"Poppet," he said when she gazed up at him quizzically, "put me down." The foolish girl had lifted him clear off his feet!

Everyone had a chuckle over that and the intensity of the kiss dissipated—for now. There was a promise in Mila's eyes that sent a tingle down his spine and made him eager to get home. She set him down.

Then Jack turned to face the others. "Thank you."

Morgan clapped him on the back, and Jack thought the fellow's hand might come out through his chest. "That's what friends do, Jackie-boy."

Jackie-boy?

They trailed past him down the steps, each giving him a little smile as they passed—as though they knew something about him that he didn't. Only Finley stopped. She hugged Mila and then hugged Jack. And when she patted his cheek, giving him a faint smile, he understood everything she didn't say. If these people were his friends, then she was the best of the lot. She understood him better than anyone ever had—until Mila. They would always be important to each other, but now it seemed she understood that he had someone that meant the world to him, and she also understood everything that came with that kind of feeling. Then she followed after the others.

"Are we going to be in trouble?" Mila asked when they were alone.

Jack looked at the broken door and the blood on the foyer floor. A handful of servants stood in the hall, dressed in their nightclothes, watching them curiously. "No. Blackhurst won't ever bother us again." Then he offered her his hand—it was just as bloody and battered as hers, the skin of his knuckles torn open. She entwined her fingers with his and squeezed.

Jack smiled at her. "Let's go home."

They made the drive back to Whitechapel at street level. Mila was silent until they were inside the house. Gracie met them at the door, and seeing that all was well, left to go back to Mrs. Rhodes's where she had secured her old room. Jack loaned her his steam carriage for the trip. Then he and Mila went into the parlor where there was still a hole in the ceiling and plaster dust on the carpet.

"It seems like I did this years ago," Mila remarked.

"You're still going to pay for it," he told her with a cheeky grin.

She smiled—a little. "Jack, you didn't need to rescue me."

"Yeah, I did." All traces of humor were gone now.

"Mila, I've been a wreck since you left. Whatever lesson you wanted to teach me, I've learned it. Just say that you're home to stay."

She swallowed, eyes wide. "I wasn't trying to teach you anything. No, that's not true. I suppose I wanted you to see that I'm a girl, Jack. A real girl, but now I know that I still have so much to learn about what it is to be human. I'm not sure I'll ever understand. I just wanted you to miss me a little, to want me like I want you."

The sorrow in her gaze broke his heart. "Real? Of course you're real. Miss you? Want you? Bloody hell, poppet. Why do you think I stopped you that day when you kissed me? I want you too much. Mila, I…" When wonder lit her eyes he was struck momentarily speechless. Gutless. *Courage, Jack.* "I love you." It took every ounce of his strength to say those words and wait for her reaction.

She stared at him.

Jack arched a brow. "Normally a girl has a response when a bloke makes such a declaration."

Mila burst into tears and sank onto the sofa.

Alarmed, Jack sat down with her. "Poppet? Are you…all right?" Seemed like a ridiculous question. Had he been wrong? Did she not feel the same? Had he ruined everything? He cursed himself for being an idiot, but then she threw her arms around him and showered his face with kisses and tears, knocking him onto his back on the cushions. He laughed.

"We have to go to the séance," she told him between kisses.

What the devil did that have to do with anything? "All right."

She kept kissing—and crying. "Because they're our friends, and Finley loves Griffin. And, Jack?" She reared up, gazing down at him with wet eyes. "I love you, too. I only went to Blackhurst's because he threatened you."

He reached up and stroked her hair back from her face. His heart was so full it felt ready to burst. "I know, love, I know. Let's not talk about him right now. Why don't you kiss me some more?" He could kiss her forever.

She grinned. It was like the sun coming out from behind a cloud. God, did she have any idea just how much she had changed his life? Changed him? The old him would have ruined his father, taken what was rightfully his and rubbed society's face in it. But now nothing was more important than being on that sofa with Mila in his arms.

"All right," she said, kissing him again. "But, Jack, there was something I was hoping we might do later."

His breath caught in his throat. "What's that?"

Her grin grew. "How would you feel about being *my* doxy?"

Jack laughed. It was difficult to laugh and kiss but somehow they managed it. And then Mila's fingers unbuttoned his shirt and Jack stopped laughing. And as they made their way upstairs to his room and fell on his bed, he realized what it was to love and be loved. And sometime just before the sun rose, Jack Dandy discovered his place in the world—and who he wanted to share it with.

Forever.

Chapter 16

Finley read the books on the Aether that Griffin had in the library. They had some useful information, but nothing that could tell them what to do with Garibaldi, which was their biggest problem. It wasn't the books' fault—not too many people who went to the Aether lived to write about it. Most of the information came from people who had been "touched by Death," as one book put it, or was speculation from people who studied various phenomenon associated with death and dying. None of it was from anyone who had spent any amount of time there.

When this was over she was going to make Griffin write a manual or guidebook so no one had to go through this again.

If they survived it. Her confidence wasn't what it

ought to be. In fact, she hadn't much at all. She had hope, and a lot of it. She even had prayers and wishes. Whether or not any of it would help remained to be seen. There was one thing she knew for certain; she wasn't leaving the Aether without Griffin, and if that meant her own death she was prepared to do it.

Of course, she neglected to mention that to Emily, or anyone else. Finley was at peace with it, though. She knew the odds were against them, especially with the shape Griffin was in. He hadn't said anything, but Emily had told her enough, and she'd seen him for herself—Griffin was dying. The truth of it brought a hot, prickling sensation to the back of her eyes, but she blinked it away while biting the inside of her cheek. No tears. Not yet.

She glanced at the clock. It was almost time for the séance. Ipsley and his friends would be arriving soon. He would once again be her anchor to this world while also being a conduit of strength for her in the Aether, drawing energy from the others. Hopefully they would be strong enough to summon and hold Garibaldi. The Machinist would know they hoped to trap him and he'd be ready, but if they could distract him just enough…

She slipped on her favorite boots—the ones she'd worn when she first took on Lord Felix—and laced them before heading downstairs. She wore her steel corset, as well. The hand-fashioned steel plates were small and allowed her ease of movement. These things were her armor; they made her feel invincible, and she was going to need all the help she could get.

It had been decided that the séance would be held in the ballroom since it was the largest room in the house outside of the cellar laboratory, and it was the room with the least amount of furniture or devices Garibaldi could use against them should his spirit manifest. All of the household automatons had been disabled and locked away for the evening, as well. The servants had been given the night off so that there was no chance of any of them getting injured in the fray.

The doorbell rang as Finley made her way to the ballroom. Wildcat ran past her and leaped over the banister, landing in a crouch on the floor below before springing up and bounding to the door. When she opened it, Ipsley and two more of his spiritualist friends stood on the step.

They were really going to do this. Finley had to stop to catch her breath—she'd blame it on the corset if anyone asked. She was scared—so much so that her palms were damp. She clenched her hands into fists as she strode into the ballroom.

The room was usually used for sparring and training, but tonight there was a round table in the center of the marble floor, with chairs around it, and the Tesla suit was set up on a table that was partially upright a few feet away.

Finley stopped. Was that a second suit next to the first? She walked closer. It was.

"I'm going with you," Sam said from behind her.

She turned and looked up into his dark eyes. "The hell you are."

He sighed. "Right, let's do this quickly. I'm Griffin's oldest friend, I'm strong enough to back you up and if anyone is going to be there when Garibaldi gets his arse kicked, it's me. It's not up for discussion, so just accept it."

She didn't have the strength to argue, and he was right on every point. "When did Emily have time to build a second suit?"

"She's been working on it ever since we got back from New York. You're not surprised, are you?"

A small smile tickled Finley's lips. "No, of course not. She'd have to build one herself just so she could figure out how it works. Has it been tested?"

He nodded, jaw tight. "The little fool tested it herself earlier today."

"What?" Finley could slap her friend for being so foolish.

"Exactly," Sam commiserated. He glanced toward the door. "Looks like everyone's here."

Finley followed his gaze as the others came into the room. Jack and Mila were among them.

It was foolish, but the sight of Jack brought those tears perilously close to the surface again. This was proof of their friendship, and how much he thought of all of them. He looked so happy with his hand on Mila's back, and the way the girl looked at him…it was almost embarrassing to witness, but oddly adorable at the same time. *Adorable* was not a word that fit Jack Dandy, but there it was.

As if hearing her thoughts, Jack turned his head and met her gaze. He grinned that self-assured grin of his that never failed to make her believe that everything would work out as it ought.

Emily clapped her hands to get everyone's attention. "Thank you all for coming. Let's get started." A woman of few words was Em.

"Do you know the plan?" Finley asked Sam, nodding at the table as the others took their seats around it.

He shrugged. "Not much. Emily seems to think it's better if we just concentrate on our parts."

"She would."

Sam's expression was equal parts sheepish and defensive. "They're going to try to call Garibaldi and hold his spirit while you and I beat him senseless and get Griffin out of the Aether."

It was almost too simple. "Then what?"

"Then they're going to try to send him on to wherever people like him go."

Hell was too good for the bastard. "Then let's die, Samuel."

Each of them climbed into a suit—Sam's was obviously the newer and larger of the two—and made all the adjustments they could on their own. Seconds later, Emily was with them, taking care of the rest.

"You be careful," she told Sam with a firm kiss on the mouth. Her voice trembled just a little, and Finley wanted to climb out of her suit and hug her. "I'll take care of him, Em."

"See that you do." There was just enough gravity to her tone that Finley knew she'd be in trouble if anything happened to Sam.

Someone dimmed the light in the room as Finley's helmet settled and was latched into place. Within minutes she felt that now-familiar chill settle over her, and then let herself drift away into darkness.

She became aware just outside of the house she recognized as the one her father had created in the Aether. Obviously he had good safeguards in place because she had focused on arriving inside the house, but Sam's accompanying her changed that.

"How do we get in?" Sam stood beside her—even taller and broader than in life. Obviously there was no deficiency in his confidence.

There wasn't any visible door, but Finley knew what to do. She walked up to the house and put her hand on the stone wall. "Papa? It's me. I brought Sam Morgan with me." The house was an extension of her father in the Aether, it made sense to her that it would recognize her, and it did. A door shimmered into existence beneath her palm, and then swung open.

"Showboat," Sam teased as they crossed the threshold.

They entered into the parlor—the only part of the house Finley had ever seen. Maybe that was all there was—not like her father had to eat or sleep. Thomas Sheppard rose from his seat at the piano where he had been playing. He immediately came over and hugged her before offering his hand to Sam. "I knew your father. He was a good man."

"The best," Sam agreed. Finley had never heard him say much about his parents but then, until recently, she'd never heard Sam say much of anything.

"Fin."

She turned in the direction of Griffin's voice. He was

on the sofa, a quilt pulled around him. And from what she could see there was absolutely no color left in him except his eyes and his hair. The shock of it was like a kick to the throat. Garibaldi had drained him, and now he just had to sit and wait while Griffin literally starved to death. In the living world he'd have more time, but time was not the same here. It moved faster in some ways and slower in others.

"Griffin." She wasn't going to let him see how much the sight of him upset her. Instead, she went to him and knelt beside the sofa so that she could touch him and kiss him—hold him. Because it might be the last time she got to do any of it.

And then Ipsley and his two friends—a black man and an old woman—arrived, wispy but visible. They stood in a close circle, holding hands, glowing with eerie silver light. Either her father had let them in, or the same rules didn't apply to spiritualists.

"We're going to begin trying to summon Garibaldi," Ipsley explained. "Once he is here we will bind and hold him within the ring of the table." It was so faint Finley could barely see it, but there was the actual table from the ballroom, with everyone around it holding hands. It was like a reflection in a window.

Her father's face was grim. "We're ready for him."

No, they really weren't, Finley thought. Griffin certainly wasn't, but it wasn't as though they had a choice in the matter. She squeezed Griffin's hand as the spiritualists began to call The Machinist.

"Finley," he said. "There's something I want to tell you…"

"Don't," she said, not caring that it might be cruel. "I'm one sweet word away from hysteria, Griffin King. Don't you dare send me over the edge. Whatever you have to say to me can wait until we get home." Her bottom lip quivered as she spoke.

He managed a wan smile. He was already so ghost-like. "Fair enough."

She gave a stiff nod, then turned her head. Just looking at him was too painful. She watched as the walls around them thinned, and became more transparent. What the devil?

"Your father is letting down his defenses," Griffin explained, his voice a hoarse rasp. "He's making it easy for Garibaldi."

Finley's attention went to her father. He looked grim but determined. If anyone could help them it was him. He'd been in the Aether for years. He knew it better than Garibaldi. He was smarter than Garibaldi.

Suddenly, a gale blew through the house—long, ragged tendrils of black smoke that Finley recognized as Garibaldi's Aether demons—his pets. They screamed around the room, whirling and diving like vultures in the middle of a fit. They skimmed around the humans, nipping and biting. Sam didn't waste any time, he punched one and then slammed two others together. They exploded into ash and fell away. One came rushing at Griffin, but Finley put herself in its path, and when it was within striking distance, she punched it hard. Ash rained down on her, sticking to her hair and clothes. *Ugh.*

"Finley!" She looked up just in time to see her father toss her a sword. She caught it with one hand. Sam had a cricket bat, and was using it to make short work of the demons. Finley jumped to her feet as two more streamed toward them. The sword swung and sliced through one, then she pivoted quickly, as though she were dancing, and brought the blade down and across another—the tip of the sword cut the air just inches above Griffin's head. He coughed on the ash.

No sooner had they dispatched of the wisps then the very foundation of the house began to shudder and shake as though something was trying to rip it right out of the ground. Crystal toppled from shelves, books crashed to the floor. The piano rattled a discordant tune. Windows began to crack.

"Enough with the theatrics, Leonardo!" Thomas shouted. "You're not impressing anyone, boy."

It seemed strange, this young man referring to Garibaldi as "boy" but in life she supposed her father might have been the elder of the two. Amazingly, the house stopped shaking and went completely still. Too still.

Garibaldi appeared—hovering above the spiritualists as if he was a puppet on strings. Finley knew better than to believe that was indeed true.

The Italian grinned. "What is this? A séance. For me? How very pathetic." He looked around the room, his glinting gaze falling on Sam. "Ah, my dear boy. It is so good to see you again. I have a special surprise for you."

The house shook again, but this time in measured beats. It took Finley a second to realize they were footsteps, and then it was too late. The huge automaton beast tore through the wall of the house, reducing it to rubble. Sam stared at it in horror.

"Damnation," Griffin wheezed, and Finley knew without asking that the machine was a monstrous version of the one that had killed Sam before she ever became part of the group. Emily had put him back together, brought him back to life, but Sam was terrified of anything metal.

Sword still in hand, Finley went to stand beside Sam. "I'm with you."

Her father came up on Sam's left. "As am I."

Garibaldi laughed. "Destroy them!" His arrogant

glee reminded her of Lord Felix with his girls. He'd been so sure they'd do as he commanded, not realizing how much they hated him. This machine probably didn't hate Garibaldi, but that didn't make it anymore impervious to harm. In the end, it was just a construct of Garibaldi's mind and will. It wasn't real metal—not really.

It still packed a mean punch—as she found out when she attacked it. It swept her aside as if she were nothing more powerful than a kitten. That made her angry. She spat blood from her mouth and attacked again. This time she went for the neck of the huge digger automaton while her father used a mace to knock out one of its legs. Sam hoisted his cricket bat and gave a mighty roar—the kind she imagined Celtic warriors made in battle. He charged at the digger without hesitation. Finley couldn't resist a glance at Garibaldi—he looked surprised. So much so that he actually struggled against the spiritual bonds that held him. She smiled as she leaped onto the machine's back and drove her sword into its neck.

Sam cracked the front panel with one swing, almost knocking Finley to the ground. It must be his rage that made him so strong here. Whatever it was, it worked beautifully. Two more bone-jarring swings and he'd opened a hole in the metal's chest cavity. He reached in as Finley worked her blade back and forth, slowly decapitating the beast. Sparks flew and gears ground to a halt as Sam yanked out the logic engine and central gearbox and threw them on the ground. Finley slid down the machine's back and jumped down.

"No!" Garibaldi shouted as his creation toppled.

Sam flashed him a grin. "Yes, you miserable bastard."

Finley grinned, as well. For one second it looked as though they had a chance. Then Garibaldi turned his attention to her. His eyes began to glow a pale blue as he brought up his hands. Energy arced between his palms, like a tiny lightning storm, swirling and coalescing into a ball of deadly Aetheric energy.

Then he threw it at her.

Finley braced herself for a blow that never struck. Stunned, she watched as the ball of energy flew past her and landed in Griffin's hand where it crackled and hummed. He was terrible and beautiful, illuminated by that light, but saving her had cost him. He had no color now except for his eyes, which were bluish-gray naturally. Still, Finley could tell that they weren't a ghostly hue. It wouldn't be long before they were.

He hurled the ball back at Garibaldi, who raised his hand and smashed the ball of energy before it even came close to hitting him. "Sloppy, Your Grace."

Finley turned to Sam. "We have to get Griffin out of here."

Sam nodded. "Ipsley, time to finish this."

The medium nodded and the silver glow around him and his friends intensified. Garibaldi squirmed above them. "What are you doing?"

Sam walked up and cracked him across the back with his cricket bat. "Retribution." The Machinist screamed, spine bowing as Sam hit him again.

Finley ran to the sofa and grabbed Griffin, hauling him to his feet and holding him up with an arm around his waist. She pulled his arm across her shoulders. "Emily's going to wake me up and I'm going to take you out of here. Do you think you can leave? Has his hold on you lessened?"

"Fin. Stop."

She didn't listen. She dragged him toward her father. "Give him another blast from your shield so he has the strength to leave."

Thomas Sheppard's gaze was sad. "I don't have any energy to give him."

She pointed at Garibaldi. "Drain some."

"Using his life force will only bind him all the more to Griffin."

Tears filled Finley's eyes as Griffin's weight settled more heavily on her shoulders. She was losing him.

"No. There has to be a way. You have to be able to do something."

Her father hoisted the shield, and shoved his arms through the straps on the back. "I can at least try to help weaken Garibaldi, but the rest is up to Griffin."

"Finley."

Still she ignored him. "Good. Do it." She dragged him toward Ipsley. The medium knew to tell Emily to wake her on her signal.

"Fin, I'm not strong enough to make it back."

A tear trickled down her cheek. "Don't you dare say that Griffin." Suddenly all of his weight came down on her. "Griffin?"

He was unconscious, and with his eyes closed there wasn't a single part of him that had any color.

Griffin was dead.

Death felt exactly like Griffin knew it would—peaceful and serene. Any moment he expected to feel warmth on his face and in his heart. He would hear his mother telling him to wake up and let go.

His mother?

He snapped to attention. He felt awake, but he knew he really wasn't. This was one more level of the Aether, or maybe a place between the Aether and whatever lay beyond death. He wasn't certain. What he did know was that it was ivory and white, and that he was standing in the middle of it, and so was his mother.

"What?" he asked.

She gave him that look she'd always used to give him when he didn't listen to her. He could see the love in her blue eyes even though she was exasperated with him. She looked younger than he remembered, and unlike the Aether she was in full glorious color from her auburn hair to her purple gown, right down to the toes of her crimson shoes. Thankfully he hadn't inherited her fashion sense.

"I said you have to let go."

"I did. Didn't I?" He looked around. "I am dead, right?"

"Not quite," she replied in a clipped tone. "But you soon will be if you don't listen to me, young man. You must let go. It's the only way to stop Garibaldi and save your friends."

"I don't know what you mean."

Suddenly, she was right in front of him, just inches away. He hadn't even seen her move. She placed a long, slender hand on the center of his chest. "Yes, you do. You've always known. It's the thing you've feared most ever since you first encountered the Aether."

Griffin shuddered as understanding dawned. She meant that he had to let go of his control. Ever since he'd first learned about the Aether and what it was to him, he'd been certain that if he lost control of the Aether it would destroy him. Not only that, but that he might have the power to destroy possibly all of London if he let the Aether in.

"What you're asking of me is suicide," he said. "Not just that, but you're telling me to kill my friends."

She smiled patiently at him. "Send them home, Griffin. You don't need them here to draw strength from them. They risked their lives for you. The least you can do for them is fight to live." Her smile faded. "If you don't do this—if you don't let go of that fear and give in to your power—Leonardo will kill them, and he won't be quick or kind about it. And he won't stop with your friends. He'll destroy the living world, Griffin, and make himself King of the Dead. He won't stop until he is a god."

The awful truth of her words sank deep into his bones. "I don't know if I can do this."

His mother lifted her hand to his cheek and patted it. "I know you can. You can do anything you set your mind to. You just have to let go."

So she kept saying. "All right."

Her smile was dazzling. "So, wake up."

Griffin opened his eyes to find Finley hovering over him sobbing. It was heart-wrenching.

"Fin."

The sobs stopped. Her big honey-colored eyes widened as they focused wetly on his face. "Griffin? You're alive?"

"For the time being."

"Thank God." This was said by Sheppard, who stood over the pair of them.

Griffin looked at Finley. "I saw my mother."

She raised her brows. "You did?"

He nodded. "She told me what I need to do. Help me to my feet."

His darling girl picked him up as though he weighed next to nothing. At one time it would have embarrassed him, now he was grateful for her strength. A quick glance confirmed that Garibaldi was still held by the spiritualists, but they looked as though their ability to hold him was weakening. Sam still beat on him with the bat, but the injuries weren't lasting. The Machinist simply had too much power—power he had taken from Griffin.

"You have to leave," he told Finley. "Get Ipsley to tell Emily to wake you and Sam up."

She shook her head. The front of her shirt, right down to the edge of her steel corset was wet with tears. "I'm not leaving without you."

"You have to."

"No."

He swore, and pulled away from her. It took every ounce of strength he had to stand on his own two feet. "Listen to me. I have a plan." It wasn't much of one, but it was all he had. "You can't be here when I use the Aether against Garibaldi. It could kill you."

"What about you?"

He had no bloody idea. "I'll be fine."

She didn't look convinced. "No. There has to be another way."

Good God, but she was the most stubborn of females. She was going to force his hand.

Griffin staggered away from her, toward the spiritualists and Garibaldi. "Sam, stop." His friend did. He was much more rational than Finley, Griffin thought. "Ipsley, let Garibaldi go."

"Griffin!" Finley cried.

He glanced at her. "Trust me." And then, "Ipsley, when I tell you to, I want you to tell Emily to wake Sam and Finley up. You do that and then you and your friends get out of here, all right?"

"Don't do it!" Finley commanded.

Griffin kept his gaze focused on Ipsley. "All right?"

The gingery young man nodded. He was little more than transparent in this realm, a fact that Griffin would like to study under different circumstances. "Good. Now, let Garibaldi go."

"Griff, are you mad?" Sam demanded.

Griffin smiled at him. "You can keep hitting him if you like." That seemed to appease his old friend.

The mediums released each other's hands, which broke the circle that bound Garibaldi. Griffin's heart pounded hard in his chest as his enemy drifted toward the floor. He reached out for the Aether with that part of him deep inside that was connected and felt a tiny spark. A tingle in his fingertips and toes. Joy spread through his veins. He could feel the Aether. It hadn't left him.

Let go. That's what his mother had told him to do. All right. Instead of trying to command and control the Aether, he imagined opening a tiny door inside his soul and letting the Aether in—like opening a window to a summer breeze. Warmth blossomed in his chest.

"Griffin." It was a whisper, but he still heard it. It was Finley, and he knew why she sounded so shocked. With that warmth he could feel life seeping back into his body. He could feel it burning in his eyes, and knew that she could see it.

Garibaldi saw it, too. "No, you don't." He threw a ball of energy at him. Griffin lurched out of the way, and almost fell. Another whisked past his head.

"Stand still," The Machinist growled. Griffin would have chuckled if he wasn't trying to stay alive.

Another ball came at him. He tried to dodge but his feet refused to move. He was still so weak from lack of food and water on top of everything else, that he couldn't move fast enough. The ball struck him in the center of his chest, knocking him off his feet.

Finley shouted, but it wasn't the scream of a hysterical woman. It was the cry of a warrior. She rushed toward Garibaldi.

"Sam!" Griffin shouted, struggling to his feet. His heart was pounding, blood racing. Underneath his fear for Finley he could feel his strength returning. His friend turned around at his shout and caught Finley in midstride, picking her up as if she were a child and holding her in the iron band of his arms so she couldn't risk her fool neck.

Griffin stood and faced Garibaldi. "That felt good."

The villain threw another ball and then another. Griffin didn't dodge this time, and he didn't fall down either. He let each sphere hit him and absorbed the energy into himself. It felt good. By the time Garibaldi caught on, Griffin felt almost hopeful.

"What are you?" Garibaldi demanded with a scowl. The Machinist held out his arms. Aetheric energy danced along his skin like electricity. What was left of the house began to tremble once more. God only knew what he was calling forth this time. If Griffin didn't act now he might not get another shot.

He looked at Sam and then at Finley. She looked terrified as their gazes locked. He gave her what he hoped was a reassuring smile, and kept his attention on her as he stretched out his own arms. The crackle started at his fingers and shot up each arm to his shoulder. Then, he felt it snake up his legs, pooling somewhere behind his stomach. It was scary as hell but he didn't try to stop it, even though every instinct demanded he do just that.

The house shook harder. Bits of ceiling fell down around him as books toppled and furniture collapsed. Was this from him or Garibaldi? He couldn't tell. The Machinist floated off the floor, his eyes glowing blue, sparks dancing on his skin. "Say goodbye to everyone you love, Griffin King." His voice echoed ominously.

Griffin only smiled. Damn, but this was incredible. It felt as though his skin were dancing. He could feel the universe in his head, hear the flapping of angels' wings roaring in his ears, and still the Aether came to him, filled him. He could feel his soul expanding, feel the pressure building as he let the energy rush in. He felt like a rag doll about to come apart at the seams.

He looked at Finley again. He couldn't take much

more of this. It was too much, and he wanted it too badly. "I love you," he told her. "Ipsley, now!"

He waited until he heard her shout, saw her start to fade. Only when he knew she was going to make it did he finally give up his control.

He let go.

Chapter 17

Finley came back into the world of the living with a scream that threatened to shatter her own eardrums. The last thing she had seen as Griffin tossed her out of the Aether were arcs of lightning sparking all around him as his eyes glowed an intense bright blue.

And then there had been nothing but light. Light that came from inside of Griffin. Light so pure and beautiful and terrible that there was no way he could have survived it.

She tore out of the suit, ripping it to shreds in her grief. She was like some sort of wild dog and she didn't care. She crushed the helmet in her hands, rejoicing as the glass cut her palms. The pain was something she could focus on. She snapped tubing and ripped off knobs and dials. Blood ran down her arms and slicked her fingers, making them too slippery to do any more damage. That's when she switched to fists.

But before she could smash anything, strong arms closed around her again—just as they had in the Aether. Sam, the Judas. She pummeled him with her fists and feet, used ever vile word she could think of against him, and still he held her. He even told her it was all right, to just let it out.

Bastard. She punched him in the shoulder as hard as she could. The impact jarred her all the way up to her jaw. Of course she would hit the arm that was metal beneath the skin. He grunted, and staggered backward, but still didn't let go. Eventually, the fight drained out of her, and she went limp in his arms, sobbing. Everyone had gathered around her and she didn't care. She had no shame; she was too heartbroken. She was numb, but inside she screamed in pain. How did anyone ever survive this sort of grief?

"Mary and Joseph." It was Emily. A collective gasp rose from around her, including Sam. She felt his partially mechanical heart skip a beat. His arms went slack around her, so it was easy to push away and turn to see what everyone was looking at.

It was Griffin. Standing there in the middle of the ballroom, clutching her father's shield as though nothing had ever happened, looking fresh as a spring daisy.

Finley almost fell down. Then her brain reestablished contact with her body and she ran to him instead. She threw her arms around him and hugged him while pressing her lips to his jaw. Tears trickled down her cheeks, but this time they were tears of joy. And when his arms closed around her she couldn't help but smile.

"I thought I had lost you," she whispered.

He kissed her hair. "I'm not that easy to get rid of, love. You ought to know that."

They stood that way for what felt like forever before the others joined them. Finley had to let him go so his friends could welcome him back. Even Jack shook his hand. Mila picked him up and swung him around as if he were a child, which made everyone laugh.

Finally, when they'd all had a chance to rejoice at his return, Sam asked what they were all wondering. "What happened?"

Griffin raked a hand through his already disheveled hair. It was a familiar gesture, one he often made, but Finley was stupidly happy to watch him do it. "My mother told me I had to let go. I thought she meant my control, but she really meant my fear. For years I've fought the Aether, tried to manipulate it and contain it. What I didn't realize was that it's in me. It's as much a part of me as my skin. I wasn't controlling it so much as denying it. Once I let it in… It was incredible. I've never felt so alive."

"Garibaldi?" Jasper asked.

"He's gone. I unleashed a wave of power that left nothing but a very small part of him in its wake."

Everyone went still. They were all thinking the same thing—Finley could see it. "What did you do with that small part?" she asked.

He picked up her father's shield. "It's in here. Thomas absorbed it. He offered to stay in the Aether and guard it, but I had a suspicion that I could bring it into this realm with me."

Finley swallowed. "My father. Is he…?"

Griffin smiled sympathetically. "He moved on. I think he went to the same place as my mother. He gave me this to give to you." He offered her a folded piece of paper.

"You brought it back, as well."

He shrugged. "It seems that I'm able to take this realm into the Aether and vice versa."

She stared at him. She wasn't quite afraid of him at that moment, but she was…in awe. That was it. She closed her fist around her father's note. Her mind couldn't make sense of all of this, couldn't understand how Griffin could be so powerful, or how he had gone from death to so very much alive in what seemed like minutes.

But then time was different in the Aether.

"So, The Machinist is done?" Mila asked. "Forever?"

"He is," Griffin replied. "I think we'll put what's left of him in a safe place just to be certain."

"Like the bottom of the ocean," Sam remarked.

They all chuckled, but there wasn't one among them who thought it a bad idea.

"You must be exhausted, laddie," Emily spoke up. "You should get some rest."

Griffin glanced around at all of them. "Actually, I'm starving. Who wants supper?"

It was hours before Finley and Griffin were finally alone. After a meal with their friends, and after the mediums had taken their leave—after Griffin's heartfelt thanks—they'd all helped seal her father's shield in a lead chest and buried it beneath the fountain in the back garden—far away from any automatons or machines, just in case. Sam had then set a huge statue of a half-naked Greek lady on top of the spot. It would take a little while before they would all truly believe The Machinist was gone, even though they knew it was true. After their connection, and with the connection he now shared with the Aether, Griffin would know if there was anything of Garibaldi left out there.

Once that was done, they separated into their pairs and said good-night. Jasper and Wildcat went off to the room they shared in the house, followed by Sam and Emily. Emily had gotten a little emotional after a glass of wine at dinner and not only told Griffin how much he meant to her, but how much he meant to everyone else, as well. When she burst into tears, Sam took her wine away and gave her a hug.

Jack and Mila took their leave after that. While Mila hugged Griffin like a long-lost sibling, Jack held out his arms for Finley.

"I'm happy for you, Jack," she whispered.

He smiled at her. It was a good look for him. He ought to do it more often. "I'm happy for you, too."

"Someday, will you tell me what you said to Black-hurst?"

His grin grew as he released her. "Maybe." Then he took Mila by the hand and off they went.

"So," Griffin said when they entered their own room and closed the door. "Jack and Mila?"

"I *know!*" Finley squealed. "Can you believe it?"

He seemed to consider it. "Actually, it makes an odd sort of sense to me."

"Oh, now that you are one with the universe and heavens and all that?" she teased.

He grabbed her by the hand and pulled her into his arms. "No. I mean that I can see how they'd make it work. He needs a little happiness and goodness in his life, and Mila is nothing but. Mila needs someone who will love her just as she is, and Jack, for all his faults, is one of the least judgmental people I've ever met."

Finley wrapped her arms around his neck. "You're spending too much time thinking about Jack and Mila and not nearly enough time kissing me."

An error he immediately remedied. And then some. It had been such an emotional few days that they were both needy and urgent. Clothes scattered as fingers stroked and touched, unable to get enough of each other. It was as though both needed some sort of physical assurance that the other was indeed real. Afterward, they lay entwined under the covers, Finley with her head in the crook of Griffin's shoulder.

"I read the note from my father."

He tilted his head to look at her. "When?"

"While you were digging the hole in the garden."

"Do you want to talk about it?"

She ran her fingers over his chest, just enjoying the feel of him, so thankful that he was there with her. "He said that he'd remained behind for so long because he wanted to watch over me, and that he finally felt that he could move on knowing that I had you to depend on."

He kissed her forehead. "That you do. Although, I thought you were going to murder me when I made you wake up."

Finley came up on her elbow. "Me murder you? I thought you committed suicide, you great idiot! You were all tragic and self-sacrificing."

He made a strangled sound that was something between a laugh and a gasp. "You heartless wench! I was trying to make a grand gesture."

"You scared me half to death."

"Only half? For a few seconds I went the whole way."

Her merriment faded into a hard lump in her throat. "If you had died I was prepared to die, too."

He frowned. "To be with me?"

She nodded.

"Finley, that's the most ridiculous thing you've ever said!"

"Oy! It was a grand gesture." She was able to make the joke because she knew he wasn't really mad at her—well, he was, but he would have felt the same way. "What I'm trying to tell you, Griffin King, is that I don't want to live in a world that doesn't have you in it." She drew a deep breath and summoned all her courage. "I love you."

Time seemed to stop. He just stared up at her. A swath of her hair fell over her shoulder onto his chest and he didn't even blink.

"Griffin? Did you hear me?"

"I did," he answered without a change in expression. "I'm just waiting to see if maybe I died after all, because this certainly feels like heaven."

If anyone else had said it she would have groaned and rolled her eyes, but she melted like butter on a stove instead. "That's so sweet."

He lifted his head and kissed her. "I love you, too."

Months ago, if anyone had told Finley that her freakish nature would lead her to such happiness she would have called them a liar and punched them in the nose. She would have given anything to be a normal girl, but now she was perfectly happy to be exactly what she was. She was content with who and what she was. It didn't matter that they had little privacy, or that they always seemed to be getting involved in someone else's problems. She had good friends—she had a family. And she had Griffin King, Duke of Greythorne. It didn't matter that he was rich or powerful. She'd love him even if he were a rat catcher.

"What do you want to do tomorrow?" she asked. "Save the world again?"

"I've had enough of that for a bit. I thought maybe we could finally go for that walk in Hyde Park."

He'd asked her to go for a walk with him before they left for New York, but they never got to do it. With The Machinist finally gone, their lives were going to be a lot quieter. Maybe. "That sounds lovely."

"And then maybe we'll take a trip to my country house in Devon."

She'd never been to Devon. "I'd love to."

He wrapped a lock of her hair around his finger. "And then maybe we could go to Paris or Venice or Athens."

Finley's breath caught. She'd never been to any of those places either. "I'll go anywhere with you."

Griffin smiled. "I'll go anywhere to be with you." As he kissed her again, Finley Jayne realized she wouldn't change a single event that had brought her to that moment, not even Griffin hitting her with his velocycle in the rain. And she didn't need to be always saving the world—every day with Griffin was all the adventure she needed.

★ ★ ★ ★ ★